Rollover

Rollover

A Dan Mahoney Mystery

Susan Slater

Poisoned Pen Press

Copyright © 2014 by Susan Slater

First Edition 2014

10 9 8 7 6 5 4 3 2 1

Library of Congress Catalog Card Number: 2014931633

ISBN: 9781464202940   Hardcover
         9781464202964   Trade Paperback

Poisoned Pen Press
6962 E. First Ave., Ste. 103
Scottsdale, AZ 85251
www.poisonedpenpress.com
info@poisonedpenpress.com

Printed in the United States of America

Acknowledgments

Because substantial time had passed between publication of the first Dan Mahoney mystery, *Flash Flood,* and the writing of the second, *Rollover,* I asked my favorite book club, University Women of Flagler's Bookminders, to read both books—the one still in manuscript form. Was Dan's "voice" the same? Did the books logically follow one another? A group of dedicated readers tackled the request and, wouldn't you know it, I'd turned a perfectly nice black Lab from book one into a fluffy golden retriever in book two! Among other things.

So special thank you's to Louel, Suzanne, Pat, Laura, Jane, Rhenda, Jo, Ronaele, Trish, Maria, Emilie, Barbara, Jean, Sherrie, and others who caught the errors. And lastly to Freda who had many helpful suggestions even though *American* English isn't her first language.

Author's Note

In 1998, the Norwest Bank in Wagon Mound, New Mexico, one of the oldest continuously operated banks in the United States, was robbed. But it wasn't a normal heist. Robbers tunneled into the bank from the outside by cutting the padlock off the bank's heavy metal cellar door and replacing it with one of their own. The new padlock went undetected by bank security who patrolled the grounds daily.

No one knows how long the tunnel took to complete, but most figure they had three days inside to pick and choose what they wanted because their effort was planned to coincide with the Bean Day Festival—held on Labor Day weekend. Even though the bank, at the corner of Nolan and Railroad Avenue, was a scant block and a half from the festivities, noise from the celebration covered any sounds from the bank.

What was taken was either exactly what had been planned or a colossal mistake. Had the robbers meant to tunnel into the steel-encased room of safe deposit boxes where they ended up? Or were they aiming for the bank's vault next to it? It's unknown because despite the offering of generous rewards, the crime remains unsolved, according to the Albuquerque Journal, September 2001.

Rollover is a purely fictionalized "what if" featuring this real-life crime written some sixteen years later. Characters are not based on anyone in the Wagon Mound community—they live solely in the author's imagination.

Chapter One

"Damn!" Dan watched the needle on the heat gauge go into the red and then hold at the top. If he thought he was seeing things, the steam that curled out from under the hood made him a believer. He coasted to the side of the two-lane highway and shut the engine off. What had the historical marker called this area? *La Frontera del Llano*, the edge of the plains. He idly wondered what Spanish was for the edge of nowhere.

He popped the hood, grabbed a rag from under the seat and got out. "Stay," Dan ordered the rottweiler who tried to follow him out of the car. He hoisted the hood touching only the side, propped it open, then wrapped the rag around his hand, and gave the radiator cap a couple of quick turns before jumping back. Wow. That was some serious steam. He wasn't going anywhere very fast.

He looked up and down New Mexico Highway 120. Not a car in sight. He was probably twenty-some miles west of Roy just past Mills Canyon, but a tow truck would have to take him to a Jeep dealer and that would be either Las Vegas or Santa Fe—another sixty to a hundred miles west. He punched 4-1-1 into his cell and watched it search for a network…without luck. He'd try again later but knew reception would be spotty. His bright idea of driving up the back roads from Hobbs didn't seem very bright anymore. There were some things to be said for living away from civilization, but not very many. That was probably the Chicago in him talking—still difficult to adjust to wide-open spaces. He snapped the cell shut. Now what?

"You think you need to get out?" Simon was whining his discontent. Dan walked to the passenger side of the SUV and opened the door. The rottweiler didn't wait for an invitation but hit the ground in one leap from the seat. "Simon…" The dog paused and looked up. "Stay close." Not that the dog understood the command; still, he paused and didn't go bounding off. Dan watched as Simon turned to sniff a knee-high patch of weeds, then weave back and forth before stopping on point where some new scent caught his attention. Dan was beginning to feel envious of not having anything more pressing to do than pee on a bunch of grass and a couple fence posts.

This little setback would probably cost him an afternoon—maybe an overnight. Today was Monday and he needed to have the investigation wrapped up and be out of here by Thursday. There was a Friday morning reservation on American for London in his name. He couldn't suppress a grin. Yeah, he was looking forward to seeing Elaine and enjoying a little downtime. Hadn't they earned it after a crazy summer in Tatum? It irked him that he'd even taken this assignment. But his boss had a point. As long as Dan was in the state, it'd be a lot more efficient—economical, Dan had amended—to just check out a claim now instead of having to come back. Good ol' United Life & Casualty still owned a piece of his soul but that wouldn't be forever. He could see the proverbial light. And at fifty-two, he was heading toward that tunnel—if his ten-year plan worked.

He leaned against the Cherokee…might as well enjoy the scenery—blue grama mixed with buffalo grass as far as the eye could see. The short-grass prairie of the southern Great Plains. Who knew that New Mexico could lay claim to such an area? Once crowded with buffalo, now cattle outnumbered people probably ten to one. He thought he'd read somewhere that, on average, less than one person inhabited each square mile of the area. He sighed. The wait could be a long one. Should he start walking? Leaving luggage in an unattended car out in nowhere didn't sound like a good idea and dragging it down the road seemed even worse.

At first the truck coming up on his left was just a speck— tough to determine if it was a mirage or for real. But as it got closer and pulled to a stop behind the Cherokee, Dan didn't know whether to be relieved or disappointed. He wasn't sure he'd ever seen a truck that old still running. But it didn't have anything on its driver—they were the same vintage.

The old man, six feet tall but stooped, slipped out from behind the steering wheel, steadied himself, and then walked toward Dan. Splotchy skin, a week's white bristly beard, matted hair that looked like it'd been cut with cuticle scissors—the old guy must live by himself, Dan deduced. Simon stopped his exploring long enough to offer a low growl, but Dan shushed him. Didn't want to spook what might be the only living being that would happen along that way for a while.

"See yer having some troubles." The old guy had the overly loud voice of the deaf. He walked past Dan and leaned in under the hood.

"Overheated." Dan offered.

"I can see that. 'Cause yer drivin' a Jeep, probably."

"I'm not following."

"Got the worst maintenance record of American cars. I'm a Ford man, myself. Jesse here's been with me since birth."

Dan wasn't sure whose, but let it slide. "Dan Mahoney." He held out his hand and waited while the man wiped his right palm on stiffly starched overalls before following suit.

"Chet. Chet Echols."

Dan wondered at the tremor. Palsy? No reason it'd be nerves. And a quilted flannel shirt? This was a beautiful fall day—not mid-winter. But circulation often left something to be desired in the elderly, he guessed.

"Any chance you could give me a tow?"

The short laugh startled Dan. "Not with Jesse. Haven't found his bumpers in six months. Put 'em somewhere—just don't know where. But I can give you a lift. Nearest gas station with a tow truck's only about twenty miles back up the road."

"I'd appreciate that."

"That yer dog?"

Dan swallowed any smart retort like whose dog would be sitting quietly by his side if not his own and simply said, "This is Simon."

"Well, I don't allow no dogs in the cab. He'll have to ride back there."

"Okay." Dan signaled Simon to jump in the truck's bed. There wasn't a tailgate but he doubted the truck would go fast enough to cause him to worry. "Let me lock up the Jeep."

Dan grabbed his suitcase from the Cherokee along with a shaving kit and put both next to Simon. "Watch." They'd been working on the command and Simon immediately sank down, nose touching the suitcase. "Good boy." He gave the dog an appreciative pat.

Chet opened the truck's passenger-side door, gingerly closing it after Dan climbed in and then held it in place. "Sorry 'bout this but I gotta wire this dang door shut. Hinge's a little rusty. Don't wanna lose ya." More laughter.

The old guy sure seemed the jolly sort but the door thing vaguely bothered Dan as he watched Chet thread baling wire through a small hole at the base of the A-post and then wrap it around the door frame. The door seemed ill-fitting and there was no need to worry about rolling the window down—there wasn't any. The dash seemed to have more wires sticking out than contained. And the front seat was all gaping holes with foam and springs poking up through the worn plastic covering. He didn't want Simon to ride in the cab? Simon had the better deal.

"Give me a minute to rev 'er up and git 'er turned around and we're off."

It was amazing the truck started, but it did and they bounced up, over the edge of the asphalt, and Chet made a wide turn to head back in the direction he'd come.

"You hungry?" Chet held out a bag of beef jerky.

"No, I stopped at Roy."

"Bet you ate at the Chill an' Grill."

"Yeah, had to."

"Yep, only place in town anymore. Used to have Sam & Ella's—"

"Salmonella?" That wasn't very appetizing.

Chet gave an explosive guffaw. "Sorry, I forget newbies to this part of the world ain't gonna know the history. Sam…and… Ella's. Husband and wife, Armijo was the last name. Made the best sour cream chicken and onion enchiladas with red on the face of the Earth." Chet paused, "I'm not saying the Chill an' Grill ain't as good—that roadkill entry on the menu sure is popular with the tourists. Tell me, you meet the cook?"

"No."

"Former lawman…now his daughter's got him flipping burgers. Bet you heard the story 'bout how he handcuffed a black bear and threw him in the back of his cruiser?"

Dan shook his head.

"Shame. Good story."

He waited for him to tell it, but Chet's attention seemed to be on the road and checking the rearview mirror. It had been a while since Dan had seen someone look behind him as often.

"You know, speaking of lawmen, I'm guessing you're one."

"Insurance investigator."

"Same thing. I gotta nose for smellin' cops. Bet yer out this way 'cause of that robbery in Wagon Mound last month."

Dan nodded, "Yeah, some people are pretty upset."

"A mite poorer, too. Can you believe those guys tunneled into that bank—God knows how long that took 'em—then spent three days jus' pickin' and choosin' their loot? Used the Bean Day parade as a cover-up. Now that's a smart bunch of crooks."

Dan wasn't sure he agreed, but was saved from comment.

"Ain't gonna find nothin'."

"Pardon?"

"Ain't gonna catch 'em. Everybody in town says it was an inside job. You know, somebody needed drug money—nobody's saying what was lost, but I understand it was plenty. Coin collection, jewelry—what'd yer client lose?"

"Don't know yet." And damned well wouldn't share that information anyway. The loss of the hundred-and-ten-year-old diamond and sapphire necklace with matching earrings designed by Tiffany was information for Dan only. Five hundred thousand insured dollars' worth of jewels that had survived the Titanic but not a bunch of tunneling bandits in a one-horse town. Who said life was fair?

He looked at the driver. Chet was the nosey sort, but jawing was socially acceptable and probably his only recreation. And he didn't seem to want to push it, accepted Dan's noncommittal answer and dropped the inquiry. They rode—Dan decided that was a misnomer, more like bounced— along in silence for a couple minutes before Chet turned his way.

"What's yer best insurance story? You know the kind of stuff that's kept you punching the clock over the years?"

Dan thought a minute. A personal favorite was solving the disappearance of the heifer Grand Champion Tabor's Shortcake Dream last summer, but that story might lead to a little more disclosure than he'd be comfortable with…"I guess my favorite is the one they tell on Jackson Pollack."

"The artist?"

"Yeah. Seems he got drunk at a friend's party one night, locked himself in their bathroom and painted the toilet seat. The family had it framed and over the years thought of it as their nest egg…until years later when a house fire took care of the nest egg."

"How'd you settle that claim?"

"That's just it. At the time Pollack's paintings were going for a million or better, but a toilet seat? And nobody could corroborate the story. Just hearsay and twenty dollars' worth of doughnut shaped wood with some smears of paint—I think they settled for around ten thousand."

Chet chuckled. "That's a good one." Another minute or two of bouncing along, then he said, "Bet you can't guess what I used to do. I'd a thought that my name might'a been familiar. Echols don't ring a bell?"

Dan ran the name Echols through his mental Rolodex but didn't get a match. "No, not unless you're that guy who landed the state's biggest wide-mouth bass last August. Over at Abiquiú?"

This brought a burst of laughter. "That's a good one. Not that I haven't tossed a few beauties on the shore before—in my time." The laughter at the double meaning was now almost maniacal but ended with Chet coughing, finally gasping for air, hands locking on the steering wheel as he slumped forward.

"Hey, watch out." The truck was drifting to the side of the road. Dan glanced at the inert driver, "Oh, shit." He scrambled to his knees and lunged to grab the wheel. But there was enough play in it that even a one-eighty jerk to the left didn't correct the truck's trajectory as it gathered momentum. By then it was too late to tuck his head between his knees. The truck slipped sideways in the soft gravel at the edge of the steep shoulder, clipped a cement culvert blowing the front driver-side tire, and they were airborne.

Chapter Two

"I should call mother."

"Not until you know something...Carolyn, for God's sake, sit down." Phillip folded the paper and put it beside him on an end table. Thank God he'd brought the paper with him, there was never anything up-to-date to read in a hospital waiting room.

"Well, at least I need to call Elaine. She left Saturday. She'll be in London by now. I need to catch her before she starts the tour."

"Carolyn, it's eleven o'clock at night in London. Call her in the morning."

"Phillip, just shut up. It's my brother in there...surgery, a head injury...I hate this not knowing."

"Well, you're not going to make things move any faster pacing up and down." Phillip picked the newspaper back up, shook it out, and began to read. He wasn't sure which was better—reading about the latest road-rage murder or watching his usually levelheaded wife disintegrate into hand-wringing.

"Thank God we were in Santa Fe when they brought him in. We'd still be on the road trying to get here if we'd been home." Carolyn dug into a side pocket of her purse and pulled out a phone.

Phillip nodded, but he wouldn't mind being in Roswell at the moment. You didn't manage a multimillion dollar electronics business and ranching operation long-distance. He watched his wife tap in a number on her cell. Of course, meeting with a few state legislators was important, too. He was still a very viable candidate in the governor's race and raising money was everything. Certainly the difference between winning and losing.

"I left a message with the tour office. They assured me they could reach Elaine before the group leaves for Ireland." She turned her attention back to the phone and pressed in another number.

"Good." Probably not before morning, he thought to himself. But he did understand Carolyn's need to keep busy. He might not be Dan's biggest fan, but he didn't wish anyone ill. And according to the docs, things didn't look good. He watched Carolyn with the cell to her ear walk into the hallway. Must be her mother.

It was a joke. It had to be. Elaine read the message again. A rollover accident, Dan in intensive care—head injury, broken wrist. Prognosis unknown. He'd just put her on the plane two days ago. He'd be with her on Saturday. But at gut-level she knew it wasn't a joke. Carolyn reiterated what had happened when Elaine called back.

"I'll get the first flight out."

Numb. She sleepwalked through making arrangements—British Airways to New York, American to Atlanta, Delta to Albuquerque. Done. She repacked, made her apologies to the tour director, tried to get a few hours' sleep, then, a cab to Heathrow, a window seat and thirteen plus hours to think. And not know.

It was a fledgling relationship barely three months old but with all the promise in the world. Dreams coming true, everything she could ever want. The summer had been brutal. Her husband of twenty years gets out of prison only to die in a flash flood, his body washed away. She buries an empty box, but then miraculously Eric shows up with all the bravado and pushy arrogance that she'd come to hate. But he did sign the divorce papers. Was she ready for another relationship? Yes, a hundred times, yes.

"Do you ever think about us?" She'd asked Dan when he dropped her off at Albuquerque's Sunport, then bit her lip.

Stupid thing to ask. Somewhere in some how-to-trip-'em-to-the-floor manual she'd just crossed over into the dating no-no's.

"No."

She poked him not too gently in the ribs.

He looked down at her, a smile pulling up one corner of his mouth. "If you can't take the answer, don't ask the question." Then he was laughing, taking her into his arms, nuzzling her neck. "You know the answer. Why do you ask?"

"Because suddenly I'm having separation anxiety."

"Hey, easy, I'll be with you in a week." He playfully bit her earlobe and then made a snuffing sound in her ear.

She pulled back to look at him quizzically, "What was that?"

"Puppy snuffs. Simon asked me to say good-bye."

Both laughing now, they walked into the airport holding hands. Maybe the question hadn't really been answered, but the last kiss didn't leave much to imagination and the feeling was mutual.

So where did that leave her now? She simply could not stand to lose this man. The torment of not knowing was new to her, absolutely foreign to her very being. She was so much a put-the-problem-on-the-table-and-deal-with-it type. And suddenly she had no control. But she had the time—free of having to report to work every day. She was six weeks into a year's sabbatical from the local university and maybe the trip to Ireland would be put on hold…again…but she was free to help Dan. Make certain he would heal and they would be together. There was some satisfaction in that.

She sighed. A person simply could not fly from the East to the Southwest quickly.

It was beginning to feel like she'd been in the air half her life when finally she walked into a restroom at the Sunport. Leaning across a sink, she stared in the mirror and did a quick evaluation. At forty-almost-six she was too old to bounce back quickly from a lack of sleep. Stress indelibly etched itself at the edges of her eyes and a sallowness replaced a normally creamy complexion.

She shook out a green-and-gold paisley silk scarf, pulled her thick dark hair back, wrapped the scarf around the low ponytail one time and tied it at the nape of her neck. Peach lip-gloss, a pinch to her cheeks, and time to evaluate. Better. The scarf gave her some color but the image staring back still looked drawn. Oh well. She headed for a stall, slipped into fresh jeans, a long-sleeved olive-green cotton sweater, and running shoes. Might as well be comfortable.

It seemed to take another eon to pick up her luggage, catch a shuttle to the rental lot, and complete the paperwork at the Enterprise desk, but finally she was on the road. It was already early Wednesday morning.

Christus St. Vincent Regional Medical Center was on St. Michaels Drive to the right off of St. Francis, one of Santa Fe's main drags. Carolyn had said she'd meet her in the lobby and was true to her word.

"Anything new?"

Carolyn shook her head and simply hugged her. "I'm so glad you've come. I know your being here will make a difference."

"Do they know how it happened?"

"I don't think so. Not yet anyway. The driver was killed."

"Driver?"

"Yeah, some old guy who was giving Dan a ride. Guess the Cherokee had engine trouble. Phillip called the dealer in Las Vegas and they towed it in."

"And the driver...died?"

"Crushed. The truck rolled at least three times. Dan was thrown clear but the driver wasn't as lucky."

"That's horrible. A simple Good Samaritan act leads to death. Poor man. Will I be able to see Dan now?"

"Of course, but I want you to be prepared."

"For...?"

"All the tubes, the machines—" Tears welled up and Carolyn didn't continue.

"I'll be fine."

But nothing ever really prepares someone to see a loved one incapacitated—someone who had been so vital, so strong. Elaine pushed open the door and stopped. "Oh." She couldn't seem to move but stayed rooted to a spot just inside the room. Finally, she stepped closer to the bed willing herself to breathe, take a deep breath, and then another.

"Will you be okay by yourself? I thought I'd go back to the motel."

"Yes, go…I'm sure you haven't slept much. Give my love to Phillip." Elaine hadn't taken her eyes off of Dan.

"Speaking of sleep, you look like you could use some, too. I asked them to set up a cot. But it doesn't look very comfortable."

Elaine glanced at the metal and canvas frame against the back wall stacked with folded sheets, a blanket and pillow. "Looks perfect. A slab of marble would probably work at this point."

"Then, I'm off. The floor nurses check vitals hourly so I'm not sure how much sleep you'll get. I'll let them know you're here."

"Thanks." Elaine walked to the cot and put her purse down next to her overnight bag. "Oh, I almost forgot, is Simon with you?"

"Dan knows better than to even ask—you can't turn cat people into dog-sitters. I'm sure he kenneled him, probably in that place I recommended in the North Valley, Canine Country Club. I'm pretty sure he said he was driving up through Albuquerque to drop him off.

"I'll call later. It would be great to have him with me…might make things easier." After a quick hug Carolyn was out the door.

Elaine stood at the foot of Dan's hospital bed. It was almost impossible to take it all in—the tubes, the quiet churning of machines, the drips from bottles hanging above him…but it was the stark, blanched paleness of what had been a tanned face that pulled at her heart. If she had a doubt, there was none now—Dan was struggling—maybe fighting for his life.

Bandages covered the right side of his head stretching from his ear, up and across just above his forehead. Someone had shaved his head—shearing dark brown wavy hair just barely peppered with silver. She almost smiled—that would pique his vanity. But it would grow back. Hair removal wasn't permanent. His right hand and arm were in a cast and tethered to the bed. Broken, she remembered from Carolyn's message. In addition, there was probably a lot of bruising that she couldn't see.

She bent over the bed and kissed his cheek. "Hey, I'm home. World's fastest trip almost to Ireland and back. Now, we've got to spend some time on you."

His eyes were closed, breathing assisted by machine. Elaine took his good hand and held it. Ice cold. She gently massaged it between her two hands to get some warmth into the flesh. "It'll be all right. Not easy, but all right. I think you can hear me so I'm going to keep talking." she paused to see if there was any change. None, but she continued to tell him about the trip over, what the group had done night before last, and, of course, her trip back home. "I'm going to rest now. I'll be right over there. Let me know if you need anything." She straightened. "I love you."

She was so exhausted that even a shift-change at six a.m. hadn't awakened her. But she was up by eight using the restroom behind the nurses' station to splash her face with cold water and put on enough makeup to keep from looking dead. The cotton pullover was wrinkled but wearable for another day. She should borrow a shirt from Dan to sleep in but she hadn't noticed any luggage in the room. Maybe it was being stored. There was probably only so much they'd allow in intensive care. She'd remember to ask.

But when she'd checked with a nurse, there hadn't been any luggage. Odd. But maybe not, if it hadn't been stolen; it would be in the Cherokee. After she located Simon and released him from his imposed prison, she'd call the dealership in Vegas.

She borrowed an Albuquerque phone book, pulled out her cell and began calling. Five kennels and no one had admitted a rottweiler. There was a little thought in the back of her head that she fought to keep from surfacing—one of those "what if's." What if Simon had been with Dan? What if he'd been in the accident, too? No. That was unlikely. If Dan had left the Chero-kee, he'd probably left Simon to guard the car until he could get back. Yes, that made sense. She dialed information and got the Jeep dealership in Vegas. But, no. No dog, no luggage. She waited while the service manager yelled back to the tow truck driver to make sure. Again, negative. She hung up and sat back.

Simon had been with him. She was certain of it. She pressed redial and got the exact location of where they had picked up the SUV. The Cherokee had been a mile from the accident site. If she were to go out there, she needed to go straight from Santa Fe to Las Vegas through Wagon Mound and take Highway 120 east out of town toward Roy. She closed the phone. Dan hadn't come through Albuquerque, he'd come up the back way—now she knew that Simon had been with him. Dan hadn't been near a kennel. She fought back a flicker of panic. Easy. She didn't have answers…not yet. She'd simply have to go find him.

Elaine spoke with the floor supervisor, briefly explaining the situation. She would be gone about three to four hours. She scribbled her cell number on a scrap of paper and asked that she be notified of any changes in Dan's condition. Plus, she had wanted to meet with Dan's doctors this morning, but would the nurse convey her wish for consultation time that afternoon? Perhaps, four? The whereabouts of Simon took precedence. She wasn't sure the nurse agreed with her, but she didn't say anything. Some people were animal-people, some weren't.

Elaine hurried back to Dan and told him where she was going and why. There was no response. She held his free hand to her cheek and thought he seemed warmer, but was she trying overly hard to find something positive? Probably. She promised to be back that afternoon…with Simon. She didn't bat an eye at telling him something that might be a lie. She simply would not think the worst. She would find Simon.

She backed the white Ford Flex out of the parking lot. The morning was beautiful—a true Indian summer. Down St. Francis, onto I-25 and north. Some of the prettiest scenery in all of New Mexico—Pecos, Rowe, Glorietta, on to Las Vegas.

Woodlands filled with piñon, spruce, and pine. Any other time she'd have stopped to explore. At least have lunch in the old hotel dining room in Las Vegas. So much history. So much surrounding beauty. But she was about forty or fifty miles from answers; there was no stopping now.

She drove through Wagon Mound and turned east onto Highway120, out past the high school at the edge of town. She couldn't stop her heart from beating faster. Please, please, dear God let there be a happy ending. She didn't watch her speed but the highway was deserted. She'd seen all of one car in twenty minutes. But she needed to slow down and check landmarks.

The guy at the dealership said she should go to the historical marker heading east, maybe twenty-two miles from town, and then turn around and come back west like she was backtracking to Wagon Mound. About a mile and a half, maybe two miles beyond the marker on her right, she'd see deep tracks that went over the edge this side of a culvert—right where the truck left the road. Couldn't miss it. She hated it when people said things like that.

But she didn't miss it. The ground was obviously more torn up after a wrecker had dragged the truck back up onto the highway, and the ruts stood out starkly against the bleached brown grass and gravel. She pulled to a stop, suddenly reluctant to get out. "What if," with its ugly possibility, pushed into her consciousness again. What if she found Simon's mangled body? What if she only had a body to take back? No. She absolutely would not think that way. Deep breath. Stiff upper lip or however that saying went, another breath; then, she pushed the door open and stepped out.

The wind was gusting across the almost flat grasslands and blew a strand of hair across her face. Chilly, she realized she should have worn a jacket. She moved to the edge of the incline and forced herself to look at the spot where the truck had landed marked by pieces of twisted metal and broken glass. It was eerie being at a place of death. She wondered what had gone through Dan's mind when he knew they were going to roll. And the driver. What was his reaction? Should someone erect a *descanso*? "Resting places" were celebrated along roads across the state with crosses where loved ones had been lost to traffic accidents. The idea had merit. She wouldn't mind bringing a cross out and decorating it with flowers.

The howl, part wolf, part frantic animal broke through her reverie. Oh my God, "Simon?" Then louder, "Simon?" She was yelling now, just his name, over and over as she started down the steep graveled slope, sliding, losing her footing, sitting back smartly on her rear before reaching the bottom more or less upright. And the howling never stopped but now ended in excited puppy yips of recognition. Simon was a bare twenty feet to her left almost covered by a parched bundle of grasses and weeds.

But he wasn't coming to meet her. Was he injured? Broken leg? Worse? She rushed forward and sank to the ground in front of him and then she saw them—Dan's suitcase and shaving kit. Of course. Perfectly safe because they had been unswervingly guarded by a dog who obviously believed if he minded his owner, his owner would never forsake him but would come back.

And it was then that Elaine couldn't hold back the sobs. Tears more than overdue...for a dog so trusting that he risked death by starvation, or worse, to do what he was told, tears for a man who didn't deserve what he was suffering and tears for all three of them—a makeshift family who had struggled enough and wanted nothing more than to be together and be happy.

Chapter Three

Once back to civilization, Elaine called a vet in Santa Fe, explained the situation and was squeezed in between a cat, Arnold, who needed stitches after a fight and a very fat Corgi, Emma, who was there for shots. Simon wasn't impressed with either animal—especially Emma who continually snarled at him showing some pretty impressive incisors. He turned his back, put his head in Elaine's lap and drooled his content. When it was their turn to see the vet, Simon checked out amazingly well—a crusted-over cut above his ear, not deep, a puncture wound in the middle of his head, likewise already healing, and a contusion above his left eye that had raised a lump but otherwise didn't seem to be causing a problem. A little dehydrated, but basically, a clean bill of health. A stop for a leash, a rawhide bone, kibble, doggy dishes, a bed and they were back at the hospital a couple minutes after two.

Elaine left Simon in the back of the SUV with a bowl of water, a bowl of kibble and unwrapped the rawhide bone. "This will hold you for awhile." But she didn't have to invite Simon to eat—he literally dove into the bowl. She left every window cracked three inches, grabbed Dan's shaving kit and the one piece of luggage, locked the SUV's doors, and hurried up the steps of Christus St. Vincent.

"I had no idea you were leaving for the day. You could have at least called us." Carolyn and Phillip were sitting in the waiting room. "I don't think it's a good idea to leave Dan without family support."

Elaine ignored Carolyn's peevishness and explained what had happened. Yes, she should have called but she was so caught up in Simon's whereabouts and welfare, she just didn't think. Carolyn seemed only slightly mollified.

"I've asked the doctor to join us. He's obviously running late. I think you need to hear this, too."

Elaine didn't say that she had also made an appointment to discuss Dan's prognosis for later that afternoon. She looked from Carolyn to Phillip. But he appeared to be staying out of any confrontation and had his nose in a *Wall Street Journal*, looking up only once to nod hello. Not that she expected a hug, but just a terse nod? She pulled a straight-backed chair away from the wall, put Dan's things next to it, and sat down.

The doctor kept them waiting another thirty minutes and then invited them into his office to the right of the admitting area. It wasn't personalized and seemed to be an office used by several docs for consultation. But it had a viewing screen for X-rays and there were two negatives already clipped in place.

"I'm Herb Zimmerman and you're?"

Elaine held out her hand, "Elaine Linden."

"Of course, the fiancée."

Elaine didn't correct him, probably gave her the privilege of a cot in Dan's room. And, fiancée did have a nice sound.

"Well, I'm going to start by saying, I'm guardedly optimistic. Here, I think you can see for yourselves." He turned to the X-rays. "On the left is the first picture taken Monday. Compare it to the one taken this morning. Notice the areas here and here." He traced a darkened area to the right side and along the internal edge of Dan's skull with the tip of what looked to be a very expensive gold ballpoint.

"I'll try to put this in layman's terms but stop me with any questions." Elaine thought his smile was a little condescending. "An epidural hematoma may occur with trauma to the temporal bone located on the side of the head above the ear. Aside from the fact that the temporal bone is thinner than the other skull bones—" Here he stopped and pointed to a life-sized plastic model of a head on the desk in front of him. After noting that these were the three areas he was referring to, he removed the frontal, parietal, and occipital pieces to show the brain and several arteries underneath. "This is also the location of the middle meningeal artery that runs just beneath the bone." The gold, monogrammed pen traced the area. "Fracture of the temporal bone is associated with tearing of this artery and may lead to an epidural hematoma. Or blood clot. If there's nowhere for the blood to accumulate, pressure builds quickly—without almost immediate attention, death is a certainty. There have been a couple pretty high-profile cases in the last few years.

"But I think we were lucky in Dan's case. He was able to make a 9-1-1 call before he lost consciousness, and he was airlifted to the hospital in less than an hour and a half of the accident. In addition to lucking out on the time side of things, there seems to be a series of smaller, tiny actually, epidural blood clots instead of one large hematoma pushing against brain tissue. These seldom require surgery but require monitoring. We're forty-eight hours in and I think doing remarkably well. Our guy's a fighter. We were able to remove his breathing tube this morning."

"So why is he still in a coma?" Carolyn asked exactly what Elaine was thinking.

A pause. "I'm going to say the very thing that you don't want to hear...I don't know. I suspect it will be short-lived. I see no medical reason for prolonged unconsciousness. But this is a head injury and all bets should be off. These things can surprise us."

And not in a good way, Elaine thought. "Can there be damage? Motor control, speech...?"

"Highly improbable because of the area affected."

Elaine waited, but Dr. Zimmerman didn't seem to want to elaborate; he was checking his notes. "Oh, I almost forgot. A Sheriff Howard called. He needs to interview Mr. Mahoney about the accident. I took the liberty of giving him your number and briefing him on Mr. Mahoney's condition." This directed at Elaine.

"That's fine. I'm sure with a death, there needs to be an investigation."

"Well, if there are no further questions…" He looked at each of them, "I'll excuse myself. Let me reiterate I think we have a lot to be thankful for—I really think this one is going to have a happy ending." A forced smile that didn't reach his eyes and he was gone.

Elaine finally broke the silence. "I need to walk Simon."

"I think we'll just peek in on brother dearest and then get something to eat. Can we bring you something?"

"No, I'll go out later. There's a McDonald's about a half mile from here—I think Simon has earned a cheeseburger."

Carolyn paused by the door. "I decided against trying to get Mother here. You know, it seems a bit premature. Not really knowing…"

"Besides it'd be tough to get her off that bridge-playing cruise to Barbados." Phillip chuckled. "That woman is a mover. Does Dan know she's still seeing Stanley?"

"My mother's love life is no one's concern but her own. You make it sound like she doesn't care about Dan." Carolyn turned to Elaine. "She's called every day for an update."

That would be twice, Elaine noted, but still certainly a show of concern.

"Carolyn, we need to go." Phillip opened the door, then added, "Elaine, I'm meeting with the state's attorney general this evening. A little strategy planning for the big run, you know. It's just a year away. I'd like Carolyn with me—think you can hold down the fort on your own?"

"Of course. Have a good evening. I'll call if anything changes." The "big run"—for governor, she presumed. Phillip always seemed to be in campaign mode. And Elaine was actually relieved that she wouldn't have to make small talk and put up with the pompous Phillip or listen to family squabbling. Families. She'd lost hers at an early age—mother and father in a car accident—raised by a grandmother. And she was never quite sure she didn't idealize what she'd never had. Being around Carolyn brought her back to Earth.

After a quick walk around the outskirts of the grounds, Elaine put Simon back in the car. Maybe after the cheeseburger run she'd take Simon to see Dan. It couldn't hurt and might really help. She was certain they didn't allow dogs, but the worst they could do is tell her to take him out. One of the night nurses seemed really sympathetic and had asked if she'd found Simon.

Maybe she was grasping at straws or maybe it was because the breathing tube had been removed, but Elaine thought Dan's color was a hundred percent better. Aside from the stubble of a three-day old beard, he looked…rested. Yes, that was probably the word that worked best…tanned, rested, and vital. He carried his fifty-two years extremely well. No one would guess there was a six-year difference in their ages. Prominent cheekbones, only laugh lines combined with crinkly ones around his eyes to mar an otherwise smooth face. And the longest eyelashes—why was it that men got them somehow as a birthright and women got them via Latisse—at a hundred and twenty dollars a month?

She dragged a low-slung leather and wood chair to the side of the bed and sank back. She just needed to rest a moment. Quiet time seemed a luxury. She never realized how tired she was until she sat down. She stretched long legs out in front, then turned on her side and tucked one leg underneath her. She raised slightly to glance at Dan before crooking an elbow and resting her head on her arm.

Long shadows had pushed into the room when Elaine awoke. Her watch said five-thirty. And her stomach signaled it was long past time to put some food in it. Had she even eaten that day? Not that McDonald's would be her usual choice of restaurant, but she had a furry dinner partner waiting on her, which greatly narrowed dining choices.

Simon seemed thrilled with the attention and a cheeseburger but was ecstatic when he realized he wasn't being left in the SUV after they got back to the hospital parking lot. Elaine clipped the leash in place, admonished him to be quiet, then led him around to a side door. So much for trying to sneak in, they almost literally ran into the floor nurse going off duty.

Elaine started to explain, but the nurse simply shrugged, "I don't see a thing. Just keep him quiet and in the room with you."

Easier said than done when it came to keeping Simon quiet after he'd seen Dan. Pulling him back from putting both paws on the bed, Elaine finally let him rest his head next to Dan's left hand and watched as Simon repeatedly nudged it with his nose.

"Easy, Simon. I don't think your master's quite ready to play yet." There was no way to dampen his enthusiasm and the squeaky whining seemed a little loud. Elaine walked to the door and shut it all the way. No need to attract attention. When she turned back, she caught her breath. There was a hand on top of Simon's head gently patting the big dog and stroking his ears.

"Hi." The grin was a little lopsided and the voice thick.

"Hi, yourself. I've spent a night on a lumpy cot by your side and it takes a dog to wake sleeping beauty?" It felt so good to tease again.

"Your nose probably isn't as cold or wet." Dan's laugh ended in a fit of coughing.

"Easy. How 'bout a drink of water?" At the affirmative nod, Elaine quickly put the bent straw in the glass on the side table and poured water from a small plastic pitcher. Hoisting the bed higher by stepping on the electric pedal on the floor, she held the glass while he drank. "Better?"

"What's better is seeing you." He caught her wrist with his good hand. "I'm sorry about Ireland…again."

"As we keep saying, it'll wait on us."

She bent down, kissed his bandaged forehead, and then pressed the red buzzer pinned to the bed sheet. "Need to let some people know you're back among us."

She took a protesting Simon back to the SUV but this time climbed into the backseat beside him. Dan's room was going to be crowded for awhile—adjusting or removing machines, running several tests—she'd go back in an hour.

"I think we've won this round, Buddy."

She caught herself. She'd just called Simon, Buddy, the name of her black Lab that she'd lost last summer. Was Simon a replacement? Well, as much as one animal could replace another, she guessed he was. She hugged him tighter and he didn't protest.

She'd get a motel for the night after one last check on Dan and picking up her luggage. A good night's sleep was in order and a shower—none too soon. They could talk plans in the morning if Dan was up to it. She knew him; he wouldn't take it easy but would want to continue to Wagon Mound and the investigation. She couldn't change him and what was another two or three days? Ireland would still be there next week.

Chapter Four

The woman standing in the doorway to Dan's room could have been a Bette Davis stand-in—with an Audrey Hepburn pixie haircut—in red…bright, almost neon, red. Stonewashed boyfriend jeans rolled to mid-calf, a black leather boyfriend jacket over the boyfriend white shirt, tail out, and silver ballet slippers which matched the big silver hoops at her ears—had she missed dressing for effect in middle school? And now at seventy-something, she was making up for it?

Elaine had never met Margaret Mahoney but had gotten an earful from a critical daughter and a much more forgiving son. And this was not a woman who was going to slow down anytime soon. No surprise that there was a boyfriend—maybe this Stanley had inspired the clothes. But how neat that she'd probably literally jumped ship to get here. Elaine knew Dan would be grateful.

"I'm Elaine." She held out her hand.

"Maggie Mahoney. Is a hug not appropriate?" Before Elaine could decide either way, she was wrapped in a bear-grip that belied the woman's slight frame.

"What exquisite taste you have, my darling son. She's just what I imagined." Maggie called over her shoulder and then took a step back to survey Elaine. "She's perfect for you."

Elaine knew her face was crimson, but at least it matched Dan's. He was sitting on the side of the bed in slacks and shirt, sans shoes and socks. He caught Elaine staring at his bare toes.

"Too many 'can you wiggle these' tests." He pointed to his bare feet. It was obvious that he was choosing to ignore his mother and her comments on the girlfriend. The turban-bandage on his head had been replaced by a four by four-inch square gauze pad anchored by adhesive tape on his barely showing stubble of hair. "Like it?" He pointed to his shaved head.

"It'll grow back. But, yes, I kinda do. You have a great-shaped head."

"Better than Carolyn's." His mother chimed in. "I had a much easier time giving birth to my son."

"That's a terrible thing to say." Elaine noticed Carolyn sitting on the cot in the corner, but no Phillip. She vaguely remembered that mother and daughter were a little challenged when it came to getting along. Guess this was proof.

"So, when are they going to give you your shoes and spring you from this place?" Elaine walked to the bed and gave Dan a peck on the cheek. Funny how even at her age, she was self-conscious in front of Mom.

"By noon if they keep their promise. I've convinced them I can recoup just as well on the outside and simply check in every once in awhile."

"How long will you be under observation?"

"A month."

Elaine tried not to react. A month? Here in northern New Mexico? Not Ireland? She realized Dan was watching her, and she quickly smiled hoping he hadn't noticed her hesitation. "Great. I'm glad they're being careful."

"Damn." The expletive came from the cot where Carolyn had dumped her purse and was pawing through its contents. "I must have left my phone in the car. Phillip's expecting a call—needs to know when to pick us up. It's a long drive; I don't want to get home too late."

The "us" must include Mom, Elaine thought. That would make sense; she was probably going to stay with them for a while.

"Here's mine." Maggie fished in a pocket of her jacket and handed over a snappy looking iPhone in a red case.

"Thanks."

The shriek caused Dan to hop off the bed and take a step toward Carolyn as the iPhone skittered across the floor.

"What the—"

"Oh my God. I can't believe it." Carolyn looked like the wind had been punched out of her as she steadied herself by slumping against the foot of Dan's bed. "My own mother. There's no excuse for this kind of lewd behavior." Spittle sprayed from the corner of Carolyn's mouth. "What if someone found you by the side of the road…found your phone—"

"Ah, Carolyn, always the melodramatic. It's called sexting, my dear. And that's a picture of my birthday present." Maggie seemed barely able to keep a straight face. "I would have assumed you'd seen something like that before. I do have a grandson. But, of course, I could be wrong."

Elaine bent down and retrieved the errant phone and there it was—the offensive picture, a stiffy with a bow on it. Stanley's, she presumed. She handed the phone to Dan.

"Hey, I've given that sort of gift before." Dan sneaked a sideways look at Elaine. Elaine quickly looked away biting her bottom lip to contain the laughter.

"You're not seventy-plus and you didn't advertise it. What happened to decorum? Don't encourage her. This is juvenile behavior. The kind of behavior that could wreck Phillip's chances to lead this great state."

"I don't think it's going to make the front page of the *Albuquerque Journal*." Dan sighed. Carolyn always wore him out—her view of the world and his had never meshed.

"Exactly. Just a little harmless fun." Maggie took back her phone and dropped it in a pocket.

Elaine held out her cell to Carolyn and couldn't resist pointing to the wallpaper, "Sunflowers. Stems covered."

Carolyn glared at her, lips pulled into a straight line. "Not funny, but thanks."

Conversation was strained until Phillip got there. Then, there were assurances of all getting together again before Maggie had to go back to Scottsdale. She was here for a week and had already said she wanted to come back to Santa Fe to shop—under much happier circumstances, she added when Dan was back in the peak of health. They'd keep in touch but maybe midweek next week? A quick hug for Elaine and more comments about how she was so "right."

Finally the room was empty, only Dan and Elaine left. A crisis averted? Or would Maggie pay for her indiscretions? Carolyn sulking, taking Phillip aside to enlist a comrade-in-arms. Elaine didn't think for one minute that Maggie couldn't take care of herself, but she didn't envy her long ride by car with the two of them.

"I like your mother."

"Me, too. I hope she'll survive to old age in spite of her daughter."

Any further discussion was interrupted by Dr. Zimmerman pushing open the door. "Well, looks like you're anxious to get out of here. I have to say you've done a real turnaround in four days. Almost like new. I'm a little reluctant to let you go, but I agree with the general populace—you can get sick in places like this." His laugh was more of a chortle. "But what I'm saying is if you follow some rules, I think you'll be fine—shall we go over them?"

He turned to Elaine. "I don't want our guy here to overexert—no foot races or *mountain climbing*." He looked meaningfully at Elaine, then chuckled and turned back to Dan. "Rest, rest, and then some more rest. Just take things easy. There's still a little swelling. No driving until I say so. Keep the bandages dry, and the cast, only take a painkiller if you absolutely have to—you probably know the drill. I'll need to see him Saturday morning." This directed again at Elaine. "Make an appointment on the way out." He turned back at the door, "I like happy endings—don't disappoint me. Take care of yourself." And with that he was gone.

"Let's get out of here."

"Shoes an' socks?"

"Try the bottom drawer under the TV."

◇◇◇

"Where to? Are you hungry?" Elaine pulled the Flex out from under the hospital's covered entrance to Emergency. Dan had refused a wheelchair ride from his room, much to the consternation of the floor nurse. And he didn't need help climbing into the SUV's front seat, even though Elaine saw the grimace before he settled back.

"Yeah. But I'm not thinking restaurant. Maybe back to the motel?"

"And that wouldn't be overexerting? I thought Dr. Zimmerman's reference to 'mountain climbing' was just a euphemism for sex."

"Can't let Stanley get ahead of me...figuratively speaking."

He grinned and Elaine couldn't help thinking how terrific it was to have him back—innuendo and all. The grin was the same, a little lopsided, infectious, probably hadn't changed any since fifth grade. The bandage gave him a rakish look—like he'd been in a really bad fight but had won. Come to think of it, that wasn't too far from the truth, she decided.

She grinned back. "Sounds like a plan."

She'd chosen a motel on Cerrillos Road—plain, not too expensive but it took pets. She carried the luggage inside while Dan turned on the shower. She looked the other way when Simon hopped onto the queen-sized bed closest to the window. There was a dog who understood creature comforts. She filled his water bowl and put it under the vanity's counter. She wiggled out of jeans and pulled the shirt over her head, dropped the silk undies on top of the pile and headed toward the bathroom.

"Glad to see you're following doctor's orders."

"Have to. Won't get this thing off for awhile." He held up his right hand with the cast already encased in a plastic bag sealed off with two rubber bands.

"Kind of a sexy outfit for the shower. But you're missing a bow." Elaine pointed.

"Ah, you'd just tell Carolyn. After you." Dan held the shower door open.

The shower felt good but it felt even better to just lean against Dan, her arms around his back, her head on his shoulder. He'd removed the bandage from his head and she could see the ten or so stitches at a diagonal above his right ear. But it was the bruising that made her pull back. Most of his right side was a dark blue-black beginning that attractive slide from puce to puke-green that denotes healing.

"Hurt?" She lightly touched a bluish-green welt on his shoulder.

"Looks a lot worse than it really is. I took the brunt of it on my right side—went through the windshield at an angle and collided headfirst with something."

"You were lucky."

"Yeah."

He bent down and kissed her, pulled back, and murmured, "God I've missed you," before pulling her into him again. "What if I wanted to take a rain check on that mountain climbing and just take a nap? Would my reputation be ruined?"

"I'd say that Superman was probably human." She kissed him again. "I'm planning on having lots of second chances."

They slept until four, ordered in, and watched a movie on HBO.

"I know it's probably back to work tomorrow." Elaine wasn't quite ready to give up having Dan all to herself. She slipped another piece of pizza out of the box between them and sneaked the crust to Simon.

"Yeah, I need to look up that sheriff—Howard didn't you say?"

"Mora County. His office's in Las Vegas."

"I'll give him a call in the morning."

The gold lettering on the door said Sheriff Lewis Howard. Dan paused, then knocked. He had been dreading this. Obviously, he hadn't known the old man who had given him a ride but still, he certainly hadn't wished him harm. It hadn't been any solace to know that asthma had brought on the coughing fit, but being pinned by the truck had killed him. Dan wished he'd been able to do something.

He was startled by the yell "Come in." It certainly didn't lack in volume. The man who got up from behind the desk was a big man—not fat, just a gym-induced solidness that made him intimidating. Something from the brick-shithouse genre that seemed to get people hired in this sort of job out here. He instantly thought of a certain lawman in Tatum.

But this man seemed to have some things going for him, according to the pictures on the wall. The sheriff with grade-schoolers at a soccer tournament handing out a trophy, sheriff at the fairgrounds crowning Miss Mora County, sheriff with a group of uniforms standing in front of new cruisers. Must be about ten years his senior, Dan thought. Ought to be staring retirement in the face. He idly wondered if someone like Lewis Howard would stay close or take off for a cabana by the sea. Dan was pretty sure he knew what he'd do in the same situation. It was tough to adjust to one-horse towns. He dreaded the "where should we live?" discussion that he'd have to have with Elaine one of these days.

"Have any trouble finding me?"

"No, your directions were great." Dan shook hands, took the proffered chair in front of the desk and waited for Sheriff Howard to return to his.

"First of all, I want to say I'm happy to see you up and around. There could have been another outcome."

"I'm all too aware of that. I was sorry to hear about Chet Echols."

"Yeah, his eightieth birthday was coming up in February. Shame. He had some good years left. Sheriff Howard blew his nose on a red square of material that he pushed back into a center drawer of the desk. Dan ruled out any emotion in favor of allergies. He waited while the man took a small spiral-bound notebook out of another drawer.

"Let's get started by you telling me what happened that afternoon."

"Anything in particular?"

"How 'bout lapse of time from when the Cherokee gave out and Chet showed up with a ride."

"Probably not more than five minutes. One-thirty to one thirty-five. I considered myself lucky to get a ride so quickly. There's a lot of empty highway out there."

The officer looked up from his notes. "You'd never met Mr. Echols before?"

Dan shook his head, "Funny, Chet seemed to think I should know him. That his name should ring a bell."

"It didn't?"

"Still doesn't. Who was he anyway?"

"An old stunt driver—right out of Hollywood. Back in the forties and fifties, he was the best. Lots of articles on him over the years…enjoyed some minor celebrity. Big in this part of the country—born in Roy. Performed in state fairs until a couple years ago. There aren't a lot of celebrities from out this way unless you include Tommy McDonald. Remember the running back for the Philadelphia Eagles? There was a deserving Hall of Famer if there ever was one. A real Roy High School Longhorn. Lived up to all our expectations."

Dan was sitting forward, "Wait, you said Chet was a stunt driver? Just don't tell me his specialty was rolling cars."

"Actually, it was." The sheriff paused to study Dan. "I don't want to suggest any conclusions that might be false—premature, that is. But let me just level with you and tell you what we've got."

Something told Dan this wasn't going to be good, but he leaned forward, the elbow of his good arm on the corner of the desk.

"About a tenth of a mile past the accident site coming back toward town, the ambulance driver reported seeing a ramp—"

"What kind of a ramp?"

"The kind you drive a vehicle up onto in order to roll it."

"You're saying if he hadn't rolled the truck when he did by passing out, he would have a little ways down the road anyway?"

"It appears so."

"Suicide?"

"We don't think so."

Dan waited. What a weird twist. He was thinking how nervous Chet had seemed. Preoccupied would be the best word. "Suicide makes sense," he said, more to himself.

"Until you realize he appeared to be following you, possibly waiting for the cut hoses on the Cherokee to strand you."

"Come on. Cut hoses? You're saying I was set up to be maimed or killed?"

"That's certainly one interpretation we're considering." Sheriff Howard got up, walked to an office fridge and took out a Diet Dr. Pepper. "Anything?" He pointed to the fridge but Dan shook his head.

"You stop for gas in Roy?"

"No, just lunch."

"Eat at the Chill an' Grill?"

"Yeah."

"Remember where you parked?"

"On the street, along the east side and a couple doors down." He waited as the sheriff sat down and made a note, then popped the tab on the Dr. Pepper and took a long swallow. "Guess I don't have to ask if you noticed anything suspicious or unusual?"

"Nothing. Empty street when I came out of the restaurant. But why me, as the saying goes?"

"I think you'll need to help me with that."

Dan sat back. He was drawing a blank. It made no sense. Unless the investigation—someone wanting him out of there or to slow him down…afraid he might find something. Plenty of people knew he would be in town on Monday—bank personnel and his client, for starters. But who knew he'd be coming along the back way? Up from an early morning meeting in Hobbs? And at that particular time?

"It could be work-related. I have no way of knowing. I haven't had a chance to even begin the investigation."

"And that would be investigating the robbery at Wagon Mound? The bank over there?"

"United Life & Casualty," Dan held out a card, "insured a necklace that was lost in the robbery…for a Ms. Gertrude Kennedy. Yes, that's what brought me out this way."

Sheriff Howard shook his head, "Whole thing's weird—you hear how they did it?" Dan nodded. "Got Feds swarming all over the place. But I don't think anyone's come up with any answers. Not yet, anyway."

Dan remembered that Chet had thought no one would. Thought it was an inside job. But Dan decided he'd just keep that tidbit to himself. He looked up to find Sheriff Howard staring at him.

"Anything else you want to tell me about that afternoon?"

Dan paused, "The old guy seemed nervous, kept looking behind him. He was apologetic having to wire the door shut on my side. If it hadn't been for that, I might have had a chance to jump clear." Dan left the impact of that fact hanging in the air and changed tactics. "But he seemed proud of the old truck… even in its condition. Said he was the original owner—"

"He said what?"

"To quote him exactly, he said they'd been together since birth…I think he meant the truck's. I took the truck to be a fifty-something Ford—hard to tell, there were some mismatched parts and others, like the bumpers, just missing."

Sheriff Howard opened a manila envelope and shook the contents onto his desk. It looked like a bunch of receipts and maybe a bank statement, Dan thought.

"When we towed the truck in, one of the guys who works in our impound area recognized it, or I should say parts of it. You're right, the truck was a composite—built from scratch at a chop shop here in Vegas and not that long ago. I think they started with the chassis and that was about it."

Dan let out a low whistle, "Who paid for that?"

"Good question. Chet himself, according to these receipts, but a Social Security check doesn't cover that kind of work. Finished product came to over ten thousand dollars."

"What about where it was done? What do the shop guys say?"

"That's another tough one. Shop's owned and run by bikers—not your Honda touring class types, if you're following me, but a few one-percenters."

"One-percenters?"

"Yeah, the hard core. Ninety-nine percent of all bikers in the U.S. are law-abiding citizens...then there's the one-percenters."

"And you're saying the chop shop is operated by...outlaws?"

The shrug said more than words. "We've adopted a 'live and let live' attitude. Everybody calls it a chop shop, but that's just because they ride choppers. I honestly don't think they're up to anything illegal. I'm a little understaffed to hassle them—besides, in twenty years we've never had a problem."

"Until now."

"If they're even involved."

"Have you talked to them?"

"Yeah. According to Jeeter Ferris—he's the owner—payment was made in advance. He gave some guy an estimate over the phone...just a ballpark...and then the rest of his dealings were with Chet. I understand Jeeter's boys at the shop did all the work."

"So you're saying they built the truck ground up with Chet giving directions?"

"Something like that. I guess Chet had some pretty narrow specs he wanted them to follow. But he wasn't lying—he and that truck had been together since birth."

"Sounds like he'd done it before."

"No doubt. I should also mention that Chet had ten thousand dollars in his bank account. Don't know if it was part of some kind of payoff or unused truck money. But his grandson says he knows his granddad didn't have anything extra...nothing tucked away...lived from payday to payday like most of the community."

"When was the deposit made?"

"Originally twenty thousand was put in first week in August. Increments of ten."

"August? More than a month before the heist? Except for the cut hoses, it pretty much rules out having anything to do with me—no way they'd know there'd even be an insurance investigation—no way they knew the heist would be successful."

"'Course that tunnel coulda been half finished by then... or more. Personally I think that tunnel'd been there for awhile. But it's a puzzler, for sure." Sheriff Howard paused. "Two many unanswered questions. I'm not trying to tell you your business, but I'd be careful. I'll keep you in the loop and would appreciate the same." Sheriff Howard leaned forward to shake hands.

Meeting over. Dan had a distinct feeling it wouldn't be the last with the Mora County sheriff.

He took the elevator down to ground level and walked out into the sunshine. Elaine was waiting for him about a hundred feet away and he had just that amount of time to decide what he wanted to tell her. Keep the details to himself or run the risk of alarming her?

"How'd that go?" She closed the novel and put it in the console as he climbed into the passenger's seat.

"Not sure. I think I left with a lot more questions than I had going in."

"Such as?"

He took a breath. Didn't he believe that honesty was the best policy in relationships? Well, usually anyway. But he found he wanted to share. Maybe she needed to be careful, too. And that made him angry. If anything happened to Elaine—

"Dan, what's wrong?" She'd turned to face him squarely.

And then he started at the beginning—didn't leave anything out about Chet and the truck and the rollover, ending finally with what Sheriff Howard had said.

Elaine was silent.

"Thoughts?"

"I'm canceling the *descansos*."

"What?"

"Not important. I'd just thought of honoring the spot where this Chet died. You know, one of those roadside crosses and some plastic flowers. But that was before I knew he attempted murder. What are you going to do?"

Dan flinched. Strong word "murder" but true, he guessed. "Be careful but not let anything that's happened get in the way of the investigation. Go in with an open mind."

"I thought you'd say that. And the first step, Sherlock?"

"I take it Watson is going to stick it out?"

"As long as you need a driver." She leaned across the console and kissed him. "And maybe even longer."

"Okay. I'll buy that," He grinned. "I guess we need to go into Wagon Mound this afternoon. See if you can find us something to rent for two or three weeks and I'll look up Ms. Gertrude Kennedy and get this show on the road."

It didn't take long to check out of the motel, gather up clothes, Simon's food and bowls, and repack the SUV. This was turning into quite the adventure and he could do with less of that. Still anything was better than the hospital.

Chapter Five

Wagon Mound was laid out like a rogue Monopoly board—Wood Avenue, Railroad Avenue, mixed with Stonewood, Bond, and Rich streets connecting to Park Avenue with a smattering of Aguilar and Romero streets thrown in. All this beneath the mammoth natural stone edifice of a Conestoga wagon pulled by a six-up team of oxen. Well, this last demanded a little imagination but the image was probably apt for one of the last great landmarks on the Santa Fe Trail.

Dan read out loud from a guide he'd picked up at LJM's Travel center—one of two gas station/convenience stores at the edge of town. "'At this very point, travelers a hundred years ago and then some could cross from the Cimarron cutoff to Fort Union. This arm of the Trail was called the Mountain Branch. In 1850 ten men riding guard on the express mail wagon were killed by a band of Jicarilla Apaches.'" Dan looked up. "Sounds like it wasn't far from here—where I-25 passes along the edge of town. Impressive. This is a real slice of the old wild west."

Elaine didn't comment but eased the SUV across the highway and turned right at the first street, Railroad Avenue. Dan continued, "Looks like the town started out as a railroad center—Atchison, Topeka and the Santa Fe—been serving the ranchers in this area since 1881." Dan turned a page, "Listen to this. 'At the turn of the last century, this area produced the bulk of the pinto beans grown in the state. One Hijinio Gonzales started the festival by cooking up beans in wash boilers behind the schoolhouse to feed the community. There's been a Bean Day celebration ever since.'"

Dan put the brochure on the dash and looked at the town as Elaine drove. It was obvious that it'd seen better times. He was struck by how many empty and boarded up homes and businesses there were. Old adobes stood crumbling in the sun next to neat little white houses with bright metal siding and roofs. One old building on a hill could have been a school or even a hospital but was now just a three-walled, cavernous shell with warnings of do not trespass.

Main Street, if that's what it was, consisted of several businesses—all boarded up. "I haven't seen a restaurant, have you?"

Elaine shook her head. "No grocery store, no restaurant, no commerce at all—but there's a great-looking high school and middle school on the way out of town. And I think I've found a boarding house—at least there was a rooms for rent sign in front of that two-story adobe on the corner."

"I'd like to take a look at the bank, Nolan and Railroad avenue… sort of get my bearings before I chat with Ms. Kennedy."

"Nolan's coming up on the right."

Elaine turned onto the street and stopped opposite the First Community Bank of Wagon Mound. She put the SUV in park and they stared through the windshield.

"Quaint." Elaine offered.

Dan looked at the L-shaped building of not more than eight hundred to a thousand square feet. Its front, probably a painted-over brick façade, sported plaster emblems like miniature coats of arms on every column—everything a solid tan, the density of color that only repeated thick coats of paint could give.

The building was flat-roofed of a period known as New Mexico colonial and probably was adobe, all but the façade. The wooden numerals eight-zero-one were attached to the building above the door and a repeat of the address in stick-on numerals on the glass in the door itself. There were no windows along the side that faced the alley, but seven foot tall windows graced the front street entrance, each encased in dark brown heavy wooden frames complete with a dark brown painted-over transom above each one. The architecture was definitely early 1900s.

"Looks vulnerable," Dan concluded. Even if the walls were solid other than the front—and he suspected they were—there was enough glass across the front to warrant an open invitation to unwanted visitors.

"But didn't you say the robbers tunneled in? Through some cellar?"

Dan nodded. "I don't see a cellar from here. Let's drive down the alley and around to the south side."

It always surprised him to find an alley in the Southwest. Alleys were a Midwestern phenomena—dirt "streets" that divided a block of houses and were fronted by backyards instead of front porches. Usually the place for garbage containers and utilities—poles and meters. And, come to think of it, cellars were not run-of-the-mill out here—another Midwestern touch.

The cellar in question on the west side of the bank was still marked off by tape. From their vantage point it looked like any cellar in a vintage home from Kansas to Indiana. Just odd to find one in New Mexico and underneath a bank. Wasn't that some kind of double-dare invite to try to get inside? Didn't seem like it'd been too difficult to hoodwink the bank's guards…or guard…there might only be one; he'd have to check—get an interview.

And he'd visit the bank later, but he'd bet anything that there was a marble counter upstairs, and an area for a couple of tellers all behind tasteful turn-of-the-century, fancy, black wrought-iron caging. Then the steel door with a combination lock leading to the room of safe deposit boxes. A couple offices, maybe a free-standing station with deposit slips, pens, and other paper necessities and that would be about it. That and the small walk-in vault, triple-reinforced and double-locked, needing a key and a combination for entry—the one the robbers didn't bother with. Just the necessities. A bank like a thousand others that appeared out this way a hundred years ago.

"Seen enough?" Elaine slipped the car in gear.

"Yeah. Think you can find Romero Street? Don't want to keep Ms. Kennedy waiting."

Elaine pulled up in front of a nicely kept two-story adobe with what looked like a fresh coat of earth-colored brown stucco. White flower boxes below each of four front windows overflowed with purple, pink, and white petunias—attesting to the fact that there hadn't been a hard frost yet this fall. A white picket fence maybe three feet high stretched across the front and around both sides and sported a sparkling white gate right in the center of the cement walkway that led to the front door.

"You didn't tell me you were visiting the gingerbread family. This is too cute—out of some book I read as a child."

"Hey, I have a good idea—why don't you come with me? Might make Ms. Kennedy feel a little safer."

"Safer? Just because her interviewer is black and blue and swathed in bandages?" Elaine turned to look at him. "You know, maybe I should."

The front door opened before they were halfway up the walk. The two women framed by the doorway were like peas in a pod—one younger but already a carbon-copy of what was probably her mother, the older with curly white hair, checked green-and-white wool flannel skirt, and matching green sweater, a starched white apron securely around her waist. The other woman, with graying brown locks just as curly but tucked under a scarf pulled back and tied at the nape of her neck, wore a solid tan wool skirt with a dark brown sweater over a crisp long-sleeved white blouse. And they were both as cute as their house, Dan decided.

"Oh my goodness, just look at you. When your office called to reschedule, they said you'd had a bit of a mishap." The older woman stepped back to let them enter. "This is my daughter, Penelope, and I'm Gertie. You can call me Gertie. I prefer to use the shortened version of my middle name—my first name being Cornelia." She paused and looked up at him over the silver rims of half-glass readers. "Well, what would you do? It was either Gertie or Corny."

"I see. That does make for an easy decision." Dan chided himself but for all the world this was exactly how he pictured Mrs. Claus—well, had pictured her as a child when Santa and his wife had been real entities in his life. "And this is Elaine Linden... my right hand until I get my own back." He held up the cast.

"And to make introductions complete, this is Bitsy." Gertie pulled a tiny long-coated Chihuahua from an apron pocket. Bitsy had the longest eyelashes Dan had ever seen on a dog. It crossed his mind that they might not be real. If a dog could wear a rhinestone tiara—which she was—why not false eyelashes? Then at the urging of her owner, Bitsy held out her paw for a shake.

He felt like an idiot but took the tiny paw between index finger and thumb giving it the tiniest wiggle up and down. "How do you do, Bitsy." All in the line of work, he guessed, but he swore the dog looked smug and withdrew her paw after the shake, dismissing him.

"Do you have a dog?" Gertie tucked Bitsy in the crook of her arm.

"A wonderful dog." Elaine spoke up and then briefly filled them in on Simon's heroics after the accident, how he defied death to guard his master's belongings. Mother and daughter nodded solemnly.

"That's such a wonderful story." Penelope patted Elaine's arm, "You must love him very much."

"Yes, I do." She caught Dan's eye above the woman's head. "Very much." Let Dan figure out if she was referring to him or Simon.

"Let's sit in the dining room. I have some pictures that your employer wanted you to see." Gertie led them to a claw-and-ball-footed round table and waited while each of them pulled out a chair and sat down. "The necklace belonged to my grand-mother—my father's mother. He gave it to my mother on their wedding day." She picked up two pictures and handed them to Dan. "This one simply showcases the piece—it's the one we've used for insurance purposes but really doesn't do it justice."

Dan studied the eight by ten glossy. The necklace was spectacular—sapphire and diamond "drops," some ten in number with a two-inch drop in the center. The sapphire in this drop was at least five carats and heart-shaped—looking like a faceted, fluffy, deep blue pillow. All drops were anchored to a platinum chain with alternating bezel-set sapphires and diamonds—not one stone less than three-quarters of a carat. The earrings were two and half-inch drops on posts, each with two-carat center stones to match.

"Beautiful." He handed the picture to Elaine and gave his attention to the other photo. Here, the necklace adorned a stunning young woman in her wedding dress. Even with the sepia tint to the photo, he could see the grandness of the necklace.

"And here's Mother on the deck of the *Titanic*." Gertie slipped another eight by ten from the pile. "You know, she kept that necklace under her clothes all the time—pinned to her corset. She was so afraid of losing it…and to think that now…"

A stifled sob caused Penelope to lean forward with a hand lightly placed on her mother's arm. "Mother, we need to have faith and trust that Mr. Mahoney will be able to find it."

Dan didn't correct her, couldn't quite bring himself to tell them that an investigator only concerned himself with the "how." How something was lost and how remuneration would be paid—not much more. He had reason to believe that every jewel in the necklace had been popped out, bagged, graded, and dispersed—most of the larger stones probably weren't even in the country. And the platinum, a melted mass already sold.

"The necklace was made in 1900 by Tiffany. My grandfather helped to design it. My father inherited it when my grandmother died, and in 1912, gave it to my mother—his wedding gift along with the fateful honeymoon. Mother was twenty-two—Father's second wife—he was ten years older. But they both survived the *Titanic*. Both among the seven hundred survivors. Father, of course, because he had a clubfoot. Any man with a disability was placed in the boats with women and children. I thought for years that my father felt guilty that he'd survived. Hastened his death, I know it did."

"Mother, you can't know that, but it would seem natural for grandfather to grieve with so many lost—over twenty-two hundred, wasn't it?" Penelope pushed back from the table. "What depressing thoughts—time to liven this party up. Would everyone like a cup of tea? It's ready to go."

Elaine got up, too. "Let me help." She followed Penelope to the kitchen.

Tea turned out to be quite the ceremony with brownish lumps of natural sugar and a plate of assorted sweets—all diminutive and looking like tooth-rattlers, Dan thought. Napkins were small with frilly edges and initials stitched in one corner, white embroidery against the slight yellowing of old linen. Dan's body was beginning to suffer sitting on hard, unrelenting wood. He shifted his weight to his left side and balanced the eggshell-thin china in his left hand. So far, so good. No spills, nothing to apologize for. But there was a lot to be said for a good cold bottle of Bud. A lot easier to grab hold of, for one thing.

"And I didn't come along for another thirteen years…" Gertie seemed to be on a roll or just enjoying an audience for what must be oft-told stories. Dan tuned back in, then shifted again, but never lost eye-contact as she continued. "In those days I was considered a late-in-life baby. My mother was thirty-five and my father forty-five. I wouldn't be late-in-life today. Did you read about that woman in her sixties giving birth? Sixties. Why, I can't imagine."

"Nor can I." Elaine filled tea cups, placing a beautifully ornate white china pot with gold trim on a trivet in the center of the table before sitting. "This is delightful. Is the pound cake homemade?"

"My specialty." Penelope appeared to blush, Dan thought. And the little tea party was "delightful," but he needed to guide Gertie back to the particulars—ask the questions he'd need for the investigation.

"Always hate to mix business with pleasure," he gestured toward Gertie with his tea cup, "but I need to double-check some details."

"Oh my, I have been rattling on. Of course, you just ask ahead. I have no secrets."

Usually when people said that, a big red flag flipped up, but not with Gertie. She was leaning toward him with rapt attention—and the guileless expression of the perfectly innocent.

"How often did you remove the necklace from the bank's safe deposit box?"

"Well, I only took it out for cleaning. And that was on a strict schedule—I never missed a date."

"And that was how often?" Gentle prodding but the old gal was eighty-five. She'd earned the right to have some lapses.

"Oh my, I forgot to say…let me get the calendar then I won't be telling fibs." Gertie walked to another room, an office Dan thought, and brought back a wall calendar showing various costumed poses of the Taco Bell Chihuahua. She backtracked to August and placed an index finger on the tenth.

"There. Notation reads…'removed from vault for cleaning.'"

"How long did you keep it out for these periodic cleanings?"

"Not long. Two days usually. This time I was running low on the ammonia mixture and had to order a bottle. I hadn't realized this when I'd gotten the necklace out."

"So, it was here longer than usual?"

"Yes."

Dan made a few notes in a forced shorthand he hoped he'd be able to figure out later. It would have been much easier if his left hand had gotten mangled instead of the right.

"Did you wear it anywhere while it was here?"

"Oh, my goodness, no. Why I'd be so nervous that I wouldn't enjoy doing anything. I wouldn't even wear it around the house."

"When it was here, where did you keep it?"

He thought for a minute she wasn't going to answer. A frail, veined hand flew to her mouth, fingers brushing her lips. She sought Penelope's okay before answering. At her daughter's nod, she began, "Well, it's deceptively simple really. We'd thought of putting it in a safe but, you know, that only advertises that you have something to put in it."

That's one interpretation, Dan thought. But under the circumstances probably a wise choice.

"So, we put it in the Barbasol can."

"I'm not following."

"Just give me a minute." Gertie pushed back from the table again and was gone longer this time. Dan slipped another lemon tart onto his plate and picked it up with his fingers—forks and left hands were a dangerous mix.

"Here we go." Gertie reentered the room, walked to the table and placed a black- and-red striped can of Barbasol in front of him. "Remember when these were so popular? Penny and I couldn't decide whether to get the Comet cleanser or the Barbasol." With that, she twisted off the top to reveal an empty can—someone's idea of the perfect hiding place.

Keep it under the sink in the bathroom and no one will ever suspect…yeah, right. Two little old ladies with a can of Barbasol—did they even make the stuff anymore? He was saved having to comment by Gertie continuing, "…you understand, of course, that this was just an overnight fix, so to speak. And I can't think of a time when either one of us was away from the house overnight."

Like burglaries didn't happen during the day. Dan sighed and decided not to enlighten them—no point doing it now.

"Do you remember when you returned the necklace to the bank?"

"Let's see." More checking the calendar. "This time—because of needing extra cleaner—I kept it out a full week."

"And the date you returned it?"

"August seventeenth. Oh dear, let me see…That's not quite right. I took the necklace down to the bank but the door to the safe deposit box room had been removed. Some problem with the hinges not releasing when the combination was entered. I had to bring the necklace back home and didn't put it back in the bank until the following morning. The bank called to let me know when the vault was ready." Gertie looked at the calendar. "Oh my, look here, I forgot to note the corrected date. But it would have been August eighteenth."

Dan made a notation and slipped the notebook back in his shirt pocket. "Anything else you can remember? Anything that you'd like to add?"

"I can't think of a thing. This is a very quiet town, Mr. Mahoney, very quiet and safe. What happened is such a shock. Why, never in a million years would I have guessed something like this would happen in Wagon Mound."

They said their good-byes. Elaine made over Bitsy and the small dog seemed to relish the new attention. Dan couldn't bring himself to perform another doggy handshake.

"I'd like to find that boardinghouse before it gets too late." Elaine pulled away from the curb and took a right at the next corner.

"What do you think?"

"About the Kennedys? There's absolutely no doubt that they're being truthful. I really feel sorry for Gertie. Eighty-five and something so precious is stolen. Certainly isn't fair."

Dan passed on making any comments about fairness, and yes, he felt badly for Gertie, too. Life at eighty-five shouldn't be complicated.

Elaine found the boardinghouse—huge compared to the buildings around it—situated on a corner maybe two blocks up from Railroad Avenue. Slick, tan stuccoed walls and tiny windows gave some hint of its age, but again, it was one of the town's better kept relics.

"Be back in a minute."

He handed her his travel plastic. United Life & Casualty was a good company to work for—all things considered. They didn't scrimp on travel expenses and he couldn't think of a time that an expenditure had been questioned. Some good things come with seniority.

Dan watched as Elaine turned halfway up the walk to wave. He was a lucky man. Beautiful woman, great companion. And he hoped that one of these days the vertigo he suffered from just bending over would go away. Wouldn't impress anyone if he swooned in the middle of sex. He continued to watch until

she disappeared inside. Then it was back to business. He took
out the notebook and began a list by writing *Gertie—interview,
completed,* followed by the date and time.

Item two was another interview, this time scheduled with the
bank president—he'd try for Monday maybe ten in the morning.
He'd also need to tour the robbery site. Not sure how long all that
would take. Then tentatively either Tuesday or Wednesday, he'd
interview the other safe deposit box holders who had also lost
items in the robbery. And he'd stop by the chop shop and talk
with Jeeter...Ferris? Sounded right but he'd check the last name.

He was purposefully leaving the FBI until last. Dan wanted
to form a picture of events on his own. It was always better to
compare notes with these guys than to sit there taking them.
Usually they were pretty helpful—he hoped that hadn't changed.
The mutual back-scratching was important in his business and
had worked to his advantage before.

Then there were other things maybe less in importance...
such as a talk with Chet's grandson, a call to the Hobbs office
to see who knew when he was heading out that morning after
the meeting and what route he would be taking...and maybe a
look around Roy. Tough to check on cut hoses at this late date,
but you never knew. If there was one thing thirty years in the
business had taught him—never, never second-guess. And to
drop the word *assume* from your vocabulary.

He looked up as Elaine opened the door and slipped into
the driver's seat.

"Here we are." She dangled an old-fashioned actual door key
from an index finger and handed him his card and a receipt.
"Three weeks, five hundred dollars a week paid in advance—I
think four hundred of that is because of Simon—a kitchenette,
queen-sized bed, all linens, private bath...it's really not half bad."

"Sounds great. Actually, United Life will think they're getting off cheap."

"And there it is." She leaned forward to point out the windshield. "On the front corner, private outside stairs, and a side
yard for Simon."

Dan didn't say anything but outside stairs translated to easy entry…of course, with Simon the warning system was no fail. And he'd just make sure he took his computer with him when he wasn't in the room. "Looks great. Where do we park?"

"Over there on the street. Our landlady's name is Mrs. Patrick. Ina Patrick. But she's not one you'd call by her first name. Nice enough but really no nonsense. I had to tell her about Simon's heroics just to get him in."

Simon's humans seemed to be milking his one good deed for all it was worth. Dan glanced at the dog who was sitting up watching their every move. Well, there had been other good deeds. Dan wasn't being fair and if this one got them in the door, then it was worth it. Simon needed a little praise.

"So what do you think, boy? Think you can be quiet and not spill your food?" At this Simon scooted forward to put his head between them.

"Let me get the car parked and get our bags upstairs. Then I'll run back to the convenience store and pick up something to eat."

"I hate to tell you this, but the choices were pizza, frozen hoagies, ham and cheese frozen pockets, egg biscuit and sausage sans and…oh yes, corn dogs."

"And the winner is?" Pretend drum roll—Dan doing a staccato series of taps on the counter ending in a flourish before realizing how much his right wrist ached.

"Pizza, and which hand do you want?" Elaine was holding something behind her back.

"Right."

"Wrong." But she brought out her left hand holding a DVD. *The Bridesmaid.*

"Hey, great." Feigned approval. Whatever happened to movies like *Cowboys and Aliens*? That one was filmed in New Mexico somewhere outside Santa Fe—surely it was on DVD by now. But he smiled; he wasn't going to disappoint Elaine who looked absolutely triumphant standing there with a DVD in one hand and a boxed cheese and mushroom pizza in the other. He grabbed her around the waist and was glad the pizza was frozen as it hit the floor. "I feel like we're living in never-ending picnic mode." She laughed and put both arms around his neck as he leaned in and kissed her…long and longingly.

"That was nice. I should leave you alone more often."

"No, never." He pulled her into him but she stepped back.

"I almost forgot. Mrs. Patrick met me in the hall…seems she got a call from the local Gestapo asking her to warn guests about recent auto vandalism in the neighborhood. She thought we'd be fine if we left the dog in the car. Simon's not going to like that."

The advice to leave Simon in the SUV overnight was probably good. Small towns always seemed to have their share of petty crime—usually cars broken into. He'd bet that the Wagon Mound law enforcement was woefully understaffed.

Still, Dan was uneasy. He was hoping that a case or two of vandalism was all it was. And it could be Ms. Patrick's way of getting a dog out of one of her rooms—at least for overnight. No. Five hundred a week was probably a small gold mine in this town—doubt if she'd rock the boat. But again, he had second thoughts about a room at the back—one that opened onto the street with stairs shadowed by a towering juniper was exactly what it sounded like—an open invitation—burglary under cover. And leaving his alarm system in the car might not be wise. Or was this just part of his overactive imagination? It was taking him a while to get over reacting like everyone who said "hello" was offering him a ride in a rigged truck.

Pizza, beer, and a movie were becoming more than just a Friday night treat—even if it meant popping a DiGiorno Supreme in the oven and watching a movie on his laptop…in bed. If you added the fact that Wagon Mound's sidewalks were rolled up at nine and there wasn't a bar, a restaurant, or a movie theater within forty miles—this kind of home entertainment wasn't so bad. He'd bet they'd do more of it. And actually, the bed part made it pretty good. And maybe *The Bridesmaid* wasn't a thriller, but you had to hand it to the actors—didn't one of them get an Oscar nod? And, he hadn't seen it—that left out most action movies.

◇◇◇

But their first night in Wagon Mound wasn't exactly without incident and now it was dawn and time for reflection. The kitchenette's window faced east and he was being treated to reds and peaches and golds being broad-brushed across the horizon. Spectacular. He poured his third cup of overly strong Peet's Kenya Auction Lot and sat down at the table. The night was a blur but he forced himself to reconstruct the chain of events. Whether or not he reported them to Sheriff Howard, he needed to sift through what had happened for himself first.

He'd taken Simon down to the SUV after the movie at about 11:30. It was a bright night thanks to an almost full moon and clear skies. If he were still a smoker, the night would have invited a few minutes of reflection and a cigarette or two, just kicking back on the stairs and enjoying the balmy autumn.

But he'd come straight back from locking the car after crating Simon in the back. When he got upstairs, Elaine was asleep so he turned off the lights, undressed in the bathroom, crawled into bed, and almost instantly fell asleep himself.

According to his watch, he was awakened at 2:45 by something—something not right, out of place, making a noise. He wasn't sure but he eased his hand under the pillow and felt the comforting presence of his .38—a nice little weapon, if he did say so himself. Nothing fancy, just accurate. He opened his eyes but didn't move his head.

He was parallel to the door, sleeping on the left side of the queen-sized bed. Next to the bed was a nightstand with lamp against the east wall, like the headboard of the bed, a chair next to it under a window on the south side and the door. The door was the old-fashioned half-glass, half-solid wood with a roller shade pulled down to meet the bottom half of the door but curled at the edges. It was this sliver of moonlight that had been blocked—just for an instant by what was unmistakably the shadow of a human form.

Dan waited and felt rather than saw that the person was still there. What was the person doing? Then he saw it. Inch by inch a piece of paper was being slipped under the door coming to rest halfway across the jamb. Now was the opportunity. He grabbed the gun in his left hand, was momentarily pleased that he'd left his boxers on, hopped up forgetting the bruising and lunged for the door.

A second lost fumbling the deadbolt with his right hand, then throwing the door open, he hit the squatting stance of a trained killer…well, that was probably overstatement, but he held the gun in front of his body, arms locked, right hand steadying the left. And he was too late.

The glimpse he got of the slight body throwing itself over the railing three-quarters of the way down the stairs, stumbling, then jerking upright only to duck back beneath the stairs was only that, a glimpse. And the footsteps quickly became muted as the person left the walkway and struck out across grass.

"Stop."

Worth a try, but like yelling at the wind. He heard the rev of an engine—motorcycle—the angry whine of a sewing machine, some kid's crotch-rocket. Not far away but out of sight. He'd seen another one of those confounded alleyways, in this case a thoroughfare, when he'd put Simon in the car. The person was probably halfway to Railroad Avenue by now—if he'd had a bike close by, he was long gone.

"Dan? What's wrong? What's happened?" Elaine was standing by the corner of the bed pulling her robe on.

"Kids, I think. Maybe those vandals the landlady warned us about—I need to check the car. It's okay. I'll be right back up." He kept the .38 out of sight and watched as she slipped back out of her robe and got into bed. Then he leaned down and picked up the piece of paper.

He waited until he got to the SUV, had quieted Simon, scooted behind the wheel, and flipped on the interior lights before taking a look at the paper he held in his hand.

GET OUT WHILE YOU CAN
IT'S NOT WHAT YOU THINK

All capital letters cut from newsprint or magazines on common white computer printer paper. Amateurish. But made to look that way? Maybe. Would there be fingerprints? Unlikely. Would he show it to Sheriff Howard? Uncertain. He reread the message. "It's not what you think." What wasn't? If it wasn't what he thought, that would seem to indicate that he actually had made some decision or thought he knew something. But for the life of him, he had no idea what the note referred to. And who knew what he thought anyway? The single line was starting to play and replay in his head. And his head was beginning to throb.

He let Simon out and watched as he watered off a few tree trunks before they both headed back up the stairs. Simon moved toward the bed but Dan signaled, "No." Dogs could sleep on the floor. He smoothed the paper and propped it against a glass on the table. Ominous message and it didn't make one bit of sense...other than the "get out" part. That sent a shiver across his shoulders.

Dan leaned back in the chair, balancing on its two legs and leaning against the counter. Sometimes Dan found himself stopping whatever he'd been doing to reflect...like now as he watched Elaine sleep and heard the snuffly snores of Simon at the foot of the bed. He smiled, enjoying a moment of true contentment. But it was fleeting. He brought the chair back down to fully rest all four legs on the floor. One minute peace, another uneasiness.

So, what was wrong? It was nothing he could put a finger on...just a vague anxiousness. Everything seemed to be a big thing. Consequences that would never have occurred to him before, now seemed uppermost. The "might happen" became the "probably would happen." Dan sighed. The simple truth was he'd found out he was mortal. "It" could happen. Death. Or life-altering injury and he had no right to burden another human being with his baggage. He loved Elaine. He loved her smile, her touch...he never wanted to lose her. He might admit to one or two thoughts of marriage…maybe. They'd only known each other four months but the feeling was there.

Yet, she'd had far too much sadness in her life to be saddled with another emotional cripple…or worse. Because he knew, one way or another, someone was gunning for him. Wanted him out of the way. And Dan didn't have a clue as to who or what or why. He only knew that he recognized the stench of fright for the very first time in his life. Since the accident, he awoke to it at night and fought it to go back to sleep. And he wasn't winning. And this didn't help. He fingered the note and read it for the hundredth time…"get out while you can."

Not him. Because now he was pissed—pissed that someone had forced this kind of control over him. Forced him to look over his shoulder and fear every shadow and bump in the dark. And pissed because he was scared shitless for Elaine—and knew he couldn't protect her…not from everything.

She had to leave. He'd approach her in the morning about rejoining the tour—fly directly to Dublin. She would have only missed a few days—a week at most. He'd stay, get to the bottom of things, at least, get his report in and join her. He'd bet the doc would release him to drive this week, or if not, maybe he could hire someone. And in three weeks he'd be ready to take off. Mission accomplished.

He awoke to the smell of fresh coffee and an unbelievably stiff neck. Why he hadn't just crawled back into bed earlier instead of sleeping at the table with his head on his arms, he didn't know. He splashed water on his face in the bathroom, brushed his teeth and still didn't feel any better. Maybe because every time he turned around he elbowed a towel rack, bumped the soap dish or knocked the toilet paper holder off its perch. The bathroom was an afterthought. The whole room could have been a molded plastic all-in-one-piece addition instead of just the shower. Tiny didn't even begin to describe the cramped space.

"Toast?" Elaine was wielding a frying pan of sizzling bacon and what looked to be tw eggs over easy as he walked to the table.

"Sure."

"You want to explain that now or wait until after breakfast?"

He didn't need to look at what she was pointing at to realize he'd left the note on the table in plain view. He shrugged, "Either, I guess." Silently he was berating himself for being so clumsy. He'd certainly lost the element of surprise. And the opportunity to destroy it.

"That doesn't look like vandals to me—not teenagers anyway. And there seems to be a certain level of knowledge of you personally."

"Yeah, I know."

Elaine put two plates of eggs, bacon, and toast on the table and sat down.

"No jam."

"What?"

"For your toast. I forgot to buy jam."

"It's okay." Suddenly he wasn't hungry anymore. "Are you upset?"

"I'm upset that you weren't exactly truthful during the night. You went rushing out with your gun drawn—"

"Just taking precautions."

"I don't like any of this. Sure there's a certain element of excitement but I don't want you in danger."

"Then that's reason to leave. I don't want *you* in danger. This is proof that something's going on that reaches beyond a simple robbery and a stolen necklace."

"I won't go."

"It's just for a month—not even that long. That'll give me time to wrap things up here—"

"Look what happened the last time I left."

"It's not safe—you just admitted as much."

"If you're in danger then so am I."

"That makes no sense."

"Doesn't it? I flew back; I sat by your side; I cried my eyes out…and you think I'll just leave again? Go off and pretend to enjoy a tour and leave you here, not knowing, fearing the worst, dreading the next phone call?"

"Elaine, it's only selfish to tell you how much I need you—want you by my side. But—"

"But what?"

"I have no right…no right to endanger your life."

"The decision is mine. We're adults—adults who love each other. I won't leave you. Besides, I kind of like whodunits. Solving them, that is."

Then she was in his arms, breakfast forgotten, and that seemed to end it. Whether he liked it or not, for better or whatever, they were together in this—and he didn't even know what "this" was. He picked her up and carried her the three feet to the bed giving up trying to unbutton any buttons with his left hand. She pulled the Henley over her head, shed panties and bra, and pushed him back on the bed to help him wiggle out of his shorts.

"Hey, our friend is back."

"Yeah, I noticed." And Dan couldn't keep the lopsided grin from spreading ear to ear. "Any ideas about what we should do with him?"

"I think I can come up with a couple."

Chapter Six

Dan was able to schedule a meeting with First Community Bank's president for one o'clock Monday afternoon. It seemed the bank stayed open until three on weekdays and until noon on Saturdays. Bankers' hours. He hadn't run into those in years, and he'd bet there wasn't an ATM...maybe not even a night deposit and definitely not a drive-through. Yeah, Wagon Mound wasn't exactly on the electronic radar. This was going to be a step back in time...as if meeting Gertie hadn't been one already.

Elaine dropped him off and went back to the boardinghouse to do laundry. He needed to get his own car back and do his own driving—he was sure the chauffeuring was getting old. He had no idea how long the interview would take but he'd need to see the area, take pictures, interview help...it'd been a month, he could only imagine how tired everyone must be of being questioned. And probably very tired of the town gossip—everyone having a theory about whodunit and why...he was sure Chet hadn't been the only one with an opinion.

He'd barely had time to admire the hundred-year-old chandelier in the foyer when a woman who introduced herself as Alice ushered him into an office lacking any customer-friendly touches. No overstuffed leather couches or chairs; no warm carpets or green plants. Some theme of Quaker austerity was being carried out in all wood mission-style benches, tables, and even the desk—the only grandiose piece of furniture in the room.

Huge, chunky, slatted wood along the sides—and complemented by an ergonomically correct Aeron chair. That had set someone back a thousand or so but good to know the bank prez cared about his posture.

Inventory of the room was interrupted by Alice sticking her head in the door to say that Mr. Woods would be with him in a moment. The moment stretched to five but who was counting? This was a starred interview in his notebook. Not that he expected any breakthrough information, but it might tie up some loose ends.

The first thing that struck Dan when L. Maurice Woods—who quickly pointed out that he preferred to be called Lawrence—finally strode into the room was how young he looked for being stuck in a one-horse town. And how underdressed the man made him feel. Red-and-blue striped power tie, white shirt, navy suit, black shoes polished to within an inch of their life… and a hanky. All this on a lanky frame that screamed basketball for the local high school and not that long ago—certainly within twenty years or so.

But he was stuffy beyond his years and overly into his position—could bank president be that big a deal in the town? Probably. Dan decided later that it was the hanky folded to two-point perfection just peeking out of the pocket that screamed affectation. But then the dress code seemed to spill over to the general workers—the tellers wore nylons, the janitor wore a bow tie, and the guard on duty had had a manicure. Wagon Mound wasn't exactly a metrosexual metropolis and all this spit and polish sure seemed overkill or just demeaning for the insurance guy. Dan wished the sweater he was wearing didn't have pilling around the cuffs.

After introductions, Lawrence remained standing. "Well let's get this tour started." A smile finally—more grimace than positive emotion, however.

"I'd like to see your check-in and out log for August. I assume those entering this area needed to sign in first?"

"Of course. Even though everyone knows everyone in this town, we follow strict procedures. After sign-in the person's box was retrieved by Stephanie there or myself," Lawrence paused and nodded to a woman sitting to the right of what looked like the door to a vault…"she would seat the owner in this alcove," a gesture to the left, "the property would then be delivered to the area. You may notice the recipient was always in line of sight."

Dan thought "goes with the hanky" but he followed suit and nodded at Stephanie who gave him an anemic smile. He made a mental note to question her…something along the line of helping him to profile Gertie—as tough and unfeeling as that sounded. He tried another smile but Stephanie quickly looked down. Dan glanced back at his host in time to catch a frown directed her way. Odd. Interaction with the investigator must be equivalent to goofing off.

"When the box holder was finished, he or she would buzz Stephanie and she would buzz me. I would then return the safe deposit box and make certain the log was signed."

Seemed like a couple extra steps, Dan thought, and a lack of trust. Wonder why Stephanie wasn't more involved? Micro manager came to mind.

"Are the logs stored here on the premises?"

"Yes. Stephanie, would you get August's sign-in log for Mr. Mahoney?"

Stephanie leaned down and unlocked a file drawer in her desk and after a thumbing of files marked by month, she separated August and placed a bagged and time-stamped log on her desk.

"Mrs. Kennedy has reported that she removed the insured items on August tenth."

"Yes, here's her signature." Stephanie had turned a few pages then scooted the log forward for him to see.

"According to her calendar, there's some confusion as to just when the items were returned—some problem with the vault's door needing repair and access was denied due to this servicing."

"I remember now. She came to the bank with…" Stephanie looked up "…her property and we advised her to wait until we notified her. We anticipated a two-day delay. In fact," Stephanie turned a page, "here's her signature on the day she removed her property and here's my notation when she returned and I informed her that the door needed to be fixed, August seventeenth."

Dan leaned forward and looked at the note.

"And here's the notation—time and date—of my call informing her that the vault door was repaired. Well, I didn't do the calling; I was on vacation but my replacement Amber Medger did—on the eighteenth. The AM notation here? Those are her initials."

"And Mrs. Kennedy returned to replace her property that day?"

"Oh, this is so silly talking about 'her property'…we've all seen the necklace and know the story of the *Titanic* and the mother, the father with the clubfoot—"

"That's enough, Miss Walters."

Well, that was going to get Miss Stephanie Walters a stern reprimand once he was gone, Dan thought. But how interesting. It was easy to imagine Gertie showing off the prized possession… and easy to realize how it could be a target. He suddenly noticed that Stephanie was rifling through several pages of the log biting her lip and appearing increasingly annoyed.

"I know it's here…I just can't seem to find…usually Amber is so careful."

"You can't find when Mrs. Kennedy returned the… her necklace?" Stephanie shook her head. Dan bent over the log running a finger down the entries for August eighteenth and nineteenth. There was a total of six names in the two-day period—three so precise and carefully crafted that the owners had evidently studied the Palmer method of penmanship. Which also indicated they were of Gertie's vintage. And then three were just a smear. He made a note of the ones he could read. A Peter (Buster) Jenkins PhD—Dan paused and reread the entry. Buster actually put his degree behind his name when signing a log to open his safe deposit box? Somehow that said something about him. Dan looked at the two other signatures that were legible—Jesus

Garcia and Antonio Romero. Maybe one of them remembered seeing Gertie at the bank that day. He made a note.

"I'll call Amber—I'm sure it's just an oversight."

"In the meantime I'll continue the tour." Again that tight smile as Lawrence motioned Dan to follow then stopped a few steps beyond Stephanie's desk. "This is it." He turned to dial the combination and apply the key that opened the safe deposit box vault. Actually a ten by ten room, windowless, cheerless—its own kind of prison, Dan thought. But it was the slight musty smell mixed with the unmistakable ethyl benzene odor of new carpet backing that almost made him gag. What a mix.

"Repairs have been made?" Dan also noted what looked like new steel shelving on the north wall.

"Yes, and no." Lawrence walked to the far corner and pulled back the carpet and lifted a piece of plywood to reveal a ragged opening in the floor about two feet from the wall. Dan leaned in and took a couple snaps of what looked like blackened edges—blowtorch? The thick metal flooring had been cut in the rough shape of a circle. Maybe high-tech laser equipment? Looked like it. Certainly made less noise than trying to blow up a steel plate like that.

"We have to have new flooring put down as you can see… this is basically cosmetic for the time being, and safety. We've made room in the bank vault for everyone's valuables. We still haven't been released to begin repairs."

Dan assumed he meant by the Feds. Things could move pretty slowly being somewhat off the beaten path as they were.

"Well, there you have it, not much to see. There are fifteen boxes in this vault—twelve were in use. One wall model safe that's temperature and humidity controlled for larger objects or those needing a special environment."

"What kinds of things were kept in there?" Dan stood in front of the two-foot by four-foot enameled door marked Irwin, the combination lock neatly cut out allowing entry.

"Oh, family Bible for the Garcias, a great-grandfather's love letters to his sweetheart from the early 1800s for another family.

Some pieces of Indian pottery…Anything that could be contaminated by plain air."

"And none of these things were taken?"

"Only one claim to date…ol' Doc Jenkins but I'm not sure it's legitimate. Odd claim…may not come to anything."

Dan waited for an explanation of what an odd claim might entail but nothing more was offered. Dan made a note to get the phone number or address of Doc Jenkins.

"Still doesn't seem like many boxes for a town of three to four hundred people."

"In my community you'll find more riches between the mattress and box springs than right here."

"In retrospect that seems like the smart thing to do." Mattresses or Barbasol cans Dan added to himself.

Lawrence didn't seem to see any humor in his remark.

"Were all the boxes vandalized?" Dan stood in front of three seemingly untouched boxes—still locked with hardware complete.

"All of the ones in use were found open. Used some kind of laser tool to cut the locks out. See here? And here? Even the big Irwin got hit."

Dan leaned closer. Well, maybe Wagon Mound had had a brush with high-tech after all. The floor and now the boxes. These incisions were neat and exact.

"The numbers indicate boxes that were in use?" Dan was looking at the small paste-on laminate numerals in the right hand corner of each box.

"Exactly. All contain the date the box was rented. As you might guess, Mrs. Kennedy's is the oldest—twenty-fifth of March, 1933. The year the number system was put in place."

Dan took out his camera again, the old 4 pixel Nikon still took great close-ups. He just couldn't get used to using his phone—somehow a phone didn't have the right to be a camera. He adjusted the Nikon and clicked a couple of shots including one of the absolute precision of the laser cuts. He was at a loss to name the tool but probably something surgical or out of a lab.

"Not everything was taken. Papers, for example, deeds, car titles, that sort of thing were found in a jumble on the floor. Even the Garcia family Bible. Several patrons only kept papers in their respective boxes...but a few kept other valuables. A gold inlaid chess set, a coin collection, a collection of 1800s railroad watches. Three patrons in all lost items of immense value."

Dan wasn't sure what "immense" value added up to—he guessed the five hundred thousand-dollar necklace would qualify. "I'd like to talk with those who lost valuables. In addition, of course, to Mrs. Kennedy."

"Is that necessary?"

"Need to make sure my client wasn't singled out. Rule out that she in some way could have invited this—hard to think Gert would try to skip out on a drug debt though." Dan chuckled.

Again, Lawrence remained deadpan. Strange man, Dan thought. Literal thinker for one thing and not prone to see humor in much of anything.

"What furniture was in the room? Table and chair?"

"No furniture, no need. We relied on Stephanie to keep an eye on things outside the vault—much better light. And it was that little bit of extra precaution. Didn't want any hanky-panky—made more sense to retrieve the boxes and have them delivered by bank personnel."

Hanky-panky? Like someone was going to sneak in with a blowtorch or better yet, stay in there long enough to pick the locks? *Control* followed by the word *freak*. Two words that seemed to fit ol' Lawrence. Dan made a mental note to check with Stephanie—soon. He took one more look around the small room. Nothing jumped out. Maybe another picture or two and then they should get on with it. "I assume the tunnel is still open?"

"With a twenty-four-hour guard. That's next on the tour."

Something about locking the barn after the horses had gone elsewhere came to mind. Dan snapped another picture of the hole in the floor, its proximity to the wall, the boxes, and the door, then he followed Lawrence out of the room, out the bank's front door and around the side. The guard on duty nodded and leaned down to unlock and remove a padlock from a heavy-looking metal door. And all Dan could think of was the root cellar at his grandmother's house. A favorite spot of his as a youngster, the farm in northeastern Illinois had gotten him out of the humidity-laden city for a month before school started. He'd had day after day to run free, fish, round up the chickens—hide in the cellar when his cousins visited. Some of his best childhood memories. He slipped the camera out of his pocket and took several photos.

"Watch your step. Little steeper than what you'd expect. Let me get the light."

Dan followed Lawrence but paused until the last few steps were illuminated. Steep didn't quite capture it and what a workout if you were carrying buckets up those stairs heavy with dirt and cement from tunneling. That would take someone in pretty good shape. Or someones. It was difficult to see this as a one-man operation. Unless you wanted to believe he'd been at it for a year or more. And, actually, who knew when it was started?

"This old boiler is a remnant from the past."

Dan tuned back in and stepped forward to inspect the hulk of an antique furnace with a blocked coal chute.

"I have no idea when this was last used. Well before my time."

Dan was guessing the thirties.

"Never seemed to be money to renovate this part of the bank. I don't think anyone even used the basement for storage. But the boiler came in handy for someone."

"So, you think only one person was involved?"

"I have absolutely no idea. It was just a comment. But if you move the boiler…" Lawrence tugged on one edge of the metal but waited until Dan gave a pull on the other side with his good hand to leverage the boiler away from the wall. "And here you have it—the infamous tunnel. Completely blocked from view if someone were to look down here."

"How long do you think they were at it?"

"I don't have a guess—not my expertise. But long enough to carve out fifteen feet of two by two-foot space. See?" Lawrence flashed a penlight around the dirt walls coming to rest at the back where the tunnel made a right turn. "That's where they went wrong."

"Pardon?"

"If they had turned left, and if they had had the proper tools, they would have been in the vault."

"And would have had access to cash and not just valuables."

"Exactly. But right past that juncture, there's another wall of two-foot-thick cement, then a steel plate and then the triple-layered steel of the vault's floor. No idea how much time that would have added to their effort or if they could have even penetrated it."

"It would have slowed them down, that's for sure."

Lawrence nodded. "So, did we dodge a bullet? Were our losses cut by blunder? Or just common sense?"

"Interesting. Impossible to know. They might have gone for both…given time. I don't suppose the bank or local historical society has a blueprint of the bank? Something that might have helped with the decision-making? I have a hard time believing someone would tunnel in—expend that kind of energy and take that kind of risk to miss the mark."

"Interest in historical preservation was slow getting to Wagon Mound. By the time there was interest, original documents were long gone."

Dan nodded. He idly wondered at the reserves. How much would a bank in Wagon Mound keep in the vault? There were a lot of ranchers in the area; deposits might be hefty. The vault could have been the primary target. And they somehow had made the wrong turn. That would make sense. Cash is a little easier to dispose of than necklaces and coin collections.

"Was there a lot of cash on hand that weekend?"

Lawrence cleared his throat, "Actually, yes. About three or four times normal deposits. Old Mr. Thompson was to close on about a hundred thousand acres that borders his ranch, the

Double Eagle. He was set to meet at the title company in Las Vegas that Tuesday morning after Labor Day. He'd sold some stock and securities and put the money here in preparation."

"And this was how much?"

Lawrence licked his lips, "Right at two million."

Dan couldn't help a low whistle. "You think anyone knew that kind of money was here?"

"Mr. Mahoney, this is a small town, we have no need for a newspaper. Everyone knew Edgar Summers was selling and Thompson was buying. The deal had been in the making for over a year."

Dan was quiet. Two million sitting in a vault, there was great cover while tunneling; they'd obviously taken their time; they probably knew the money was there...yet, the money wasn't touched. A right turn instead of a left. It made no sense. Something wasn't right. What was he missing? Could they not have had the tools to go through the triple reinforcement below the vault? No, anyone with laser cutters, blowtorches, and patience could have turned left and made it worthwhile. And anyone with any sense would have done a drawing of the interior. First. And deduced where everything was. It was as easy as just walking in the door upstairs to know where the vault was located. They had to have known their right versus their left.

So why the safe deposit boxes? There was no way the jewelry and other heirlooms offered a greater profit when fenced. Doubtful the black market would have coughed up even a hundred thousand for Gertie's necklace. Yet, he supposed it was possible, jewels taken from their settings, bagged separately...easier to grab, safer maybe—

"Were the bills marked in any way?"

"Good grief, no. This is Wagon Mound, New Mexico, we hadn't had a robbery in over forty years. And that one involved a guy buck naked—wrapped himself in a bed sheet, then lost control of his costume when he bent over to pick up some loose change." Lawrence tapped his temple with an index finger. "Absolutely loony."

"I'm just trying to make sense out of it. Trying to apply some logic."

"Not sure 'logic' and criminals ever go hand in hand." Lawrence snapped off the penlight and put it back in his pocket. "So, there you have it. Unless, you're going to crawl back and take a closer look."

"My crawling days have been curtailed for a while." Dan held up the wrist cast. "Might be a little difficult."

"Well then, let's go back up to my office. You requested the names of the other two patrons who lost valuables?"

Chapter Seven

Dan was back at the room to go over his notes and set up appointments for the rest of the week. Elaine had dropped him off and then took off for Las Vegas for some serious grocery shopping. Eggs, bacon, and frozen things past their expiration dates had gotten old…literally. He'd forgotten what a fresh veggie even looked like. It was amazing how elastic a month-old carrot could become without hydration. But this life wouldn't be for long. He had enough work for the next three days and then if the doc released him to drive—which he was pretty sure he'd do—he'd wrap things up and be outta here within a couple weeks.

So, what was first? He needed to chat with the other box holders who had reported losses. That should probably be next. And a quick call to the sister office of United Life & Casualty in Hobbs—find out if anyone had known his itinerary that morning. It was still tough to believe someone had set him up with Chet Echols. There was a chance that it had all been a mistake. Wrong place, wrong time. Yeah, the cut hoses were a stretch to call a mistake but there was a chance that someone got the wrong car. But that didn't explain the "it's not what you think" note.

He sighed. No, he had to assume that he was the target for someone wanting to keep him from any kind of investigation. Which reminded him—he needed to see if other insurance investigators had run into the same things—had there been any incidents, attempts to discourage them, too?

He looked at his notes. Ferris. He needed to stop by his chop shop in Vegas. Trace the money behind the truck's overhaul, if he could. Maybe even call Chet's grandson and verify his granddad's bank statement. And just chat. Sometimes it was the casual, off-the-cuff comment that opened things up. Worth a shot. Cover the bases before he contacted the Feds. He put the notebook back in his pocket. A lot of running around. He really needed to get back behind the wheel.

But first things first. He pulled his cell out and dialed the Hobbs office.

"Becky, Dan Mahoney here…got a minute?"

"Of course. It's so good to hear your voice. How are you doing?"

"On the mend…there's every reason to believe that black and blue won't be permanent skin colors."

"Thank goodness! We all have been so worried. How can I help?"

"Do you know of anyone who might have known my schedule that morning—*when* I was going to get to Wagon Mound or which route I was taking? Besides you and Fred, of course." It was a mom-and-pop office, two people with a typist/file clerk on call when needed. But they were efficient and had handled all the paperwork on the Billy Rowland Eklund case he'd worked on in Tatum. That last morning had been a check of the details and signing off.

"Other than the bank you mean?"

"What bank?"

"The one you're investigating. The one with the robbery."

"The bank called?"

"Yes. The president's secretary. Actually, not the secretary herself but her assistant. Said she'd tried to reach you and leave a message but your voicemail box was full."

Lies numbered one and two, Dan noted. "Do you remember a name?"

"I made a note. Alice…something…no, no, that was the secretary. I talked to Amber somebody. I don't think she gave a last name."

"That's okay. Do you remember what she asked?"

"Well, they were planning a little welcoming get-together for that afternoon and it would make a difference which way you were coming. That is, the back way would get you there quicker but up through Albuquerque would be an easier drive—more four-lane."

Lie number three. "And you told her I was taking the scenic route?"

"Yes, up through Roy. I remember you saying that you'd never seen the lesser prairie. And I mentioned that you'd gotten away early.... She was so sweet and the party sounded so thoughtful. I did wonder though if they weren't just trying to present the bank in the best possible light. You know, didn't want any more bad press. Did I do something wrong?"

"No, not a problem." Time to change the subject. Dan asked if there had been any feedback on the Eklund papers from Chicago, inquired about Fred's bum shoulder, and then said his good-byes. He snapped the cell shut and sat there.

Amber. Another name for his list. Did this tie in Lawrence Woods? Or was this Amber even the Amber who helped out Stephanie? Odds were that it was but would she have used her real name? It'd be nice if every answer didn't lead him to a new question.

He opened his cell and dialed the bank. Stephanie was answering phones and he asked her to reserve lunch on Wednesday—his nickel. He had a few questions and would appreciate her giving him some time. They decided on noon and sack lunches from the convenience store—yes, ham and Swiss would be fine—and then they'd find a quiet spot to talk, somewhere outside if the weather was good.

Chapter Eight

"It's two blocks. I don't need a ride. I think it's important that my chauffeur have a day off."

"But I'll feel guilty."

"Yukking it up with my mother and Carolyn, you won't give me a second thought."

"I wish you'd reconsider and come with me."

"Carolyn has to be taken in small doses. Besides, I'm anxious to get out of here. If I stay and continue the interviews, we'll be that much closer." He pulled her into a hug. "Mom'll understand. Enjoy your lunch, but don't believe everything my mother says about me. Now, go…have a fun day."

He watched Elaine pull away from the curb. He'd made an appointment to see Doc Zimmerman in the morning. A couple days early, but the doc seemed to be on his side. Dan couldn't wait to pick up the Cherokee—hopefully in the morning on the way back to Wagon Mound. They'd had to order a part but now it was ready to go. Just sitting there waiting on him.

He gave Stephanie a quick call to double-check her sandwich preference and make sure she was still planning on company. Stephanie had agreed to meet on her lunch hour but had forgotten that she'd also promised to watch phones while Alice Nedderman kept a dentist appointment in Las Vegas. So Dan jogged the half mile or so to the convenience store, bought two soft drinks, two ham and cheese sandwiches wrapped in cellophane plus barbecue chips, and pulled a chair up next to Stephanie's desk at twelve sharp, hoping the sandwiches wouldn't turn out to be some kind of trichinosis fix.

"I'm so sorry about this. It's nice to get away. There's a park… well, sort of a park about two blocks over. I'd hoped we could walk over there."

Parentheses reads "get out of here" and maybe out of earshot, Dan thought. But he didn't see Lawrence, just the guard and a teller. They would pretty much be alone, but that didn't stop Stephanie from whispering.

"I want you to know that I'll help any way that I can. I can't stand to think of Mrs. Kennedy's loss. She is such a dear. And, oh my goodness, what a beautiful heirloom…with all those memories." Stephanie leaned forward, thin hands folded in front of her on the desk. After a couple bites, the ham sandwich had been pushed to the side.

"Thank you, Stephanie. Let's start with some basics…" Dan looked at his notes. "How long have you worked for First Community?"

"Oh dear, forever, I guess…since high school. Well, to be exact, twenty-four years."

Age, early forties, Dan noted. And time hadn't been particularly kind if the lined skin and prematurely gray hair were any indications.

"You must have started at about the same time as your boss."

Stephanie looked confused, "My boss? Actually, I've had five over the years. I inherited each one as the bank changed names. First it was Farmers and Stockmen's Bank, then Citizens Bank, Western Bank, Bank of New Mexico, Norwest, and now First Community—I guess that's six bosses, isn't it? "

"Lawrence, Mr. Woods, hasn't been here that long?"

"Oh no, less than a year. He was a part of First Community— came with the new name. And I don't think I'll ever forgive him for these." She poked a leg out from under the desk and pointed at her nylons. "I could spend a small fortune keeping myself in these. I guess I'm just not cut out for panty hose."

Dan looked up from his notes and couldn't think of one thing to say...one appropriate thing, that is. So, he tried to put on a sympathetic face and nod knowingly. Stephanie didn't seem to notice and went right on.

"I'm going to tell you this and you absolutely cannot tell anyone where you heard it...."

She paused and Dan couldn't help himself but tensed as she lowered her voice almost below a whisper and leaned closer, "The bank's in trouble."

Then she quickly sat back and looked around.

"What kind of trouble?" He leaned closer and mouthed the words.

"Not enough assets and after this last debacle..." she paused to point in the general direction of the vault, "he's..." again a look around, "under investigation."

"By?"

"Feds." He was now having to read lips.

"They don't think he had anything to do with...?" He followed suit and silently made a circle with his index finger that took in the vault.

She gave one of those "who knows" kind of shrugs that lifts eyebrows and shoulders at the same time and took a bite of sandwich.

Dan sat back. Wow. This was a new kettle of fish. Good ol' two-point hanky on the hot seat. Of course, this was...or could be...speculation by a disgruntled employee. He'd remember never to make a subordinate wear panty hose.

"How do you know?"

"I...I opened a summons or something like that—it looked really official and was from the government. I sometimes act as his secretary when Alice is gone. She's getting implants, so she has to be away a lot."

Dan figured teeth, not breasts, but didn't ask. He had guessed Alice to be on the barely sunny side of sixty when he'd met her last week, but you just never knew anymore...wasn't Jane Fonda in her fifties when she went for the silicon? He remembered

Carolyn going on about it—like it was some insult to women in general.

"He doesn't know that I know. He'd be so upset—that's why you can't say a thing."

"Not to worry. I didn't hear it here." Dan made an index and thumb twist of the two fingers in front of his mouth—lips sealed. He felt foolish but the gesture seemed appropriate. Then, he smiled what he hoped was encouragingly, before asking, "What do you think of the allegations? Do you think he's capable of setting something like this up?" He wasn't sure just what part the bank president could play or what he'd get out of it, but it offered an interesting new twist. "It's not what you think," popped into his head.

"Honestly? I wouldn't put anything past him. I remember the word 'mismanagement' was used…'failure to stay within guidelines'…that sort of thing."

Or scapegoat, if Lawrence had inherited a weak bank to begin with. Dan made a few notes, mostly questions to himself, and finished his sandwich. Stephanie followed suit and they sat quietly sharing chips.

"He was starting to act so strangely."

"How's that?"

"Well, for one thing he took over one of my jobs for no apparent reason. He said it was a bank procedure that he'd been lax in enforcing. We were getting ready for inspections, so, maybe he was telling the truth."

"What was that?"

"Supposedly, no one could be left in the vault. That is, all boxes had to be removed, brought out here and the owner would sit in that alcove just behind me to go over their belongings."

"What had you done in the past"

"I had the combination and master set of keys and could remove the boxes and place them on the table in the vault."

"Let me get this straight, at one time box holders could sit in the room and do whatever it was they needed to do?"

"Exactly. No one was going to steal anything. There was no way anyone could get into the box of someone else. They only had a key to their own property."

"That doesn't sound too unusual. Certainly, the light was better out here." If he remembered correctly, that had been Lawrence's point.

"I agree. But there was no reason to cut me out of the loop. He changed the combination and re-keyed the locks. After making certain all the box-owners had a new key, he kept the masters. I didn't even know where they were."

"Seems like overkill."

"At first I thought he didn't trust me. Just to be spiteful, I didn't wear nylons for three days—told him I had a rash." She leaned back in her chair and crossed her arms.

The look of smugness said it all. If that's what it took to "act out" in order to feel better about the slight, it certainly was harmless.

"And he never gave you back the keys or told you the combination?"

"Never. Imagine my relief when the break-in happened. I wasn't even questioned."

"Sometimes things happen for the best. Oh, I forgot to ask, did you ever check with Amber...," he glanced at his notes, "Medger about the date that Mrs. Kennedy returned her necklace?" Now might be a good time to ask a couple other Amber questions, he reminded himself.

A sigh and a shake of the head. "Amber's getting married and I swear her mind's a sieve. I even had to remind her of the dates she sat in for me."

"I'll use the date that Mrs. Kennedy remembers." Dan wadded his sandwich wrapper and threw it in the trash beside Stephanie's desk. "No pressure but I'd appreciate your keeping an eye out. We both want to do right by Mrs. Kennedy. If something catches your attention...if you remember something that might have impacted the robbery, I'd appreciate a call." He scribbled his cell number on the back of a company card and laid it on the desk.

Then, a stroke of genius…maybe…"Could I have Amber's number? It would look better if I had her statement about the missing signature. Company's a stickler about details. I don't think it means anything but it is a blank that needs explanation."

"I can but it won't do you any good. Amber's long gone."

"I'm not following."

"Took off over the weekend with the fiancé. I think they're going to his home in Alabama. No, maybe it's Georgia. I don't remember exactly. But her mother was in this morning, fit to be tied. Amber and her got in a fight before she left. Amber said she had enough money and didn't need any help and would marry who and when she pleased."

"Where did Amber work?"

"No place in particular. She did odd jobs…sat in for me, baby sat…for awhile she did those 1-900 phone-sex calls. Middle of the afternoon when her mother was at work."

"Was the boyfriend from here?"

"No, a biker. They'd only met at the Bean Day Festival."

"How old is Amber?"

"Nineteen, I think. This was her second year out of high school."

Dan couldn't think of any more questions. He was trying to keep from dwelling on phone-sex in the middle of the afternoon and those who would be most likely to do that sort of thing. As he left, he repeated his request that Stephanie call him if she remembered anything else.

Chapter Nine

"No swelling…no lumps or bumps that shouldn't be there." Dr. Zimmerman was examining his head and, Dan thought, trying to make a joke. Maybe old Zimmerman was a phrenologist a couple centuries out of time. "Your X-rays look great. No trouble sleeping?" Dan shook his head. "Appetite good?" A nod. Dan followed the penlight with his eyes, tried not to flinch when the staples came out, stood on one foot, then the other, bent over, straightening quickly—all at the direction of the watchful doc. "You understand that the okay to drive is not an okay to overdo it?" Again, a nod.

"Let's get you in a soft cast for that wrist and that'll do it for today. I'd like you back in two weeks. But, of course, if there's anything in the meantime, any questions, changes…I'll expect a call." Dan was waiting for a reference to mountain climbing but it didn't come.

Elaine was walking Simon when Dan joined them in the parking lot.

"Keys, please."

"Oh my God, you passed." With a shriek she was in his arms and he swung her around before he kissed her lightly on the mouth, then held her. The second kiss was longer, the kind that makes an embrace tough to pull away from.

"This whole thing has been a nightmare. I can't believe it's over."

"Not quite in the rearview, but close." Then he realized she was crying.

"Hey, no tears. We've won."

"I've been so afraid."

"That's past. I'm going to be all right. We're going to be all right."

Dan tipped her head back and wiped away two drops that threatened to slide off her chin. "I love you. This is the start of a life together." The next kiss wasn't so chaste and lasted long enough for Simon to start whining, tired of his forced inactivity.

Dan laughed and took the leash. "Haven't you seen enough of this parking lot?" But Simon was intent on another round before going somewhat willingly back to the SUV.

They decided to make an afternoon of it. Lunch at the Santa Café, the restaurant that Carolyn had chosen for the girls' lunch with Mom; some window shopping on the Plaza, then back on the road, stopping in Las Vegas to pick up the Cherokee.

Yeah, life probably couldn't get much better than this, Dan decided as he headed the Cherokee toward Wagon Mound.

"Well, we know you'll have to be here another two weeks. So it makes sense that I go home, turn in the Flex and bring the Benz back. We don't need two rental cars. And Jason emailed this morning. He wants to spend a couple days of fall break at home. I may not have a chance to see him again before Christmas. After last summer and the problems with his father…well, I just can't say, no."

"Hey, no apologies. That's great."

"If I take off today, I'll be back next weekend. Think you can stand to be without me that long?"

"It'll be tough." Actually, it would be; he'd miss her but he was busy and could understand her need to get away—stir-crazy probably didn't adequately capture it. And he and Simon could batch' it. What was a measly week when they'd have the rest of their lives? And she'd be safe—away from whatever seemed to hang over this investigation—hang over it and threaten them.

◇◇◇

As much as he'd prefer to be following up leads connecting Chet Eckles to the rollover that almost killed him, Dan figured UL&C would rather be paying him for investigating the robbery. Would expect that to be his first order of business. He could do the other in his spare time. So he called each of the three numbers that Lawrence had given him linked to safe deposit box owners who had lost valuables, and made appointments to discuss their losses. All seemed older—he'd guessed correctly about the Palmer method of handwriting—one elderly man who lived with his wife; a second senior who lived with his daughter and her husband; and the last, a single man, the Peter Jenkins who put PhD behind his name. The appointments fell into place—all seemed willing to talk. Two appointments for that afternoon and Dr. Jenkins in the morning.

A car was almost overkill in a town of three or four hundred but Dan took some extra turns down Park Avenue, around the high school and over, coming back up Railroad before turning onto Romero Street—it felt so good to be behind the wheel. Like when he was fifteen and had a learner's permit and his parents would only let him go around the block by himself.

He made a right turn onto Romero...interestingly, Ernesto Romero lived on Romero. Must be a family link there. And in a town this size it probably meant a lot to get a street named after you.

Mrs. Romero met him at the door with a finger to her lips. "He's asleep. He always naps until one. I'm his wife."

Dan glanced at his watch. He was five minutes early.

"Would you like a cup of coffee?"

"Thank you, that sounds great." He followed her to a small but immaculately neat kitchen that smelled of the cinnamon and sugar used to dust biscochitos and was warmed by a wood-burning stove.

"Would you like a cookie? These are my grandchildren's favorite." She opened a round tin and set it on the table between them before sitting down. "I'm sorry. I'm forgetting my manners. I'm

Rose." She smiled and held out a hand. "Oh dear, the coffee." She quickly got up, mixed two cups of instant coffee using water from a copper kettle on the stove. "Be careful, it's very hot." Then she placed a small ceramic pitcher of milk on the table next to a matching sugar bowl and gave him a napkin and spoon.

Dan was saved any small talk by the appearance of a grizzled elderly Hispanic man, awake but seemingly grumpy. And yes, it was exactly one o'clock.

"I won't take up too much of your time—I appreciate your willingness to talk with me." Dan stood up and offered his hand.

"Anything that will help us get our things back is not an imposition," Mr. Romero sat down heavily, ignoring Dan's offer of a handshake. He spoke with a slight lisp caused by missing lower dentures. Rose placed a cup of coffee in front of him and then seemed to fade into the background.

"I hope I didn't mislead you. I'm representing Mrs. Gertrude Kennedy." Dan put a company card on the table. "It's routine in matters like this to interview others who have had similar losses—losses under the same conditions, that is."

"You saying you're not from the bank?"

"That's right. I represent a private party."

"Well then, I don't think we have anything to say." Ernesto Romero abruptly pushed back from the table, picked up his cup of coffee and left the room. The nap hadn't improved Mr. Romero's attitude, Dan noted.

"I'm so sorry. There's no excuse for bad manners. Let me walk you to your car. We can go out this way." Rose motioned toward a door at the back of the kitchen. She slipped a shawl from a hook and wrapped it around her small frame.

They walked in silence along the side of the house before Rose offered any explanation.

"He's been ill. Not really himself." She paused and Dan stopped to stand beside her. "I don't know if I should be telling you this...."

"Is there something I can help you with?"

She looked at the ground for maybe a breath longer then, "I'm so worried. I don't want him to get into trouble."

"I don't understand."

"The things he said were taken? Well, I know for a fact that he sold his grandmother's pearls and the antique derringers last year. And the railroad watches? Well, there never were any. Mr. Mahoney, he's lying. I don't think anything of real value was taken from our box. We only kept the deed to the house in there and a cameo brooch from his grandmother. And we got those back. I didn't look, but I don't think there was anything else."

"Were any items insured? I mean, maybe there were things you didn't know about. If he can prove that he lost—"

Rose shook her head. "No, not with a company like you're with. My husband thinks the bank will make good on any reported losses. But it's my understanding that they won't."

"You're correct. The Federal Deposit Insurance Corporation or FDIC doesn't insure safe deposit boxes. It's possible that people with losses could file a class-action suit but I'm not aware that that's been done."

"So, if I don't say anything and let this go, nothing bad will happen—I mean nothing because my husband's lying?"

"I would say that's correct."

"Thank you for understanding." A small hand placed on his arm, a pat, and then Rose was gone back around the house.

Dan sat in the Cherokee and finished his notes. Times were tough—especially out here. Rose and Ernesto were probably on a fixed income. Could he blame the old guy for trying to get a couple extra bucks? Not really. His next appointment was only three blocks away. A quick call to see if he could come early and he was off.

A young woman opened the door introducing herself as Emily. Her father was burning leaves in the backyard. She told Dan to go around the house, and she'd tell her father he was there.

Emily didn't seem overly hospitable but then this was an intrusion on a person's time. Even out here where things moved fairly slowly. The acrid smell of burning leaves assaulted his nose and eyes before he'd rounded the last corner. But there was the man he needed to talk with.

Miguel Sandoval wore a bandana tied firmly over his mouth and nose and, silhouetted against the fire, looked like some errant bandito from hell as he fed the flames.

"Mr. Sandoval?" A nod. "Is it possible to take a few minutes of your time?"

"You talk to Emily. She can help." This said as he pulled up one side of the bandana before tugging it back down and turning to throw another box of leaves on the flames—cardboard box and all.

The smoke was getting to Dan and a spasm of coughing forced him to back away and retrace his steps to the front door. He knocked and waited. He was afraid no one would answer just as it opened. This time Emily didn't try to cover up her hostility when he handed her his card.

"You're not even from the freaking bank. So why do I have to talk to you?" The card landed at his feet.

"You don't. I'm hoping that you might share what you lost in the robbery. Every bit helps put together a picture of what was taken and maybe why."

"You work for old lady Kennedy?"

"I represent Gertrude Kennedy, yes."

"Well, you came to the wrong place if you expect me to help. We don't have no thousands in precious jewels…my mama's wedding set is gone and her sterling baby spoon—that's not even enough to make a claim over. So why don't you stick to bothering the rich and leave us alone?"

Before Dan could answer, the wail of a small child from somewhere within gave Emily an excuse to slam the door—even without the baby, she would have slammed the door in his face; he was pretty sure of that. For whatever reason, he was Mr. Unpopular. He took a deep breath and walked back to the car.

So, what did he have? A bogus robbery report and a hostile young woman who suggested her loss wasn't even worth reporting. And maybe it wasn't. The real question—had she lost anything? Could a wedding set and a silver baby spoon warrant paying for a safe deposit box month after month? Judging from the modest home, that would seem to be ill-spent extra money that might be better applied elsewhere. Odd. But then who was he to judge the sentimental value of something? He could only hope his meeting in the morning with Peter Jenkins, PhD, would be more fruitful.

He and Simon enjoyed a plate of bacon and eggs…one on the floor, one on the table. It didn't hurt to spoil a good friend every once in awhile. And, yes, he missed Elaine already. And not because he'd had to fix his own breakfast—he was used to that—he missed her presence. Rolling over in bed at night and throwing out an arm netted him air…the kind of emptiness that always startled him awake. But he wouldn't be alone for long.

They needed to have that conversation about permanence. And where they wanted to live…and if she would want to continue working…or did she even want to sell her house and move to a city? Baggage. Not the emotional stuff that could weigh a person down, but the concrete, real stuff…decisions that were a hundred times easier at twenty-something. Before the collecting began, of a life established before meeting the right person—because he had no doubt that she was the right one. But it wasn't going to be easy.

There was his apartment in Chicago—two bedrooms, living room, dining area—all completely furnished. There was her house in Roswell—three bedrooms, living room, office, game room, dining room—again, full of furniture. What do you do with two sets of dishes and two coffeepots? Let alone blenders and juicers and flatware?

And ten years from retirement, where did you live? That perfect fishing spot on the Chama or the Jemez in New Mexico? Or maybe just buy a cabin and spend weekends until…but she was younger…twenty years from retirement. It made his head hurt. Sometimes when he warned himself not to get his hopes too high, he'd run through this scenario. And try to face reality. And he'd always come back to admonishing himself not to let "things" like furniture get in the way of a life together. He didn't want to get dumped because of a La-Z-Boy. He could only hope that Elaine felt the same way. Besides he hadn't even asked her to marry him…yet.

Dan talked Simon into staying in the apartment by unwrapping a new chew—this one a beef-flavored former pig's ear, his favorite. Dan then topped up his water bowl, admonished Simon to "Be good" and he was out of there.

The drive out to Doctor Jenkins' ranch on a crisp fall day was at once relaxing and invigorating. Drying fall grasses, piercing blue skies, outcroppings of rock shimmering in the morning sun…the five miles flew by. Dan almost missed the tall, double-wide, black iron gate with carefully cut out silhouettes of prairie chickens across the arch. Prairie chickens? Actually, grouse might be the more correct word. But what a weird symbol for out here. He'd seen a lot of ranch gates with iron cutouts of cows and cowboys, the curved horns of Texas cattle, even brands were common, but never perfectly crafted tufted birds. He opened the gate, drove through, and shut it behind him.

The drive to the ranch house covered at least a couple miles. This was a big spread. Whatever Doc Jenkins did, he had the land to do it on. Probably ran a few head of cattle, but Dan hadn't seen any. He saw the house in the distance, along with a couple of oversized barns and various other buildings, and headed in that direction.

Men with guns always unnerved him. And the man standing on the porch was cradling a shotgun. Dan slowed the car and stopped in a graveled area about fifty feet from the front steps, opened his door, and leaned out.

"Doctor Jenkins?" Was that a nod? Dan couldn't tell but the man didn't put the gun down. "We have an appointment for this morning. I'm with United Life & Casualty."

"Mr. Mahoney, isn't it?" Finally, the gun was placed on a chair by the door. Dan pulled closer to the porch and got out.

"Sorry about being inhospitable—too many lowlifes out this way. By the way, call me Buster."

Interesting that driving a year-old Cherokee, wearing pressed chinos, and a long-sleeved checked shirt could brand him as a lowlife. Maybe it was the lack of hair. But a couple weeks' growth—a good quarter inch—surely kept him from looking like a skin head.

"Coffee? Beer?"

"A little early for a beer…how 'bout coffee?"

"You got it." With that his host turned on his heel and the screen door banged behind him. Dan noted that the gun remained behind so he followed Buster up the steps, through the living room and into a spacious kitchen at the back of the house.

"Pull up a stool. This is as good a place to talk as any."

Dan agreed. The room was spotless—gleaming appliances everywhere and not ones from Walmart. Kitchen Aid for the small stuff and Wolf and Viking for the larger. Walk-in freezers, double-doored fridges—Dan wondered if there was a Mrs. "Doctor" Jenkins or if good ol' Buster was the gourmand.

"Lived out here long?" Dan couldn't quite see Buster as part of the locals.

"Land was an investment before it was home. It's taken awhile to get it right."

Ducking an exact answer of time, Dan noted. "I'm assuming it's a working spread…cattle? Sheep?"

"Prairie chicken." Buster put a mug of something awfully black in front of Dan with just the hint of scum near the edge; then scooted a sugar bowl and creamer his way. Judging by the coffee, Buster was not the cook in residence.

"Prairie chicken?"

"Um hm. You must have seen the gate? Had it specially done."

"I'm guessing there's a story here?" Dan poured a healthy dollop of cream into his cup only to watch tiny white chunks pop to the surface. Oh boy. How was he going to get out of drinking this curdled mess?

"I oversee a government grant to save them. They thrive in grasses, the more variety, the better. They were just about extinct in these parts. Haven't been any in decent numbers since the thirties. But the emphasis on bringing the short-grass prairie back paved the way for saving its inhabitants." Buster took a sip of beer. "Home brew. Oughta try it."

"Don't mind if I do." Dan carried the cup of vintage coffee to the sink and quickly dumped it when Buster turned to pull another unmarked beer bottle from the closest fridge.

"This one's frosty." Buster leveraged the top off using an opener hidden beneath the counter. "Just the way they should be. But I bet you didn't come all the way out here for a beer and a chat."

Dan chuckled. He was beginning to feel a lot more comfortable with the shotgun out on the porch. And Buster without firearms was affable enough. "No, I didn't. I'd like to ask you some questions about what you lost in the heist. I understand you have a claim?"

"I have a claim but I didn't lose anything, per se."

"I don't understand."

"Follow me. Let me show you something." Buster put his beer on the counter and walked toward the living room but this time turned down a hallway and led Dan into a five hundred-square-foot office. Three computer screens seemed to all be churning out graphs or lists of numbers. File cabinets lined one wall and shelves of books another.

"Looks like you do some serious work here."

"Know anything about the government? They give you some money to do something and you'd better account for every penny. We're the biggest save-the-prairie chicken operation in the U.S. I'm in the process of getting all this info online, but it's taking forever. I've got some help with data-entry, but it's not enough."

"Out of curiosity what sort of records do you keep?"

"Well, this cabinet contains the results—weights, number of eggs, hatchings, males versus females living to maturity—for twenty-five pair raised on blue grama. No supplement feeding. While this cabinet same criteria, different forage." Buster tapped the side of an even larger cabinet. "Another part of my research covers grasses—we're losing a lot of the natives—fires, drought, the expansion of civilization. Prairie chickens and a tough, lush groundcover go hand in hand. But I didn't drag you back here to talk chicken. That's my real passion." Buster pointed to the wall above the desk and then continued to turn in a circle pointing to the other three walls. "Comics. For every cover you see mounted in those glass cases, I have the full original in a safe deposit box in Albuquerque."

"I've got the feeling I'm looking at a lot of money?"

"A couple million."

"Really?" Had Dan heard correctly? He certainly had no idea.

Buster nodded then added, "Bet you don't know when the first speech bubble appeared."

"Got me on that one."

"*Hogan's Alley*, 1895 by Richard Felton Outcalt. I have comics from each of the five ages—Platinum, 1835 to 1937; Golden, 1938 to 1955; Silver, 1956 to 1969; Bronze, 1970 to 1979; and the Modern age, 1980 to the present."

"And the bank heist involved a comic?"

"Yes. I had sold a 1938 Superman to a trader in Boston. I put the comic hermetically sealed and packaged for shipping in the vault in Wagon Mound. Lawrence Woods was overseeing the transaction—verified that the book was there and was going to oversee the wire transfer and subsequent shipping."

"Which I assume was never done?"

"It was slated for Tuesday—the day after the holiday. But that morning when the discovery was made, the transfer was halted."

"Why? You said you didn't lose anything."

"Might as well have. Someone broke into the case, removed the comic, then sat down on the floor and read it. A pristine copy now has a folded back front cover and a tabbed page—like the kid was interrupted while reading and just tossed it aside. Do you believe that?"

"You said, 'kid.' Do you believe that a young person or persons tunneled into the bank?"

"Who knows? Do you see an adult taking the time to read a comic in the middle of robbing a bank?"

"What is the comic worth?"

"In pristine condition, $330,000."

"And now?"

"I've sent it to authenticators for assessment. The price could go as low as fifty grand."

"So your claim is—"

"Lost revenue because of altered condition occurring during the break-in."

"Possibly in the amount of $280,000?"

"Correct. Needless to say this has caused me a great deal of consternation—let alone disappointment for the buyer."

Dan nodded, "I can understand that. But kids...doesn't add up."

"I think the fact that someone took the time to read it when he did, indicates addled thinking—drugs, maybe? And, if so, then tunneling in there could have been all about money to keep them supplied."

"A possibility. Makes sense that they took the wrong turn altogether—got into the room of safe deposit boxes and not the vault. Amateurs might do that." But that didn't explain the sophisticated laser equipment, Dan mused to himself. That was one bunch of tech-savvy kids.

"How 'bout another?" Buster pointed at Dan's empty bottle.

"No, thanks. Good stuff, though, but I need to get going."

"Would you like to see some real chickens?"

"As opposed to those over the gate?"

Buster chuckled, "Yeah, you could say that. Back of the house here is one big incubator. Come on, I'll show you."

Well, why not. It wasn't like he had anything really pressing. And Dan was a little curious. Hatching prairie chickens? Sounded interesting.

"First building is just one oversized greenhouse. The government is paying the big bucks to preserve the prairie grasses...find a sustainable fertilizer, grow more drought-resistant, bug-free strains—those are their main concerns."

"Any luck?" They were walking between the house and a Quonset hut-shaped building of about a thousand square feet. Dan stood to one side while Buster unlocked two padlocks. There it was again, that attention to safety by locking everything up.

"Actually, a cross between *Andropogon gerardii* and *Schizachyrium scoparium*—in layman's terms "big bluestem" and "little bluestem"—is giving us a stronger version of the parents. So far, it seems to be outperforming blue grama."

Dan followed Buster into the structure. Growing-tables in precise rows stretched from front to back each holding fifty to a hundred small containers with green shoots poking up. Dan waited while Buster pressed several buttons on an electrical box and watched as panels in the ceiling slid open.

"These are about ready to be transplanted but need to be hardened off before it's back to nature." Buster picked up a small planting cup from a table near him. "Shoots need to be over six inches high. This is just one of over two thousand samples that need to be planted before the first frost."

"Impressive." And Dan meant it. This was one well-run operation. "That's an interesting plant." Dan pointed at the corner nearest him. "Another hybrid?"

"Not exactly, but it is part of the research model. Trying to find cheap hardy chicken feed. This plant also makes good hedge-row cover. But it's underrated. Lost its popularity. In my day and maybe yours, too, a tablespoon of this plant's tonic kept a lot of children healthy."

"Castor oil?"

"One and the same. More than one generation of grandmothers swore by it." Buster pointed to a side door. "Go through there and you'll see a fairly successful cross of native juniper with ornamental juniper. We'll be ready to set out seedlings with the grasses end of next month. And one greenhouse over, you'll see an array of houseplants. Originally, we'd hoped to finance a part of all this by supplying local nurseries. But we're just a little too isolated to make that kind of operation really worthwhile."

Dan didn't know anything about greenhouse growing, but what he was looking at was a huge undertaking. "You can't do all this by yourself."

"Got about half a dozen workers come by four hours a day. We're between shifts at the moment so the place's empty."

Something told Dan he was glad he wasn't there to check green cards. But maybe if you worked on a government project you were given some kind of immunity. Dispensation for working with prairie chickens? The government was involved in more bizarre things, he was sure.

"Think we've seen about all there is to see here. Let's check on those chickens. Follow me."

Dan fell into step behind Buster but stopped just inside the door to the third Quonset hut. Breathtaking. Cage after cage all with automatic waterers and tube-filled food dishes. And incubators lined the walls. Fifty? More? Dan knew there were a lot. But it was the pens on the floor in front of him that had made him stop.

All baby animals are cute. Something his grandmother would say every time he tried to make a case for bringing that "cute" baby squirrel in the house to raise or a "cute" kitten found in the ally. But just being cute wasn't enough to get his grandmother to allow an expansion of his critter collection. More than once the saved "cute" one was taken to the vet's or a wildlife rescue center. But prairie chickens, now that personified cute! Grandma couldn't have turned those down. Pen after pen of feathered fluff from about walnut size to rounded grapefruit, some with mothers in attendance, some not, spread out before him.

"Kinda takes your breath away." It was obvious that Buster was proud. "Every pen you see is slated to be released one flock at a time over the next two months. They're banded and a few have radio transmitters. The tracking will begin in November."

"Is this your first release?"

"First release of this quantity. We've had two years of relative success with smaller samples. Now it's time to increase the numbers."

"Awe-inspiring. Thanks for the tour." He followed Buster back through the greenhouse and then the kitchen.

"Oops. Don't want to be running off with this." Dan held up the empty beer bottle.

"Let me take that." Buster took Dan's empty and set it in the sink. "You know where I live if I can be of any further help."

"That the latest in prairie chicken formal wear?" Dan pointed to a rhinestone tiara on the counter. For all the world it looked like a Bitsy castoff.

A laugh. "Kids. My granddaughter visited last weekend with her two—turned the place upside down looking for this." Buster slipped the tiara in his pocket.

As they walked past the shotgun on the porch, Dan wondered if it was kept locked up when kids were around. He could only hope Buster was as diligent with his grandkids as he was with a couple thousand baby birds.

The five miles back to town gave him time to reflect—in hopes that some of the pieces were ready to fall into place but something wasn't adding up. Two days of interviews and the only thing taken was apparently the one thing of greatest value in the vault—Gert Kennedy's necklace. That made sense until he thought of the amount of time and work it took to get to it. Well, there was the comic, but its value obviously wasn't known and it wasn't taken. But kids? Druggies? "It's not what you think." So, where did that bit of wisdom fit in? And why try to keep him out of Wagon Mound? Keep him from doing his job? Pretty drastic to try and kill someone over an insured necklace. And his job was cut and dried unless someone thought he might uncover something else, giving that someone a reason to—

His cell vibrated against his chest from the inner pocket of his jacket. Elaine. She had said she'd call before she left Roswell. But it wasn't Elaine's number.

"Hello."

"Mr. Mahoney? This is Penny…Gertrude Kennedy's daughter. I need to talk with you."

"Okay. Now's a good time." He was on the road but hadn't seen a car in ten minutes.

"I don't mean over the phone. Could we meet? I'm on my way to the bank. I'll meet you out in front in ten minutes." Click.

She seemed to know that he'd agree. He could only hope that there wasn't a problem, and that Gertrude was okay. He was rather fond of the old girl.

He pulled up across from the bank and almost missed Penny, only recognizing her after she'd gotten out of the vintage Jag. Now that was worth a pretty penny—not to play on words or anything. But it wasn't just the car, the Penny in front of him looked different. Once again she was dressed in a no-nonsense, cuffs at the wrist and lace at the neckline, shirtwaist. But her head was uncovered and her hair had been straightened. He wasn't sure how that was done, but now the unruly curls were soft waves that framed her face and just touched her shoulders. And the sunglasses? Straight out of Hollywood. Still the Jag didn't quite fit. But why did it bother him? Because he hated to be wrong and he'd have bet his life on her driving something Asian and cheap...a KIA maybe? Nothing with the sleek, eye-catching dark green lines of the car that had pulled to a stop in front of him. But she was headed his way and he leaned over to open the Cherokee's passenger-side door.

"Thanks so much for meeting with me." She climbed in, turned toward him and plopped an oversized bag onto her lap. "I see you like my car." She slipped off the oversized, tortoise-shell sunglasses.

He hadn't realized he was still giving the Jag the once-over. "Yes. A true classic." But then he gave Penny the once-over, too. Those eyes...was that makeup? She looked pretty good to just be going to the bank.

"My father's pride and joy. I think he loved that car more than my mother....Um, that's a family joke." She colored slightly which made him think that maybe it wasn't a joke. Then, suddenly she just looked flustered.

"I don't know where to begin." She fumbled with the clasp on the bag. "I suppose I should just get it over with and answer questions later."

She certainly had his undivided attention. She rummaged for a moment in the bottom of the bag before pulling out a drawstring purse or maybe it was just another smaller bag, Dan wasn't sure.

"I owe you such an apology. I never saw this coming but everything is our fault—" Penny was struggling with the knot, picking at it with short blunt nails. Finally it gave way and she reached inside slowly drawing out her hand.

Dan didn't need to be told that he was looking at the real thing. The diamonds and sapphires caught the sunlight and sent prisms of light dancing across the dash.

"Where…?"

"Under the mattress in the guest room. Mother sometimes would put it there if she had it out when someone came to the door. It was only ever a quick fix—never permanent. I was putting the flannel sheets on the bed for winter when I found it."

"The pictures don't do it justice."

"No, they don't."

Dan waited and watched Penny struggle with what she wanted to say next.

"Your mother—"

"Mr. Mahoney, Mother doesn't know I've found the necklace. She's…she's beginning to have problems, forgetting things, confusing names and dates."

"All signs of being eighty-five, I'd imagine."

"I'm afraid it's a little more. The doctor called me after her checkup last spring and wanted me to take her for testing. He told me he suspected the beginnings of Alzheimer's. Of course, she'd have none of it."

"Pride and the elderly can be a tough combination."

"More than that. I think the dementia is becoming dangerous…just yesterday she left eggs to boil, went out in the yard to weed, and forgot them. Took us hours to air out the house."

"What will you do now?"

"With the necklace? I've already talked with Mr. Woods. He's willing to look the other way…say the necklace was misplaced, put back in another box after the robbery. Then it will be 'found' and Mother contacted. Mother doesn't need to ever know what she did. That, of course, depends upon you and the insurance company." Penny's left eye involuntarily twitched.

"Sounds like a plan." And he meant it. The last thing he wanted to do was cause additional worry for the two women.

Penny's sigh of relief was audible as she grabbed his hands and just held on, "You'll never know how much this means. Mother's failing is so very difficult."

"I can only imagine."

"And now you can leave. Take that wonderful Ms. Linden on a trip to Ireland after all." Penny sat back and fairly beamed at him.

Everyone liked a little romance…boy gets girl, girl gets trip to Ireland. But there was something vaguely bothering him… yes, he now had no reason to prolong his stay in Wagon Mound; certainly, he wouldn't be on the UL&C payroll after his report. But there was something…something that rankled, flew in the face of right versus wrong. A man lost his life and his own had been threatened. No, it wasn't what it seemed, but unavenged death…was old Chet counting on him?

"Mr. Mahoney?" Dan jerked back to the present. "That's right isn't it? You really don't have a reason to stay. I can't believe that Mother's dementia came so close to taking your life. I know she'd never forgive herself if she knew. And the fact that she was standing in the way of Elaine's happiness. Bitsy loved her—Mother and I just know she's a wonderful person. The right person." This delivered with hands clasped to chest and a wink.

"I'm sure Elaine would appreciate the vote of confidence and you're right. A day or two to wrap things up and I'm gone." But, then again, maybe not. Taking away his reason to be in Wagon Mound still left questions. Lots of them.

"Well, again, my apologies. Better get going. Just holding this thing gives me the jeebies." A quick smile, an awkward, moist handshake, the oversized glasses perched once again on her nose, and Penny was out of the Cherokee and across the street. He watched until she was safely inside the bank. And then he just sat there. *What the hell?* was about the only coherent thought to drift to the surface. Just plain what the hell? Then he put the Cherokee in gear and turned toward I-25. A visit with Jeeter Ferris was long overdue. Now that he had a clear conscience about working on company time. Company time had just been erased.

The trip to Las Vegas took an hour and allowed some time to reflect. He wasn't going to lead the witness but he wanted access to any paper trail.

What had been done to the truck, and when. He figured he was owed that much. A quick check in the phone book when he gassed up at the edge of town put the chop shop about four blocks from the center of downtown. He wasn't going to call first. This was a workday; somebody would be there. Better to not give anyone a reason to overthink what Dan might want.

He had to park on the street and walk back to the chain-link entrance. Didn't look like the brothers were lacking in business. The array of half torn down bikes and cars filled the side yard and extended around the back.

The office seemed to be the top floor of the two-story metal-sided barn-like structure in the front corner of the lot—if he could trust the word "office" above the arrow pointing up the outside stairs. The door above him opened before he could reach the bottom step.

"Help yuh?" Complete with red-and-white bandana rakishly pulled low touching bushy eyebrows that matched a handlebar mustache that brushed his chest, the mountain of a man towered above him—and it wasn't just one story's worth of stairs with Dan being at the bottom looking up. This guy was big.

"Looking for Jeeter Ferris."

"Found him. Should I know you?"

"Probably not. Dan Mahoney. I was Chet Echols' passenger when he rolled his truck. I think you put that truck together for him."

"Yeah. Been expecting you actually. Some ol' coot try to take *me* out, I'd be hot—wanna know the where's and why's of that one, fer sure."

"Are you saying you can help me?"

"Well, maybe I wouldn't go so far, but come on up. I'll tell you what I know."

Dan followed Jeeter up the narrow wooden stairs and settled in a folding chair facing a huge, pockmarked wooden desk with carved initials under a skull and crossbones on the corner nearest him.

"I appreciate you taking the time."

"Not a problem." Jeeter rummaged in the desk's file drawer before drawing out a grease-stained folder. "This should help." He opened it and spread a stack of receipts across the desk. "And this." He handed an envelope to Dan.

"What—?"

"Initial contract."

The letter was on regular paper—could have come out of a copy machine—no letterhead or other identifying marks. No marks on the envelope and past the time when there'd be any viable fingerprints. It was short and to the point. A movie producer by the name of Martin St. Martin would be sending one Chet Echols Jeeter's way by the end of the week. This Mr. Echols would map out what he would be needing in the way of a pickup to be used in various stunts on the set of the movie *Cowboys and Werewolves*, currently being filmed outside Roy, New Mexico. Mr. Echols had been instructed to begin with a budget of ten thousand. More would follow as needed. Receipts would be turned over to Mr. Echols every thirty days.

"And I take it Chet showed up that week?"

"As promised."

"What kinds of things did he ask for?"

"Well, it wasn't our usual job. That's fer sure."

The door to the office opened a foot and the man who stuck his head in looked startled that Jeeter had company.

"Sorry, catch ya later." He ducked back and the door quickly closed. Dan barely registered another red-checked bandana and handlebar mustache.

"Let's see where was I?" Jeeter paused then opened the middle drawer of the desk. "Here's a list of parts we ordered. Suppose I should have handed these off."

"Can I make a copy?"

"You can have the original. No good to me."

Dan glanced at such objects as bumpers, right fender, left headlight rim, doors…"You know the door didn't fit—didn't line up with the hinges on the passenger side."

"Told me to leave the door that way…said he'd need to wire it shut anyway."

"And you didn't ask why?" Dan stared hard at Jeeter, then turned away. "Sorry, but I'm just trying to figure out why a whole bunch of red flags didn't fly up."

"Mostly 'cause I don't know my ass from my elbow when it comes to stunt autos. He coulda told me he wanted chrome duel exhaust pipes mounted on the hood vertical and I'd done it."

"Yeah, I'd be the same way. But didn't he talk about the stunt? Say exactly how he'd use the truck?"

"He was talkative all right but mostly about past movies—past stunts. Can't say that he offered anything about the current one."

"Did you ever talk to the producer?"

"Yeah. Twice. He called to set things up, said to expect a letter." Jeeter pointed to the sheet of paper in Dan's hands. "Then later on he called to ream my ass about spending money on a tailgate."

"Odd. Sounds like he was the one pulling the strings. At least Chet kept him informed. Where were the calls placed?"

"LA prefix—I know that 'cause I used to live out there."

"Same number both times?"

"Yeah. Gave it to the cops but apparently it traced to a pay phone."

"And this Martin St. Martin? Did the cops question him?"

"Got me there. 'Fraid this is the end of my knowledge."

Dan stood. "Thanks again for your time. Would you mind if I had a copy of this? I'm assuming you want the original?" Dan handed him the letter.

"Yeah, better hang onto that. Give me a minute or two."

"Not a problem."

Dan sat, fingers lightly drumming on the steering wheel, before starting the SUV. Where to now? Jeeter wasn't as much help as he'd hoped but he could always question the producer himself. In fact, that sounded like a pretty good idea now that he was basically on his own time. The fact that nothing was stolen was eating away at him. It'd been a very expensive wasted trip…if he'd wanted to have a near-death experience, he probably wouldn't have chosen Wagon Mound, New Mexico, to have it. He turned the key in the ignition and pulled into traffic.

If he started now, he could get to Roy before dark. It looked like rain but he'd take a chance that the movie crew would still be there. He guessed it was called "on location" and he remembered reading that the movie wouldn't "wrap" until the end of the month. If this Martin guy was around, maybe he'd feel like chatting. And he'd just bet that Simon would like to take a ride. No fun being cooped up in one room all day, pig's-ear chew or not.

After stopping for directions, Dan drove the length of Roy's Main Street and headed out of town. The set was hard to miss—cars, trailers, a crane, several facades of old-time buildings propped up to form a street from a time long past. Dan pulled in beside a chain-link gate manned by a woman in a baseball cap, yellow slicker, and holding a clipboard. She didn't let him get out of the car but came running forward and leaned down when Dan lowered the window.

"You the replacement for Harry?" She was staring at him in a slightly disapproving manner but backed up two steps when Simon stuck his head out.

Dan had no idea if he was supposed to be an actor or just the guy delivering supplies. "No, I'm here to see the producer."

"Martin?"

"Yes."

She checked the clipboard, "Your name?"

"I don't have an appointment."

"Then you're probably shit out of luck."

"Would you mind seeing if Mr. St. Martin might have a few minutes?"

"And what is this concerning? If you're trying to hand off a script, they have to go through me first."

"Script? No, I'm not a writer. Mr. St. Martin's name came up in my investigation." Dan handed her a card.

"Are you saying there's some kind of claim? The studio—"

"No. This involves a stunt driver—Chet Echols."

"That son-of-a-bitch cost us three days' shooting."

"How was that?"

"Ivy? Is that Harry?" The man coming toward them wore a maroon silk nubby jacket, tan tassel loafers, and white linen slacks...White Linen Dan repeated to himself...it was after Labor Day but did that rule just apply to women's shoes? Appropriate, or not, he bet Roy, New Mexico, hadn't ever seen anything quite like that. "The toilet in the third trailer is still overflowing." The man planted himself in front of Dan, arms akimbo. Which might have been intimidating if the man had been taller than five feet four inches.

Ivy took a step forward. "Martin, this is...," She checked Dan's card, "Dan Mahoney. He's an insurance investigator and wants to ask you some questions."

"Call Harry's office again. We can't put up with this another night." Martin turned back to Dan. "Questions? About what?"

Dan started to explain but got to the name Echols and Martin St. Martin exploded. "That cheat. Despicable. Couldn't tell the truth if his life depended upon it. I suppose I have a few minutes. Park over there." He waved toward an open spot next to the fence. Dan parked, got out, but left a very disappointed

Simon whining to follow. Martin was already walking away but he paused on the steps of the fourth trailer and left the door open for Dan.

"Just move that junk." Martin waved Dan toward a chair stacked with what look like scripts. "The name Martin St. Martin isn't familiar?"

Dan shook his head. What was it with everyone out here thinking he should know them? *Déjà vu* all over again. He set the stack of loosely bound paper on the floor and sat down.

"Executive producer of last year's Oscar winner…picture of the year?"

"Oh, congratulations. 'Fraid I don't keep up."

"Doesn't matter. Said to myself the minute I saw you—TV sort." Martin perched on a stool next to a kitchen counter and had leaned forward to waggle a finger in Dan's direction. The effeminate posturing on Martin's part was vaguely irritating. But then anyone who still drank cherry cokes—the trash basket was overflowing with cans—probably was harmless.

"He cost me ten thousand dollars and another twenty-five in shooting delays."

"How so?"

"Said he needed a little something up front—"

"He worked for you?"

"We'd signed a contract but he'd rolled the truck before he did a day on the set. Wait, you're that guy who was with him. Of course, I remember your name now from the papers. Wrong time, wrong place."

"That about sums it up. But back to the money—you didn't have the truck built? Through Jeeter Ferris in Las Vegas?"

"The cops went over this a hundred times. Someone used my name, apparently knew Chet was working for me, and fabricated the rest."

"But someone paid for that truck to be built. And ironically it cost ten thousand. Are you saying that Chet had the truck when you hired him?"

"Absolutely. Horrible piece of shit but he was only going to roll it. It wasn't exactly right out of a dealer's showroom, but it didn't need to be."

"Was he working with anyone from your crew?"

"He and his grandson were a team. Didn't seem open to outside help."

"His grandson?"

"When it came to the money, I only dealt with him."

"Do you happen to have a name and address?"

"Ivy can get it for you. Is there anything else?"

Dismissed, but he was probably through here anyway. "No, I can't think of anything. Thanks, this has been helpful."

With an address, name, and phone number in his pocket, Dan headed back to Wagon Mound. A little voice kept urging him to give up trying to solve Chet's involvement in his own death, let alone the near miss on Dan's life. Nothing had been stolen. He was off the clock. Elaine would be back in two days—and they could be out of there. Still, the unknown, the "it's not what you think"…tough stuff to turn away from.

Chapter Ten

The three days with Jason flew by. There was a girlfriend—maybe he could bring her home over Christmas? School was great. He was starting to lean toward journalism but maybe languages and didn't those two go together anyway? Elaine smiled. His excitement was contagious. And she was so relieved to see him happy. The summer had been brutal, devastating to any vestige of family they might have had left. It was time he started out on a life of his own. And wasn't she trying to do the very same thing?

She checked her list. Return rental after she got the Benz out of the shop—new tires, belts if needed, run a diagnostic—all the things she'd planned on doing after Ireland. But now it was housework and laundry. Thanks to the girlfriend who shortened Jason's stay by a half week, she'd be ready to leave for Wagon Mound ahead of schedule. Maybe she'd surprise Dan. They'd talk that evening but she wouldn't have to tell him she was leaving in the morning.

She didn't get the early start that she'd hoped for—not after stupidly stopping by her office. A textbook she'd used for ten years was suddenly out of print. They needed to get the replacement into this year's budget. And the phone message from the publisher who had signed on to do her book of poetry—he was having second thoughts. He thought they could salvage everything with a collaboration—hopefully with a famous name—and still get the book out in the spring. Could she set aside some time for the three of them to get together? He needed to know by Friday. She checked the date on the message slip. She was already two weeks late.

Finally she was on the road. One o'clock instead of seven, but she was moving. She'd be there by six.

Daylight-saving time didn't help the traveler and she suspected it wasn't on the side of the farmer either—not anymore. Throw in a light drizzle and the quickening dusk made driving a little challenging. But she only had five more miles to go. And wasn't this pizza and a movie night? She'd stopped in Las Vegas and picked up one of each. It had turned into more of a joke, but still something they looked forward to. Friday nights were even marked on the calendar with a big P & M. On really good nights Dan would add a big S and draw a heart around the letter. Schmaltzy, but she loved it. He was sexy and tender and a listener. She could not ask for anything more.

Her headlights caught a sparkle of light on the left-hand side of the road. Elaine slowed and was almost stopped when the twinkle suddenly made a dash across the road in front of her.

"Bitsy."

Elaine was sure of it—or a prairie dog wearing a tiara. She quickly pulled to the side, threw the car into park, grabbed her shoulder bag, and jumped out. The tiny dog stopped, acted like she was going to come to her then darted forward. Visions of a distraught Gert made Elaine follow. If Bitsy didn't get hit by a car, there were coyotes, bobcats…owls…the poor little thing was defenseless out here.

The drizzle had stopped but keeping the small dog in sight was difficult in waning light. And calling her name seemed to make no difference. Bitsy would pause, look back, and then run forward usually at an increased rate. Finally, she veered sharply to her right and disappeared in tall grass. Elaine didn't even slow down but plunged ahead squinting to keep the faint ripple in the grass in her sights.

When the grass leveled out to stubble, there was Bitsy sitting, waiting on her but staying some thirty feet away. Then she was off again. Elaine called her name but Bitsy ran on. She was treating it like a game. Poor thing had no sense of the dangers. Elaine hurried forward, up and over a low ridge, across an open sandy area. Bitsy was heading for a wooded section and Elaine entered the bramble just as she lost sight of the bouncing bit of rhinestones about ten inches off the ground. Low branches were swatting Elaine and scratching her face while thorny vines tore her clothing. Now what? There was no going further.

Maybe if she just waited, Bitsy would come back and check on her pursuer. Of course, catching her might prove impossible. She listened. A slight breeze made it difficult to discern between small dog trotting through underbrush and branches rubbing together overhead. She really needed to get out of the woods. There was very little daylight left and it would be difficult enough to retrace her steps to the highway. She'd just have to hope for the best and pray some dog-God would protect the Chihuahua. Pushing branches aside she turned to go back the way she came.

Now the inky edges of darkness were coming together quickly. Amazing how soon after the sun set, the world took on a totally new look and sort of turned in upon itself—enveloped everything around her in shades of shredded gray and midnight blue. Was she lost? She honestly didn't remember that pile of sharp-sided rocks that suddenly towered above her to the right at the edge of the woods. But the clearing was welcome. The woods had been closing in on her—so close, so dark.

The screams pierced the gloom with a suddenness that took her breath away—bloodcurdling over and over knifing through the half-light. She turned searching for the source and saw movement across the open space at the edge of the gloom. A half a football field away several figures were going in and out of a boxcar. Well, maybe not a boxcar, maybe the back of a transport, an eighteen-wheeler. Hadn't they heard? Why weren't they going to help?

In the fading light, moving in unison, all dressed in white. She watched entranced and suddenly realized the screams had stopped. As suddenly as they started, there was nothing. How eerie. She was rooted to the spot. But the screaming. A woman? Probably. Should she investigate? Or go back to the car? There was something just plain creepy about this place. Her skin prickled and some little voice inside whispered she was seeing something she shouldn't. *Ignore. Leave.* The voice inside her head was fairly shouting now.

She turned but stopped again to get her bearings and that's when she heard it. A riding lawnmower? Out here? No, of course not. An ATV. Someone out for a joyride but at this time of day? And it was coming straight toward her. Was she paranoid or was it coming too fast for the objective not to be finding her? Someone had seen her. But how could that be? She veered to the left and sprinted toward the stretch of tall grass. And so did the machine behind her. Overactive imagination? No. She was being chased. And it was not a good feeling.

Think. How could she elude a machine? Turning and standing her ground was not an option. If she could doubl- back to the outcropping of rock and climb high enough and quickly enough, she doubted the ATV could follow. She quickly darted left and poured on the speed—didn't she win some medals for just this sort of thing in the past? That was past with a capital "P". She hadn't run track in thirty years. She was thankful that she was wearing sneakers and not a pair of hooker heels trying to impress Dan.

The rocks loomed ahead of her now and the grass seemed to be thinning. Breathing hard, she kicked it up a notch and scrambled up the first group of granite boulders, the ATV screeching to a halt behind her. She didn't turn to look but from the cursing there was one guy in hot pursuit not doing too well on slippery, rain-wet granite.

When she reached the top, she gulped in air but didn't stop, just slowed enough to get her bearings. She thought she saw headlights in the distance and assumed she wasn't far from the highway. She zigzagged around an enormous rock jutting out of sheer granite and started downhill. The steep-sided ravine caught her by surprise. Elaine tumbled, struggled to regain her footing then stepped into a crevice that held her ankle tight. She pitched forward feeling ligaments twist, scraping both knees and the palms of her hands, but the ankle continued to tether her to a crack in solid rock. She knew she was making too much noise, but her ankle was beginning to swell. The pain made her dizzy and she bit her lip to keep from crying out.

There was no seeing, let alone escaping, the strong hands that slipped a pillowcase over her head, pulled her arms backwards, and tied her wrists together behind her back.

Chapter Eleven

It was making his head hurt. If you added the fact that the necklace wasn't really stolen and that the other box-holders probably were lying, and the tabbed page of a comic was the only legitimate claim, then nothing was taken…a fifteen-foot tunnel, laser equipment, sophisticated planning for nothing? And that call he'd made earlier on the offhand chance he'd connect with Amber turned out to be a real dead-end. Her mother was still irate over Amber's leaving—didn't expect her back, hadn't talked with her. She could just rot in hell. Heavy stuff from a parent but probably did mean Amber wouldn't be back any time soon.

He thought of popping the cap off a second Bud but opted instead to take Simon around the block before bed. It was already eleven and Elaine hadn't called—probably too busy with Jason and didn't want to bother him so late. Friday night without pizza and a movie wasn't any fun at all.

He slept fitfully. Dreams of tunnels circled around and around finally dumping him down a chute to land in a pool of cold water. And he sat bolt upright. This was driving him nuts. Maybe if he looked at his pictures again—the ones he'd taken of the vault. He moved to the kitchen table and his computer. There were a number of pictures of the bank—outside, inside, the tunnel, but he had put all the snaps of the vault in one folder. He opened it and started to flip through the thumbnail captures stopping often to blow one up to normal size.

Then he went back to the beginning and moved the photos to make a panoramic sweep when viewed one after the other. First shot, walking in the door, second, third, and fourth turning to the right continuing to the back then up the left wall—safe deposit boxes, hole in floor, standing humidified safe, then back where he started. He leaned his elbows on the table and studied the picture of the room.

There was something about the boxes themselves. He looked closely at the ones with doors open and let his eyes move slowly to the last row—three boxes still locked, untouched as if the person or persons knew they were not in use. But who would know that a box without a dated sticker was empty? Probably only an insider. But if nothing was taken…?

What if…no, it was too bizarre, but still, what if no one tunneled into the bank to steal something out but tunneled into the bank to put something in? But what? What would be safer in a bank than anywhere else? A place where no one would look. What could be so important, maybe so dangerous that it needed to be kept where no one would look for it?

Crazy? Yes, but in a strange way, it felt right. Think. He knew he was close, on the right track, anyway. The three safe deposit boxes that hadn't been in use, still locked without pasted-on identifying patron numbers—that was a place to start! Had anyone even thought to open them? Dust for prints? He doubted it. He'd bet they'd just been ignored—assumed to not be a part of the investigation. For the first time he felt he had a legitimate lead.

The minimum of six months' work of tunneling was just a little too much work. For nothing. Put the whole scenario outside the realm of normal. Whatever it was, it was big. And the necklace? He wasn't sure how it fit in. Had it really been misplaced? If he didn't know the players, he'd say it smacked of opportunism. Take advantage of what looked like a robbery and claim a loss. The necklace didn't have to be related to what happened at the bank but wasn't it a little odd that Penny only found it now—hadn't torn up the house looking for it before on the offhand chance Mom had forgotten a hiding place?…

But why? Why not just continue with the claim and get the entire five hundred thousand? Was it found to get rid of him? He'd been the monkey wrench in the works all along. It wasn't surprising that somebody hadn't wanted him to show up. It's not what you think. How true! Shouldn't he be looking at Gert or Penny? Both, maybe, or Lawrence Woods?

It was tough to shut his mind down but sometime before dawn he drifted into dreamless sleep. Tomorrow just might be the start of the end to all this. Even on a Saturday he thought he could get Woods to open the vault—the vault that might hold some answers because he'd be looking for something no one else had—evidence that something had been put in, not taken out. It still sounded bizarre. Would anyone believe him?

He'd expected a call from Stephanie but not at 5:43 am and not with her crying and screaming, hysterically trying to tell him something about bank president Woods. Dan dropped his cell once before sitting up and swinging both legs over the edge of the bed.

"Stephanie, take a deep breath. Easy…that's it." He waited until the sobs quieted to hiccoughs. "Now, tell me what's happened."

"I'm at the bank. I came in early to catch up on bookwork… Oh, Mr. Mahoney…he's dead. I opened the door and there he was swinging in the air…from the antique chandelier."

"Stephanie, I'm on my way. Call the sheriff, a doctor, and emergency services. And it might be best if you step back outside." Dan had the cell tucked between chin and shoulder and was already pulling on jeans. "Try to stay calm. I know this is a terrible shock. I'll be there in five minutes."

In fact it was more like three minutes when he jogged down the middle of Nolan Street and up the sidewalk to where Stephanie stood.

She was shaking and pale, just on the edge of shock and chattering teeth but still clutching the cell phone. She managed to point over her shoulder.

Dan didn't go inside but looked through the door's glass partition. The less touched at the scene, the better. And it was apparent that Lawrence Woods had been dead for a while. Bluish swelling already appeared around the edge of the rope, puffing up his neck under his ears. His first thought was to marvel at the strength of the chandelier. Must be anchored to a main cross beam. The twisted cable that held it in place looked substantial—overkill for a mere lighting fixture. They didn't build things like they used to.

Was the dead bank president prominently on display in the foyer of his bank some kind of message? Was Woods making a statement? Dan sat down on the curb, motioned Stephanie to join him, and put an arm around her shoulders.

"I'm sorry you had to find this."

Snuffling, and a nod. "The local police should be here any minute but it'll take the EMT guys a while."

It took almost an hour but finally the little group on the curb had enlarged to include several early-rising curious neighbors, the sheriff, the emergency crew with the ambulance, and the coroner. Dan introduced himself, told the sheriff and the coroner what he knew, then followed the group to the door of the bank but stayed outside.

Dan instantly liked the coroner. As a rule and by lot, they all weren't the type you wanted to be buds with, but Clayton Asher was a winner. Droll, nothing in-your-face lewd or sickeningly in bad taste, and with a seeming respect for the human being. Dead or alive.

"You want to step over here?" Clayton looked up from kneeling on the floor next to the body. He was putting instruments back in a black bag and peeling off latex gloves. "I'd like to give you a heads-up before I have the guys give Mr. Woods a ride to town."

Probably talking to the sheriff, Dan thought but he walked in that direction anyway.

"Looks pretty cut and dried to me. Suicide's always hardest on the family. I'll get a list of next-of-kin from Stephanie." Sheriff Howard looked over the coroner's shoulder.

"Appearances can be deceiving. I won't have any final word until I do some testing but a preliminary exam suggests the hyoid is broken."

"The what?" Sheriff Howard was now leaning over the body.

"Bone in the throat. When it's broken, it usually suggests that it was done manually—result of a scuffle or pressure applied from behind—leaving all the rest of this as a cover-up. The killer doesn't realize all this is wasted effort."

As if on cue, all three of them glanced upward. One end of a three-quarter-inch, tight knit cotton rope—the kind used for leading horses—dangled from the ornate brass fixture. "Plus the chair here." Clayton pointed to a wooden high-backed chair on its side about three feet away. "Cane seat's busted out along the back. The lab boys can determine if that's a new or old break. My guess is new. I'll even go so far as to say there were two people on that chair—one dead, one alive."

Dan heard the sheriff suck in his breath and quickly exhale. Disgust? Certainly disappointment. Suicide had just turned into murder and a heck of a lot more work. He felt sorry for him. And maybe just a little sorry for himself. Dan thought Lawrence might have had some answers and this probably proved that Dan's suspicions had been right. He turned to go. This was not the time to get someone to let him into the safe deposit vault. That would have to wait.

"Mr. Mahoney?" The sheriff was walking toward him, "If I could have a minute?"

"Sure. What's up?"

"I'd be more comfortable in my cruiser…more private. I'm right outside the door."

Dan looked at the sheriff but he averted his eyes…Uh-oh. Not good. He followed the man to his car. Sheriff Howard took his time settling behind the wheel before turning toward Dan.

"I don't know why I didn't put two an' two together before this but when I tried to leave a message for you at the hospital a couple weeks ago, the doc said he'd pass it on. I think he said your fiancée." Dan nodded. "I believe the name was Elaine

Linden." Again, Dan nodded and watched the sheriff lick his lips before continuing, "I think this Ms. Linden got herself in some trouble last night."

"You have the wrong person. Elaine went home. Roswell. She won't be back to Wagon Mound before this evening—probably won't be leaving Roswell before noon today." Yet, a flicker of dread sparked somewhere deep within.

"Look, I usually push this off on the women—"

"Push what off? What's happened? Accident?" The dread now raced full blown up his spine threatening to paralyze his brain. "Tell me. Just spit it out." He was fast losing patience with the man beside him.

"Here's what we know. A late model Mercedes Benz was found on the shoulder of Highway120 about five miles west of Wagon Mound city limits at a little after six last night—"

"Last night? That's twelve hours ago."

"As I said, I didn't make the connection until now. If I remember correctly, y'all were driving a Cherokee. The plates on the Mercedes were gone and we traced it through the VIN. Up until then we didn't have a name. And that info sent us to Roswell."

"Did she have mechanical difficulties? A flat tire?" No, she would have called him. This wasn't making sense.

"Won't know that. The car was pretty well burned—"

"Burned?" Now his mouth was dry and his hands felt like ice.

"Listen, this is why I'm retiring the end of this year. I can't take this shit any more. The car was burned and there was a woman's body on the front seat—"

"What are you telling me? Where's Elaine?" He hadn't meant to shout.

"Calm down, man. Forensics hasn't had a go at this yet. I didn't bother Clay at home last night—time we got the car towed and the…body…to the morgue, it was almost midnight. Now this." A wave of his hand took in the bank. "Look. I'm sorry. Real sorry. I don't have the right words. And I sure as hell don't have the answers. Plus, I don't have the manpower to go in six directions—there's pretty much only me out here."

Dan turned away, tried to steady his breathing, and glanced out the window. Doing whatever you shouldn't do to the messenger came to mind and he vowed to give the sheriff a break. And he reminded himself that there was no definitive information… not yet anyway. He watched Clay follow the gurney holding Lawrence Woods to the ambulance. Two EMTs snapped the legs flat, scooted the gurney forward, and the coroner climbed in before the driver slammed the doors shut. With lights flashing, the ambulance took off.

"Do you have a number for the morgue? I'm going to ask Clay to wait for me. I need to get some firsthand information—you know, just make certain…." Dan shrugged his shoulders and gave up trying to look strong.

"Good idea. I'll call him. Come on, I'll give you a ride home."

◇◇◇

He was numb. He couldn't put two coherent thoughts together—it wasn't Elaine. That's all he could think of. It wasn't Elaine. Once again, he tried her cell but snapped his phone shut the minute her voice-mail came on.

Action, he had to do something, prove something…but how? And what?

He couldn't allow himself to think, even allow a "what if" to push its way in.

Or he'd lose it. He had to have hope until he knew beyond a doubt. He was flying toward the edge of a cliff with nothing to slow him down.

He grabbed his billfold and car keys and let Simon out. The dog rushed to the Cherokee and waited not too patiently by the passenger-side door until Dan opened it.

"Hey, in the back." Simon quickly obeyed.

The ride was uneventful. Fast, but there was no one patrolling at that hour of the morning. Seven on a Saturday morning, and Las Vegas was just waking up. Like a robot he maneuvered the car through town. Left turn, right turn, a couple stops and he turned into the parking lot. Before him the low squat, block, building looked forlorn. There was one lone pickup which was probably Clayton's. Dan pulled in beside it, left windows down a few inches and admonished Simon to "be good."

The front door of the building was open and he stepped inside. "Anyone here?"

A yell from the back, and Dan was on his way down a long hall eerily lit by flickering fluorescents. Tight budget, Dan guessed. The building could use a little paint. Another shout of "back here," and he quickly walked to the last door on his left. The spotless room fairly gleamed with shiny metal tables, refrigerated storage units, sinks and pull-down track lighting—somebody was putting the County's money in the right places. Clayton was waiting just inside the door.

"Sheriff Howard filled me in. I'm sorry. I hope I can be of help."

"Thanks. I appreciate you meeting me."

"There's probably no reason to view the body…I've uploaded a series of pictures I took last night. We can view those online. Have you seen burn victims before?"

Dan shook his head. He'd investigated countless fires—damaged houses, belongings, but never a human being destroyed by fire. "I think I need to see…there might be something…some clue that in the flesh—"

"There's not much of that. I just want to warn you. You sure?"

"Yes."

"The body's in a fridge. I'll get it." Clayton walked through double-doors at the back of the room.

Dan held the doors open as Clayton returned pushing the unwieldy gurney into the room. Clayton maneuvered it into position directly under the overhead lights and snapped the wheel-locks into position. Clayton looked at him once. Checking for a sign—a last chance to back out?

"I'll tell you what I know. Let me get my notes." Clayton walked back to his desk, returned with reading glasses and notebook, put both on a side cabinet and began unzipping the body bag.

Dan felt wooden. Visions of Elaine laughing, hugging Simon, leaning out the car window to kiss him good-bye—he couldn't stop them. Was he prepared to see a human body melted like a candle? Flesh peeled back, nose gone—he turned away.

"You OK? Let me get you a chair."

"No, go ahead. I'd rather stand."

Another one of those "you can back out if you want to" glances and Clay stepped away from the table. "I'll just give you a rundown of the preliminaries. Stop me whenever for more detail. And if we need to reference the body, we can." He cleared his throat. "Female Caucasian, dark hair, five feet nine or ten, undetermined age—"

"Ballpark guess?"

"Tough to be exact. There was nothing even extraneous to give us a clue, no clothing, no—"

"Wait. She was naked?"

"No evidence of clothing burned or otherwise. Cause of death was most likely smoke inhalation. I'm not seeing any other obvious life-threatening marks—nothing made by a knife, a bullet…no broken bones. My guess is she was bound from the placement of her feet and hands, and a melted nylon residue in close proximity to the extremities—not unlike clothesline."

"Whoa. Naked, hands bound…what the hell? She was alive when she was placed in the car?"

"Pretty sure of it."

"Makes it sound like she was removed—taken from the car and then returned."

Unbelievable. Dan's brain was reeling. This was sickening. What kind of monsters were they dealing with? What could be a reason to commit such a heinous crime? Burn a body? But why would Elaine have stopped in the first place? Gone somewhere with her killers? Did she know these people? Or person?

"Look, I know this is pretty brutal. Want me to go on?"

"Yeah."

"Let's see…other bits of info…I'm going to leave out all the measurements; don't think you're interested in the length of the right and left femurs." Clay glanced up and Dan shook his head. "…full dentition, a couple fillings, epoxies, not amalgams, one cap, front left canine or eye tooth." He looked up, "Otherwise her teeth are in great condition. We'll know more after a dental workup. And that, most likely, will be our definitive marker when it comes to identification. Let's see if there's anything else…" Clay turned several pages of notes, then paused and backtracked a page, "Don't know if this will be of help but this woman has never given birth—"

"That's it. Elaine has a son." The flood of relief almost buckled his knees.

"Natural birth?"

"I…I don't know." He felt like the air had been punched out of him. Up, then slammed to earth. "No, wait." He wasn't thinking, a C-section would leave a scar. "She doesn't have an abdominal scar." He knew he blushed, but they were adults. "Did you see a scar?" He stopped, deflated, "I mean if you could tell." The impact of "burned beyond recognition" jolted him back to earth.

"Sorry, don't think that marker's available to us anymore. But if you can find out that her son was a natural birth, I think we have something to go on. Pretty definitive stuff, too. Look," Clayton turned to a computer on his desk and brought up a picture—a picture that caused Dan to take a couple of deep breaths. "Here and here…according to the sub-pubic angle and the pelvic inlet, the area would have widened and possibly tilted after bearing a child. There is no indication of any widening. We've got a pretty narrow set of hips here."

Dan fished his cell out of side pocket and hit the speed-dial number for Carolyn. He knew he'd have to explain later, but for now expediency was everything.

Carolyn picked up on the third ring. "Don't ask questions, just answer one."

"What's going—"

"I mean it. This is important—was Jason's birth natural? No C-section, right?"

"Of course not, we did it the old fashioned way. We were in the hospital at the same time. Now, tell me—"

"Later. And, sis? Thanks." He snapped the phone shut. The rush of relief almost toppled him. He steadied himself with the edge of the table.

"Confirmed."

"That does it then. I'm gonna go out on a limb and say this isn't your girl. You know earlier when you asked about age?" Now, he had Dan's attention. "Without a lot of testing, but relying on experience and a fairly well-developed sixth sense, I'd say our gal here is late teens or early twenties—not someone in her mid-forties."

Chapter Twelve

It's not Elaine. It's not Elaine. He couldn't stop repeating it. He felt light-headed—too much stress, overpowering grief, steeling himself for the worst, then finding out the opposite. Or maybe he was just getting older—couldn't take the emotional roller coaster. He let Simon out and walked him around the grounds. He knew he'd have to face the fact that just because she wasn't the body on the table inside didn't mean that she was okay and not in some equally precarious danger, waiting for him to find her. My God, what had he gotten her—gotten them—into? And what should he do next? Where did he start? Because he would find her. That was a promise. He hustled Simon back into the SUV and headed to Wagon Mound.

He slowed five miles before the town's outer limits. The Mercedes was gone but now the scorched ground where it had been was surrounded with crime tape. Things sure seemed to work on a *mañana* schedule out here. No one had even been at the site when he'd passed it an hour earlier. But it was Saturday morning and only nine thirty.

Dan pulled in behind the second cruiser and parked on the shoulder. Sheriff Howard was talking with a highway patrolman while two men in jumpsuits were running old-fashioned metal detectors over the area—each walking parallel to the other but fifty feet apart. Sheriff Howard waved him over and met him with a hearty handshake.

"Just got off the phone with Clay. Boy, am I glad he had some good news for you. You don't know how relieved I am."

"Thanks. Me, too." Not proved beyond a doubt but very, very probable. Something to hang on to and Dan needed that. "You need to organize a search and rescue. Elaine's out there somewhere—"

"Got the boys on this another half hour, but I don't think we're going to find anything. I'll put in for a statewide S&R when we know for sure that Ms. Linden is missing."

"Know for sure? What more do you need? You're losing valuable time. It needs to be done now."

"With all due respect and understanding your situation, I have rules to follow. Twenty-four hours before I can make a move. Best I can do."

Dan knew he wasn't going to get anywhere. Rules. How many lives had been lost in the name of following orders? But he kept his mouth shut. He wouldn't gain anything by antagonizing the sheriff.

"When was the last time you heard from Ms. Linden?"

"Night before last."

"And you didn't know she was heading out yesterday?"

"I'm betting it was supposed to be a surprise."

"We don't know if she even made it this far. She could have been carjacked anywhere along the way and the car brought here."

"True. But why here if she wasn't driving?"

"Yeah, doesn't add up."

"I take it you haven't found anything...any hints as to who?"

"Could have been robbery; we haven't found a purse or luggage. There's a scorched box of pizza and what was probably a DVD that was on the backseat."

"Friday night." Elaine was planning on being with him last night...almost made it.

"Pardon?"

"She was in the car at this point. She left the car—was taken from the car—whatever, but she was here."

"What tells you that?"

"I'll make a bet that she picked up the pizza in Las Vegas— she wouldn't bring frozen food from Albuquerque or Santa Fe. We've rented DVDs from that store at the edge of town before. I'll call 'em."

Dan retrieved his cell from the SUV and let Simon out after clipping his leash in place. A quick call supported his claim— Elaine had rented *Eat, Pray, Love* at around quarter to five, Friday night. His first reaction was he didn't mind seeing the DVD in a melted state—then admonished himself. He'd watch *The Wedding Planner*...hell, he'd watch *Under the Tuscan Sun* looped non-stop if it meant having Elaine with him.

"We're gonna wrap it up. I'm not going to know what direction to take until we get that poor girl ID'd. And I got that bank president needing attention. But I want you to know I'll do everything I can as quickly as I can to find Ms. Linden. Want me to keep you in the loop?"

"Absolutely. I'll do the same."

Dan watched the little group of law enforcers pack up their equipment, pile back into separate cars, two pull U-turns and head back to town while the sheriff continued to Wagon Mound. By now Simon was more than ready to be let off leash to stretch his legs.

Helpless. He hated that feeling. But no one said he couldn't do some investigating on his own. This was where Elaine disappeared. She had been here. He could feel it. But how cold could a fifteen-hour trail be? He just shook his head. Frigid, probably.

He started with the scorched square of grass at the edge of the road and walked around it. No gauging now what direction she had taken when she left the car. What wasn't burned was trampled flat between hauling the car off and the metal detecting search team that just left.

Had the Benz had engine trouble? He doubted it. She had said she was going to get it serviced—even new tires. No, more than likely, something made her pull over. Had she hit an animal? He quickly stepped to the edge of the highway and scanned both the asphalt and the embankment for a furry or feathered body. Nothing. Where did he go from here? It wasn't like there was any kind of neighborhood to canvas—the old standby questions, *what did you see* or *what did you hear* didn't make it out here.

When Simon came up to stand beside him, he was so lost in thought that the bag in the dog's mouth didn't register—not until Simon dropped the tan leather Coach shoulder purse on his foot. Dan quickly stooped to pick it up, wiped a trail of saliva off the strap, opened it and immediately fished out Elaine's billfold. Fifty dollars in cash, cards, change, gas receipts—nothing had been taken. This wasn't a robbery. He didn't know what it was, but he could eliminate a hold-up. And she had gotten this close to Wagon Mound.

Now the question was how could he find the spot that Simon had found? He wasn't thinking when he let the dog go. He should have leashed him and then with dog under control scoured the area. But praise was in order now. From the look of rapt attention, Simon was sure this feat must be worth a treat or at least some pats on the head.

"Good job, Simon." If a rottweiler could beam, then the dog fairly glowed. And for a fleeting moment, Dan wished Simon had some retriever in him. There was just no way that Simon could lead him back to where he had found Elaine's purse. Then he thought of something. Where was her phone? He upended the bag spilling everything on the ground: lipstick, tube of gloss, grocery list, house keys, two pairs of sunglasses, Kleenex…no cell.

Of course, it could have been on the seat in the car but if it had fallen out—he quickly pulled out his cell and dialed. Tough to tell, but he swore that he could hear a jangling tune from somewhere over to his left. Faint. Barely discernible. He dialed again. This time Simon gave a low "woof" and bolted.

Something about trying to follow four legs on only two… Dan paused twice to retry the number and was rewarded when the sound appeared closer. But, of course, Simon got there first, up and over a jumbled mass of boulders he was hopping around at the edge of an arroyo when Dan got to him. Then Simon disappeared over the edge and plunged down a six- foot incline.

The grass at the edge was bent, some dried stalks broken leaving little doubt that something or someone had slipped over the edge besides Simon. Now the answering cell was just below him—still hidden in underbrush but probably within fifteen feet. He took a step forward, slipped, lost his footing and sat down sharply. Broken Juniper branches, flattened grasses and weeds—someone had done the exact same thing, fallen and struggled to get up.

He just sat there staring, then stood balancing against a boulder. The spot was remote, well off the highway. He moved to retrieve the cell phone below him neatly planted in a clump of blue grama. What had happened here? Why was Elaine in the arroyo in the first place? He stood in one spot and looked around. What caught his eye was how beaten down the grass was around and below him. Much more damage than one person could do. Slipping and sliding, he kept an eye on the ground and made his way to the flat, sandy, arroyo bottom.

Looking back up, he recalculated and figured the steep side to be more like twenty feet—a hefty climb, or fall. But there was every reason to believe that either for better or worse, the boulder broke Elaine's fall. She didn't reach the bottom on her own judging from the footprints and tire tracks in the arroyo, she had help.

Damn it. Someone had rescued, then abducted her. The same folks who put the nude body of a teenager in the Mercedes? He hoped not. There were satanic overtones to killing someone by fire—somehow beyond any other means of death, fire was torture, or at the very least, a nasty cover-up. And this looked to be the former. What would people like that do to Elaine?

He was jolted back to the present by the low keening sound of Simon who was still sitting above him beside the boulder.

"Yeah, I know, Boy. This isn't pretty." He motioned for Simon to "come"—another one of those newly learned signals—and reluctantly, the dog obeyed. "Let's see where these tracks lead."

It was obviously an all-terrain vehicle. Only an ATV could maneuver around the boulders and get good traction in the thick sand. An arroyo was dangerous in the best of weather and deadly during the monsoons. The same torrential rains that had deposited the boulders and debris that he was skirting, could take the life of a human being in the blink of an eye—carrying that person at a rate of over thirty-five miles per hour hell-bent down one of these watery avenues.

He squatted and checked the tracks. The crustiness of the top layer of sand was indented suggesting a much heavier vehicle would have broken the surface and sunk in. Which also might mean only a driver onboard. If there were two people, the second was a lightweight, until the ATV turned to go back the way it came. Then the back wheels dug in perceptibly deeper—not by much but enough to account for a hundred and thirty plus pound passenger.

He followed the tracks until the ATV went up a lower sloping side of the arroyo and the tracks disappeared on the asphalt. What now? He could just about prove that Elaine had gotten out of her car to follow something—something that she'd hit probably. She'd never leave a wounded animal. And in following it, she fell down the arroyo, was injured, then rescued by one or two people on an ATV. No, rescue was the wrong word. He had no warm, fuzzy feeling that her saviors meant anything other than harm.

The tuneless melody from his cell made him hurriedly reach in his pocket. He flipped the phone open. Elaine? "Mahoney, here." He deflated like a balloon when he heard a man's voice. How long would it be before that rush of adrenalin and hope at every ring would subside? Every minute without knowing made it that much more difficult.

"This is Sheriff Howard. I need to have you meet me at the bank."

"Sure. Is there something I can help with?"

"Hope so. Otherwise, just need to pick your brain."

The sheriff wasn't long on words and abruptly hung up. With everything else going on, Dan had pushed Lawrence Woods from his mind. But he was another piece of the puzzle…or puzzles. Dan couldn't even figure out if everything was connected. But he didn't have a good reason to think that it wasn't.

"May have a match with that girl that was burned." Sheriff Howard met Dan at the curb in front of the bank.

"That was quick."

"Well, should say I'm putting two and two together…nothing definitive but just got a missing person's report. Mother of a girl who worked part-time here at the bank."

"Amber Medger?"

"Yeah, you know her?"

"Not really. I wanted to talk with her about a couple times she filled in for Stephanie." Dan wasn't going to mention the call to the Hobbs office…about her knowing his route and ETA… how she could have set him up.

"Her mother filed a missing person's report this morning. Seems the girl ran off with a biker few weeks back…was supposed to have gotten married. Apparently, that fell through and she came back home only to disappear again. No one's heard from her for the last four days. I think she's our dead mystery woman."

"Amber?" Both men turned. Stephanie had walked up behind them.

"Sorry you had to overhear. That information isn't for general distribution. And, I may of misspoke. We don't have answers." Sheriff Howard looked contrite.

"But Amber? She wouldn't hurt anyone. She just wanted a chance at life." The tears were starting, and Dan moved to put an arm around Stephanie. The morning had taken its emotional toll on her—it would on anyone.

"The sheriff's right. No one knows anything for certain." Dan hoped his smile was empathetic.

Sniffling, then a quick smile of gratitude as Dan fished a Kleenex out of his jacket pocket, and Stephanie blew her nose.

Sheriff Howard touched her on the shoulder, a half-hearted sort of squeeze, but Dan was glad to see him break his stiff façade. "Stephanie, if you have the extra time, I'd like you to answer some questions about the vault. Show me a thing or two about security."

Good, Dan thought, give her something to do, take her mind off of her friend—and her boss. The three of them went back into the bank. The sheriff paused at the vault door before stepping into the room.

"Did you happen to notice when you opened up this morning, if this door was open?"

Stephanie shook her head. "I didn't get past…get past…." She turned sideways and pointed toward the foyer.

"I'd like to know if you see anything different here. Take your time."

"I don't need any time, sheriff, the fact that the door is open at all says that Mr. Woods had to have opened it…and those boxes—there's no reason they should be open."

Dan looked over Stephanie's shoulder. Hot damn! The three unused security boxes with their doors standing wide open. Well, maybe not unused, just unmarked without the name of an owner on the list in Stephanie's drawer.

"I don't want to step on toes here, but I'd really recommend going over each of those boxes with a fine-tooth comb." Dan expected some objection from the sheriff but only got a, "Why?"—and a piercing stare.

"Well, I have a theory." Quickly, Dan filled them in on how the necklace had been misplaced, not stolen, and that other customer's claims turned out to be bogus which led to an epiphany of sorts. What if someone had tunneled into the bank to leave something, not take something out? Something so unusual, or valuable that it took a bank vault to hold it. You have to admit this would be a perfect hiding place."

"That's a new one." Skeptical. But Dan could see that the sheriff was rolling it around. "No bright ideas on just what this was?"

Dan ignored the hint of sarcasm. He knew how it must sound. "No. I only believe they didn't even try to reach the two million sitting in the next room. This is where they wanted to be. And I've got a feeling that the tunnel had been there for a while. Maybe, Woods knew about it. Looked the other way."

Sheriff Howard stared at Dan, then shrugged and turned to Stephanie. "How many people had access to this vault? Knew the combination and had keys to the boxes?"

"As I explained to Mr. Mahoney, that was one of our new rules. Mr. Woods took control of the vault first part of the summer. I checked people in and out, but he was the only one who could retrieve their belongings."

"Any explanation as to why this change?" Sheriff Howard was taking notes.

"No, he said it was new bank-wide policy. A vice president or above was the only authorized person. We don't have a vice president."

"Let me get the boys back down here. I'm taping off the room—no one goes in or out. We'll see if your theory holds water." Sheriff Howard flipped his cell open, then turned to Dan. "Oh yeah, with this new info I'm authorizing a search and rescue—might be premature but then again, might not be."

Dan nodded. He didn't get the feeling that the sheriff held out much hope. For that matter, did he? But as long as he was here he wanted to look at the check-in book again. He had nothing particular in mind, but maybe there was something he'd missed—some notation by Amber that would somehow indicate duplicity. Yeah, a long shot but he'd do anything to not go back to the apartment. He couldn't just sit there staring at four walls and thinking and not knowing.

"Stephanie? Do you have a minute? I'd like to look at the vault sign-in sheet for August again. Actually, let's make it June and July, too."

Stephanie looked pleased to be doing something and gave him a weak smile as she went to her desk. After unlocking the lower drawer, she set the logs for the three summer months on top facing him.

"Can I help you look for something?"

Dan sighed. "If I knew what I was looking for." He pulled the logs closer. "How often did Amber sit in for you?"

"I guess a lot over the summer. My grandson was ill and I took several long weekends to go to Albuquerque."

Dan opened the June log and leafed through. There were three long weekends—Friday/Monday combinations starting the second week. He reached for July and found four Fridays that Amber had sat in. During August, she was in twice—only one of those a long weekend.

He opened each log to the first date that Amber's initials showed up and let his eye run down the entries. It wasn't until he'd compared the second and third days that he saw it. Coincidence? He leafed back through the pages when Stephanie had been there—then turned back to Amber's fill-in times. No. This didn't add up.

"Stephanie, how often did Emily Tapia request her safe deposit box?"

"I don't remember any times. She never came in. Paid for their box on a monthly basis but never checked on it."

"Wouldn't you say it's interesting that she came in every single time Amber was on duty?"

"Really?" Stephanie turned the logs to look. "She and her dad had one of those manuscript-sized boxes. You know, like the post office? It could hold several folders."

Yeah, Dan thought, manuscript-sized to hold a silver baby spoon and her mother's wedding set. Things that she needed to look at nine times over the summer.

"Just to make sure her visits started in June, check another three months like March, April, May of this year."

He watched as Stephanie leafed through the additional logs. "Not one visit. Not even the times Amber was here. What do you think it means?"

"I wish I knew." Dan shook his head in puzzlement. No immediate explanation jumped to mind. But the start of an idea was just sparking somewhere in the recesses. What if Emily was a "mule"? Maybe Emily made the deposit and Amber took it from there. Delivered money? Picked up drugs? Depositing drugs or money beside the silver baby spoon and wedding set for Amber to…to do what? Drugs made sense. It wasn't farfetched. In fact, it made perfect sense—out here, off the beaten path. Still, it was dangerous work. Amber should have stuck with talking dirty in the middle of the afternoon. But how did Amber get into the safe deposit box? Maybe the bank president…?

He thanked Stephanie, waved good-bye to Sheriff Howard, got in the Cherokee and sat there thinking. What if ol' Lawrence Woods was involved? There it was again, another "what if." And what did that leave him with? He dug out his keys. He couldn't put off going back to the apartment forever. He started the Cherokee and made a U-turn.

Inactivity was crazy-making. Dan went over his notes. Took Simon for a walk, went over his notes again. Could the death— he needed to amend that to murder—of the bank president and the part-time worker be connected? If he didn't know that Amber had set him up, the answer might have been "no." But she was a player. Former player. But how much had she known? Had she been paid to look the other way when Emily visited the family box? And what did she see then? Was she on the same page as Lawrence? Somehow in cahoots? Whatever her level of knowledge, someone saw the need to silence her.

So where did Elaine fit in? What could she know? What could she have seen? Had she been silenced too? Somehow, maybe out of the sheer need to survive and not give into any worst-case scenario, he refused to believe that. She was alive and she was out there somewhere—somewhere in a part of the country that boasted an average of less than one person per square mile. Proverbial needle in the haystack.

He whistled for Simon, opened the Cherokee's back door and then slipped behind the wheel—and just sat there.

"Where to?" He watched the dog in the rearview cock both ears. "Think we should go back out and look around?" This time there was a woof and a shake of the head that sprayed saliva across the back of the driver's seat. "Okay, back to the wilds."

Maybe it wasn't that he expected to find something and more like this was the last place that he knew Elaine had been and there was comfort in that. Whatever, he let Simon out and walked the trail once again from the burned outline of the car, back through the brush, down the arroyo, up the dry bed, back up the side following the ATV tracks and back to the Cherokee.

Nothing. Nothing he hadn't seen before and no epiphany. It was a long shot but as long as he was out here, he might as well see if ol' Buster saw or heard anything. He was less than a mile north and west. It wasn't out of the question that someone might have noticed something. A burning car would have been noticeable at a distance further than that. He had no idea if Buster had ranch hands that stayed late in the evening but guessed there might be. It was improbable that he worked that sized spread 24/7 all by himself.

The gate was unlocked and Dan let himself in. At the end of the drive this time there wasn't a man with a shotgun, just one furiously barking Chihuahua…with a rhinestone tiara.

"Bitsy. Get in here." Penny Kennedy stood at the edge of the porch.

"What a nice surprise. What brings you all the way out here?" She deftly leaned down and scooped up Bitsy.

At least this Penny was the one he remembered. Eye makeup and straightened hair must be reserved for bank visits. "I'd like to talk with the doc." Dan explained the events of the last twenty hours leaving out the dead girl in the Mercedes. But mentioned the car fire. Dan had purposefully left out the part about an ATV, too.

"Oh my. That lovely Ms. Linden. And you think she may have gone for help and gotten lost? Or worse? Oh dear, it's so dangerous out here.

Animals…" She looked up, "I'm so sorry. I know Doc Jenkins will just be beside himself to think it happened on his property. He was away over the weekend. I don't expect him back before tomorrow."

"Were you here on Friday?"

"I only worked until mid-day and then came back this morning. I don't work much during the week—only weekends. I do filing and correspondence for Dr. Jenkins. This is my little mad money job. I don't like to leave mother alone for very long."

"What about ranch hands? Is there a full crew here today?"

"Oh, my goodness, no. The boys live as far away as Albuquerque. They're out of here Friday afternoons by two."

"So, no one was here late last Friday and no workers are here today?"

"No, the place is quite deserted."

"Thanks for your time. I'll catch up with the doc first of the week." Dan turned to go, then paused, "How is your mother?"

"She's been better this week. Of course, finding the necklace just gave her a new lease on life. That necklace is her life if you know what I mean. And that sweet Mr. Woods, God rest his soul, was a dear to cover for her."

"I'm glad things worked out." No wonder the town didn't need a newspaper—Woods was already news before lunchtime. He idly wondered who of the curbside spectators was the town crier. No mention of murder. That must be under wraps. "I'll keep in touch."

"Please let us know about Ms. Linden. Mr. Mahoney, I know this is going to have a happy ending. I can just see the two of you in Ireland, come spring. An Irish spring." A trill of laughter, and a wave.

She was still waving in that somewhat simplistic, chipper way that she had even after he'd turned the Cherokee around and headed back toward the highway.

Chapter Thirteen

Two figures in bulky hazmat suits complete with hoses connected to wheezing air pumps mounted on their backs pushed open the door. No ray of sunshine streamed in over their shoulders. Must be night. Again. Elaine shifted her weight to the side that didn't hurt which was a toss-up, both hips felt bruised and stiff. And her right ankle throbbed. Wherever she was, it was humid and cold. Humidity? In New Mexico? Must be some temperature controlled building…amend that to closet. She only had the luxury of seeing around the edge of the blindfold—but the walls seemed close. Maybe a ten by ten space.

Then it struck her. She was in a walk-in cooler of sorts—the sound of the heavy door thudding into place, bolt locks noisily sliding across when her captors left, the clammy metal walls. And the sound of a generator that came on now and then and refreshed her air supply. She only knew the cooler opened to the outside because she had seen sunshine frame the doorway. Yesterday? Maybe only this morning—she had no way of knowing. At least both of her captors carried flashlights or that was her guess as beams of light skirted the edges of the blindfold.

The first white suit leaned over her and prodded the area around her ankle while the other stood behind her and pointed a beam of light at the area. She hadn't meant to cry out but the pain was swift and blinding. She must have twisted her ankle. She remembered leaving the car to get Bitsy, but the rest was a blank. White-suit applied what was probably a bag of ice, and not too gently lifted her leg to rest on a pillow. Elaine willed herself to pay attention. Was this a woman? The shadows seemed to outline one smaller or shorter person and one taller one. The person closest to her was now ripping gauze. A long string of it was tucked under the turned back cuff of the white suit and between the latex gloves and the cuff, Elaine could just make out a tattoo. Something very black, maybe the image of a tree trunk…there was no way to see more without giving away that she could see at all. Impossible to tell what they had in store for her. Should she feel heartened that if they patched her up, they probably weren't going to kill her ? Not yet, anyway. Maybe they were just saving her for something.

She also smelled food and her stomach did a somersault. How long had it been since she'd eaten? White-suit untied the straps around her wrists but didn't touch the blindfold. Neither did she. She sat there rubbing first one wrist and then the other waiting until the person closest to her had secured the bag of ice to her ankle with strips of gauze. Finally both shuffled to the door and left, slipping the bar into place from the outside.

Tentatively she untied the knot behind her head. The generator whirred on and a single light bulb suspended from a cord in the middle of the tiny room began to glow. Elaine looked around. Her luggage was stacked against the closest wall. There was a porcelain pot in the far corner. She thought her grandmother would have called it a slop bucket, ten feet away was a covered tray and six one-gallon plastic bottles of water. The bathroom and dining area seemed a little close together. A blanket and a narrow, rolled cotton mattress completed the furnishings. Spare. No, bleak was more like it. Tears threatened to spill over her lower lids; she blinked and willed herself to have strength. Giving into feeling sorry for herself wouldn't get her anywhere.

On the first attempt at standing, her right ankle refused to hold any weight. She sat back sharply on the floor and gasped with the sudden searing pain. Was she going to faint? She willed herself to stay alert and didn't move until the dizziness passed.

She gingerly untied the gauze strips holding the ice pack in place and let the bag fall to the floor. Her ankle looked badly bruised but possibly that was the extent of her injuries. A test circle to the right and then to the left hurt but proved nothing was broken. Maybe not even badly sprained. This was good news but only if she thought she could get away. And that seemed hopeless.

So, first things first, she crawled to the tray of food. A stack of sandwiches, a dozen in all, each individually wrapped from a convenience store—with contents like ham, ham and cheese, tuna salad—well, there was one she wouldn't eat. Two unopened bags of chips, a jar of peanut butter, six pop-top cans of soup and a box of Raisin Bran. No utensils. No condiments. She reached for a sandwich, a ham and cheese on rye. Safer than the tuna salad but the rye was a little too dry. And who knew where they'd been or how long they'd gone without refrigeration.

But why so much food? Unless…she put the sandwich down…this was it. What she was looking at was the allotted stores for whatever period of time her lockup would entail. So, like those miners who survived in a Chilean mine, should she eat half a teaspoon of food a day…just in case she didn't get rescued for some time? And shouldn't there be some relief in knowing her captors weren't coming back? Or were they still there and just ignoring her? She put the sandwich back in its plastic tray and pulled the cellophane in place. The severity of her situation quashed her appetite. How long could she survive? Who would know where to look because just plain where was she?

Saturday night, twenty-four hours in, he called Jason. No, he didn't need to come out. His mother would not want him to miss classes. He'd keep him in the loop and call with the least bit of new information…police suspected car problems and then becoming disoriented walking for help—looked like she tried to take a short-cut through a wooded area. No, no evidence of foul play…got a full complement of law enforcement working on it. No, there wasn't anything he could do. Dan would call the minute anything changed.

Dan hung up feeling like a coward. But how do you tell a kid the truth? That you're scared shitless his mother's dead? Burned car, possible injuries…not things you throw out lightly. And you add a rollover and the murder of a bank president and temp employee—it took some strong-arm persuading and a few fibs to keep Jason away with what little information he did give him. And he could only hope it was the right thing to do—the thing Elaine would have wanted.

By Sunday morning he knew he had to do something or go crazy. Inactivity was torture. Thirty-two hours and no news. Absolutely nothing. On the positive side there were no new burned cars or bodies. Clay called him from the lab with the definitive news that the young woman was, indeed, Amber Medger. Amber, nineteen, a whole life ahead of her. What did she know to die so brutally?

He knew if he expected the sheriff to keep him in the loop, he better contribute to that loop himself. The info wasn't all going to slide downhill in one direction. It wasn't that Dan was keeping secrets—Emily's odd preoccupation with viewing family keepsakes or Amber's possibly setting him up might not be considered trade-worthy but he'd bet the sheriff didn't have much more. Something might be better than nothing. And he needed to know what he was doing to find Elaine. He'd give him a call.

He wasn't sure he'd ever really understood—empathized with maybe was a better term—the vacant stares, the abject pain etched around mouths and eyes, the begging for help on TV when a loved one had disappeared with cries of "Please, call. Tell us what you know. Help us find Cindy, Carol, Tammy, Emma, Sofia…" Reporters gathering around, the questions—is there a person of interest? Do you suspect the husband, son, boyfriend, next door neighbor? And it always came back to: what will you do? How will you cope? What would you like to say to your loved one's captors? What would you like to say to your loved one?

How did these people go home? Make their beds, open the fridge, turn on the stove, put dinner on the table? How could you go about your life if you'd lost a part of yourself? How was he going about his life? His cell vibrated in his shirt pocket.

"You were right." Sheriff Howard didn't bother with "hello." "Got some fresh prints off of those empty boxes—running 'em through the system now. Prints and some kind of residue in one of the boxes that's on its way to the lab. Got a deputy hand-carrying it. But the feds are back involved. The demise of the bank prez was on their territory. So to speak. That puts me back in charge of what's happening locally. One murder and one missing person." A clearing of the throat and a softer tone, "I thought you might like to do a fly-over with me. I got volunteers and mounted deputies doing a fine-comb of the area looking for any trace of Ms. Linden. Nothing yet. But when you can't find anything on the ground, taking to the air sometimes works. Meet me in Las Vegas in an hour. Airstrip south side of town."

Perfect. A capital idea. He quickly walked Simon and put him back in the room. "Sorry, pal. I know this is getting old. But it won't be for long." God, he hoped he wasn't lying.

Sheriff Howard was standing beside a Bell 206 and it looked like he was the pilot. "Used to do this for a news team out of Albuquerque. Every once in awhile the state lets me borrow one of theirs. I've decided they think it makes up for being undermanned. I don't complain. You take perks where you can get 'em out here."

They took off flying south above trees, past Glorietta before turning right and making a wide circle, then continuing east and a little south.

"Not sure what we're going to be able to see but it saves us a lot of useless ground searches. You don't strike me as someone who enjoys spending all day in the saddle."

Dan nodded. The summer in Tatum had given him more hours astride a horse than he'd care to duplicate. He shifted in his seat just remembering the stiffness, then took the binoculars handed him to scour the terrain below. Trees, trees, and more trees rose up to greet them. The forest was dense with an end of year over growth that obscured paths. But the color was phenomenal—dark green interspersed with golden Aspen and touches of red scrub oak.

"Pretty out here. But I take it this isn't home?"

Dan shook his head, "Chicago." He waited but that seemed to be the extent of the pilot's interest. "What are we looking for?"

"Anything. Anything that catches your eye; anything out of place."

"I got a feeling in this remote area you might run across a certain cash crop being cultivated?"

"Yeah, and that's when I need backup. Those boys don't take kindly to losing a couple million dollars of hard work."

"How often do you find a crop?"

"Couple times a year. But most of the growing has moved inside—I've seen some cracker jack set ups under lights. Much less time from planting to harvest. 'Course there are more meth labs than anything else out this way. Cheap, easy drug to make. In the old days I-25 was known as the cocaine corridor. Shipments came up from Centro America. Columbia, mostly. Now that's sharing the spotlight with the homemade."

Drugs. A little bell was going off somewhere in his brain. He had a feeling he'd been right about Amber and Emily. Big money to be had. Might be a reason to check a safe deposit box nine times in three months. His idea of Emily as mule with Amber in on the action made sense. A little pick up and distribute, collect and hand off money. But that didn't explain the tunnel. It was obvious that Emily was able to walk in the front door of the bank and do business—didn't seem to be a reason to be covert. Was Amber an accomplice? Was that why she was expendable? But what was making him think the two were connected? That the tunnel had anything to do with drugs? Guess he had to start somewhere. And he didn't know that they weren't.

"What's that?" A glimmer of something shiny. "To the right." Dan aimed the binoculars. Whatever he saw seemed to quickly disappear but as Sheriff Howard circled, both could see trampled grass, a couple white garbage bags, and what looked like a collapsed tent. "Hunters?"

"Shouldn't be. All this is private land. I think you met the owner. Buster? Ol' Doc Jenkins?"

"This is his land?"

"Far as the eye can see, as they say. Some of it's government grant land because of the chickens, but the doc owns a fair piece."

"And no one hunts on his land?"

"Never have. Doesn't mix with what he's trying to do—providing specialized plantings of native grasses. And re-introducing the endangered prairie grouse. Last thing he needs is people camping in the area and maybe grabbing a chicken meal on the hoof."

"Good point."

"Look, I'd like to check it out. But I can't keep this baby in the air past sundown—don't have the instrument rating for night flying. And it could take awhile. I'll take the chopper in and come back here while there's still light left to look around. You up to riding shotgun?"

"Sure." What else did he have to do? Let the hours gnaw away at him? The hours without Elaine—without even the whiff of a clue as to where she could be…no, shotgun looked pretty good about now. And he needed to share a few things with the sheriff.

The Crown Vicky was cruising at eighty, but compared to the chopper, it seemed like they were crawling. It'd take them at least forty-five minutes to get back to where they saw the campsite if that was what it was. Big difference between "as the crow flies" and an Interstate.

The sheriff listened intently to Dan's tale of faking a promised welcoming party by the bank in order to get information on his whereabouts. Amber was the only one from Wagon Mound who knew what route he'd take. Sheriff Howard pursed his mouth and tapped an index finger on the steering wheel.

"Shame. Looks like Amber could have been of some help."

"Yeah, maybe on a lot of fronts." Dan told him how Emily Tapia had visited a mostly empty safe deposit box nine times—all on Amber's watch.

"Emily Tapia? I think you mean Emily Echols. Least it was Echols for a couple years."

"Any relation to Chet?"

"His grandson's wife. High school sweethearts, then the baby, then the marriage—a lot of those 'have to's' don't last. I heard she'd moved back in with her father and the boy was out at his Granddad's place."

Dan's mind was racing. A connection, sort of, that hadn't been there before. At least at the very simplest of levels, two people who happened to be related had something to do with the bank job...and the rollover. Then he shook his head—just too farfetched. One didn't necessarily support the other or vice versa. And Emily wasn't an Echols any longer or at least didn't use that last name. He'd wanted to talk to Chet Echol's grandkid in person...still might be a good idea.

"Tim used to help me out as a part-time deputy, plus the occasional security guard gig—worked all the high school games when they didn't interfere with his other jobs. Good kid, just couldn't survive on not being able to rely on a steady paycheck."

"You know what I'm going to ask. Was he ever on the bank's payroll?"

"Yeah, he worked relief. Don't know how often."

"What about the weekend of the robbery?"

"Nope. Tim was long gone by then. Finally went to work full time in Las Vegas. Ford dealership. Got out of security and law enforcement all together and started a small engine repair business on the side—set it up out at his Granddad's place. Kid can fix anything. That dealership got a gem of a mechanic." The sheriff concentrated on the highway. "Still, takes a lot of money these days to support a family."

Dan was quiet. Was it one more piece of the puzzle, a connection along with grandfather and ex-wife that was too important to overlook? Dan's gut was telling him he was on to something. He made a mental note to definitely look up the young Mr. Echols.

Suddenly Sheriff Howard braked, made a right turn and took the cruiser off road—up then down and over a low embankment. Dan braced against the dash. Note to self: never buy a cruiser at auction. These babies were put through their paces.

"I think the site's about five miles in. This is an old ditch road—back when this land was irrigated by water backed up from the Gallinas River—before it empties into the Pecos. But that was the old days. Irrigation was stopped years ago. Droughts were just too unpredictable. Never knew if there'd be enough water for crops. No snow-pack, no run-off, no irrigation."

"Tough making a living out here."

"Young people are leaving—can't wait to get out. You probably noticed half of Wagon Mound is a ghost town."

"What about you? Retirement can't be that far off."

For a minute Dan wasn't sure the sheriff was going to answer.

"Yeah, it's closing in. Some days I think I'll just work 'til I drop, then I go online and check out a sailboat or two."

"So what's going to win out? Sense of duty or the good life?"

"I lost my wife little over a year ago. Up until she got sick, it was sailboat all the way—the Bahamas in winter, nice little place on the Intracoastal the rest of the time. But dying can be expensive."

"I'm sorry."

"It's life. No regrets."

Dan thought the *c'est la vie* shrug lacked conviction. And until last summer Dan could have said much the same thing—retirement in ten years, fishing on the Chama during the summers, winters spent skiing. And now? He'd been gearing up for "the talk"—the "where do you want to live after we're married?" Yeah, married. Sometime in the last couple days, he knew for certain. He couldn't see the rest of his life without this woman. And now she was gone. He suddenly had more in common with the sheriff than he would have guessed possible.

The woods came up suddenly. One minute Dan was looking at open fields, the next a wall of trees. Sheriff Howard nosed the cruiser into a cleared space and stepped out.

"Should be straight in from here. Maybe a mile."

"Are we on Doc Jenkins land now?"

"Starts at the ditch. In the old days, ditches were boundaries—and water was shared." The sheriff walked to the back of the cruiser. "Just need to get some extra fire-power." Dan followed him. The spacious trunk looked like most people's garages—no room.

"Is that Hazmat gear?"

"Yeah, just part of a one-man show. Department keeps a few suits. I like to keep one handy. Had a bad spill right outside Rowe about a month ago. Actually, a load of fertilizer heading up this way."

The first half-mile was easy—not a lot of underbrush, early fall wildflowers, golden aspen overhead. Dan was lulled into suspending the nagging, paralyzing worry—what could be bad about a day of glorious sunshine without a cloud in the sky? The first shot tore through his reverie and jerked him back to the present.

"Let's go." Sheriff Howard wasn't waiting on him but plunged into a thicket and scrambled to the right. "Came from over this way."

Dan had barely caught up when the second shot rang out. This one came from the left. Closer.

The sheriff stopped, "Shit. Warning system. Whatever we saw from the air was a little fresher than I thought. I'd feel a lot more comfortable with a posse behind me. Let's go back. No need to take chances and we're going to lose our light in another hour. I'll recruit help from Santa Fe County in the morning. Need to go at this like we know what we're doing."

A change of plans because he was there, Dan wondered. Shouldn't endanger civilians. Or worse yet, let a chivvy put you in a compromising position. And it was a little disconcerting. Warning shots? Suddenly the woods were less than friendly. And all he could think of was Elaine. Could armed men be holding her? Out here in nowhere? But the sheriff was right, it would be stupid for the two of them to continue on their own. Warning shots were just that, a warning.

"You know we're going to find her."

Had he been reading his mind? Dan watched as the sheriff expertly maneuvered the cruiser back up onto the highway.

"I don't know what to think. I don't know what to do."

"Posters. Flyers with her picture. Blanket the earth."

"You really think that helps?"

"Hell, yes. And you never know. People pay attention around here, a stranger sticks out. Post a few in Las Vegas, along the road, here in town. All the way to Santa Fe wouldn't hurt. A picture of her car, too, if you've got one."

"You really think she could still be close by?"

"Been wondering. They tell us to think like the perp. But we don't know what crime has been committed yet—not to Ms. Linden, anyway. Can't think she was carjacked just so her car could be used as a crematorium. And why abduct Ms. Linden in the first place? Wrong place/wrong time? Did she see something she shouldn't? You might have noticed there's a lot of this that doesn't add up." A wry smile and a sideways look at Dan.

Dan decided this was as good a time as any to share the "it's not what you think" message. He'd expected to get a dressing down for concealing evidence, but the sheriff just seemed lost in thought.

"And you didn't see who left it?"

"Well, you're not going to be too overweight if you're jumping over the banister halfway down and landing on your feet. Takes some agility. I thought it was a kid—but guess it could be anybody slightly built."

"And you heard a bike start up and take off, but didn't see it?" Dan nodded. "So, might have been related, might not. Still got the note?"

Dan reached for his billfold and took out the now much-folded piece of paper.

"Put it in the glove box, I'll look at it later."

Simon met him at the door and after a quick jaunt around the block, Dan set up his laptop on the kitchen table and started to hunt through his pictures folder. There they were—a couple good head shots of Elaine and one of her standing by the Mercedes from last summer—exactly what he needed. He downloaded them to a flash drive, typed out copy that pleaded for information, saved that to the same drive, and got ready for bed. He thought the makeshift Post Office at the back of the convenience store offered electronic copying. He'd check in the morning. Posters or in this case flyers—oversized with pictures required paper big enough. He hoped they had supplies but more than that he hoped it would prove to be more than just busy work.

The knock on the door had even caught Simon snoozing. Dan shushed the big guy and checked his watch. Six-thirty. This better be important; he didn't think he'd even dozed off before three. Didn't seem to be any way to shut his mind down. The "what ifs" were rampant. He slipped on slacks and opened the door only to have a microphone thrust in his face. Simon saw this as a threat and lunged before Dan could grab his collar.

The woman with the microphone shrieked and jumped backwards knocking the guy holding the camera two steps down the stairs her microphone flying into space and the guy's camera clattering to the first floor landing.

"Did you get dog pictures? That animal is vicious and out of control."

"This one?" Dan pointed to Simon sitting by his side. "Dan Mahoney, and you're…?"

The woman, somewhat past her prime, stopped brushing off her jacket and held out a hand, "Mollie Barton, KOAT News at Six."

Dan ignored the hand. "How can I help you?" As if he didn't know. Was this what happened to aging newscasters? Gave new meaning to "out to pasture."

"We're following up on the Elaine Linden story." She leaned over to pick up a notebook. "Sheriff Howard has referred to you as 'a person of interest'…what do you have to say to that?"

Dan could only hope the shock wasn't showing on his face. Keep smiling. Act like it was the dumbest thing he'd ever heard—and, well, wasn't it?

"Sorry, but that's a new one on me. I think you'll have to follow up with the sheriff. Now if you'll excuse me."

"I doubt the sheriff would call you that without a reason? What is your relationship to the missing woman?" Turning to look down at the man on the landing, "Bob, get a shot of this." A step toward Dan. "What connection did Ms. Linden have to Amber Medger? "

"You want a shot of this, you'll need another camera."

Bob sounded thoroughly pissed, grabbed up the camera, clomped down the steps and took off toward the news truck parked at the curb. Dan used the distraction to turn Simon and step quickly back inside. He knew he slammed the door a little too hard but "person of interest"? Where the fuck did that come from?

He dialed the sheriff's number and waited through the twenty or so prompts only to get a "this office is not open" message. Dammit. Seven a.m. Of course, no one would be in. He wished he'd gotten the sheriff's cell number—he deserved to be up at this hour, too. After all, he started it all by talking to the press. Press? Not exactly Katie Couric out here. But his biggest worry was the story hitting national news. All he needed was for Jason to hear about this "person of interest."

By ten o'clock he'd pretty much blanketed the town with flyers—mailboxes, telephone poles, fences—what tape wouldn't hold, staples did.

Was he holding out hope that it would help? Yeah. He had to believe in something. At least he could take Simon with him; the walk was doing them both good. Two more calls to the sheriff and a voice message but no call back. Maybe it was for the best; it was giving him a chance to cool down.

"Yoo hoo."

Dan had just put a flyer under the windshield wiper of a parked car and looked up to see an elderly woman hurrying toward him—as quickly as arch-support, lace-up oxfords could propel one.

"Mrs. Kennedy. This is a nice surprise."

"Oh my, I was afraid I wouldn't catch you. Gertie, please. Mrs. Kennedy is my husband's mother." A wan smile and several more deep breaths. "I really want your opinion on something. Do you have a minute? We just need to go back to my garage."

Dan nodded. He was about finished putting posters around town then it was out to see Chet Echol's grandson—no appointment, just a drop-in visit. His usual surprise factor. He'd be more likely to find things out that way. Or not.

"They're coming today to put a safe in. And I have absolutely no idea where it should go. The house isn't built on a slab, only a crawl space and partial basement. But I can't get up and down those stairs. Penny suggested the garage. But I don't know. I could get to it there, but the garage is detached from the house. Do you think it would be, well, safe?"

"Let's take a look." By now they were walking up the driveway toward a side door. He held the door open; Gertie stepped inside and flipped on a light switch.

"Over here in the corner. This is the spot I've picked." She motioned him to follow. "The safe is six hundred and seventy-five pounds and will be bolted to the cement floor. Not that someone couldn't take it if they were determined but it would be discouraging, don't you think?"

"I would say so." The wall looked solid; the area wasn't close to a window..."Will you be keeping the necklace here?"

"Yes, of course, after what happened, I'd never trust the bank again. Do you think that will be all right? I mean with your company?"

"I'll need the specs on the safe, but I think it will be acceptable."

"Good. I know I'll feel so much better and it will be right here. It's like having Mama living next door." Gertie was beaming, then sobered. "I can't get over feeling so guilty. The accident, Ms. Linden…then the suicide."

"Suicide?"

"Poor Mr. Woods. There were rumors that he didn't like it in Wagon Mound and that maybe the bank was having some difficulties…then the robbery. I don't think my necklace was the only thing misplaced. There's talk…No, not his finest hour."

Dan waited for a "tsk" or two but Gertie seemed lost in thought. He guessed the suicide story was the better one to circulate. The town could probably take only so much excitement—in the way of killings. He turned his attention back to studying the corner, "Are you going to have them set it up higher? Make it easier for you to see the keypad. If it's placed on the floor, you would be bending down. I don't think that would be comfortable."

"Oh my, I hadn't thought of that. You're right. This way I'd have to kneel down. That wouldn't do. The height is an important consideration."

"I think it would be easy to build a cement block platform and still bolt the safe itself to either the floor or to it. With the safe elevated, you could set a chair in front and work the combination easily."

"Oh that's just perfect. Yes, of course, so much easier. How can I thank you?"

"If they're delivering the safe today, you probably need to call and tell them what you've decided. The masonry will have to be completed first."

"I'll call right now."

Dan turned to go; it was time to get back to distributing those flyers. But then he stopped and just stared, "New hobby?" Dan pointed to a purple Ducati resting on its kick-stand.

"Oh my goodness, no." A giggle, "That belongs to our neighbor…well, he used to be our neighbor. He's moved recently and needed a place for some stuff until he gets his new place set up. Sweet young man and his wife. They had the cutest baby. Bitsy just loved that baby. But they went their separate ways. Like so many young people today. Gave up and moved on." Gertie paused lost in thought. "Maybe you know them? Tim and Emily Echols? Oh dear, of course, you knew Tim's grandfather, Chet Echols. You know, sometimes I think poor Tim just had too much on his plate. Too much responsibility, too much sorrow."

Dan nodded staring at the sleek machine. He was hearing the echoes of a crotch rocket tearing off down the alleyway and him standing there holding a note—"It's not what you think." Was it his imagination or did the Echols family have one or two too many ties to murder, attempted murder, and just plain suspect behavior. Now he knew he'd have that talk with the younger Echols.

The double-wide had seen better days. Or maybe it was the junkyard clutter of bits and pieces of cars and trucks and ATVs that reached as high as the porch railing. A school bus and a Karmann Ghia on blocks completed the picture. The four dogs that rushed the Cherokee from a hole in the trailer's skirting gave him pause until he realized he was outside the range of their chains if he backed up a couple car lengths. He watched the dogs stand there looking at him. Mangy, flop-eared, with missing teeth…How many dogs did you have to have on the front porch to snag Redneck status? There was a joke in there somewhere.

Dan wondered if anyone had ever done psych profiles on junkyard owners—they had to be hoarders. This place looked like a set for a reality TV show. And it fit from what he remembered of old Chet; this matched the rough beard and chopped up haircut. He sure as hell hadn't been visited by those guys from the Publishers Clearing House. This was poverty or very close to it. Would ten to twenty thousand tempt the owner to do something outside the law? Dan thought he was looking at the answer to that.

He left the Cherokee out of range of the dogs and got out. No sign of life but there were two good-sized garages in back and with no safe way to knock on the front door maybe he'd take a look at them first. Then he noticed the man standing at the edge of the trailer cradling a double-barreled shotgun. Damn. What was it out here with men and firearms in the way of a greeting?

Dan stepped to the front of the SUV hands in plain sight. "I'm looking for Tim Echols."

"Found him."

Tim reminded Dan a lot of his grandfather—both with lean and sinewy builds, both about six foot, only this one was clean shaven and wearing some pretty expensive biker leathers. The Ducati must not be his only ride.

"I'm Dan Mahoney. I—"

"I know who you are. If you think you're going to sue me because my grandfather lost control of his truck—"

"Hey, nobody said anything about a law suit. True, I'm looking for answers. And I think there's a chance you might be of help, but that's it."

A pause, Tim seemed to be deciding something—whether or not he could trust Dan? Maybe. Finally, a shrug and with the gun still cradled in his left arm, he motioned Dan to follow him.

"My office is back here." Dan waited while Tim leaned the gun against the side of the nearest metal building and pulled a ring of keys out of his pocket. "To be truthful I haven't even started to go through Granddad's things in the house. Can't bring myself to do it quite yet."

"Things like that have a way of waiting on you."

A chair, two filing cabinets, and a desk defined the area Tim called an office. A cot with a comforter and two pillows filled an opposite corner underneath two ropes holding jeans and t-shirts. He wasn't kidding when he said he hadn't gone through his Granddad's things—he didn't even live in the trailer. Strange but grief could make people do odd things. Things outside the norm.

Dan took the folding chair Tim offered and set it up close to the desk expecting Tim to sit opposite him. But Tim leaned back against a file cabinet to Dan's right and didn't sit. What was that they said about the power in a conversation going to the tallest? Was the posturing supposed to make Dan uneasy? Hard to say.

"First, let me offer my condolences. I liked your grandfather. I'm sorry for the way things played out. You and I both know there's reason to believe that I was targeted—your granddad was hired to scare me or maybe get rid of me—"

"Hey, this sure sounds like you're working up to a lawsuit."

"Just curious about the money trail…twenty K deposited to rig an old truck—actually build it ground up. I would like to know who wanted me out of the way."

"I can't help you there. Last I knew Granddad was working for that movie outfit." Crossed arms seemed to close that avenue of questioning.

"I understand you have a Ducati for sale."

"Not any more. Sold it."

Dead end. Real or faked? Dan couldn't tell—maybe if he tried a new tactic. Something less threatening. "Were Emily and Amber Medger friends?"

"You son-of-a-bitch." Tim hit him straight on, both hands on his shoulders, full body coming down from a standing position. The momentum pushed Dan, the chair and Tim sprawling backwards across the floor.

"Hey…?" Dan rolled to a crouch.

Tim stood above him with fist cocked, then dropped his hand and didn't appear to want to follow up after the first burst of anger subsided, "Just get the fuck out of here."

Dan stood ready for another onslaught but Tim pushed past him and strode out the door. Dan noticed he picked up the shotgun on the way to the trailer. Dan might not have gotten any answers but he was convinced that Tim Echols knew a lot more than he was sharing. So much for thinking the Emily/Amber angle was less inflammatory. What was with that?

Chapter Fourteen

It was back to the waiting game. Flyers were out; he was fresh out of people to question. He'd put in a call to Sheriff Howard but was almost glad when he didn't reach him—he was still smarting over that "person of interest" comment. So, what to do? Might not be a bad idea to check in with Stephanie. She'd been rocked pretty hard by all this and he'd offer lunch if she felt like it. And activity kept him from thinking….But she turned him down. The bank had been closed since Saturday morning and would remain so for a week at least. In the midst of all the sadness, she thanked him, but said she was treasuring the time at home. He understood.

Then she asked if he would like to go with her to offer condolences to Amber's mother? She was feeling guilty not even contacting Mrs. Medger. She'd appreciate the company. She was having trouble working up the nerve to go alone. He'd be glad to. He'd meet her at the bank parking lot; they could go from there.

Actually, it wasn't much of a ride. Andrea Medger lived about a half mile from the new high school on Highway 120. He pulled up in the driveway and went around to open the car door for Stephanie but she'd already hopped out and was halfway to the porch.

Andrea was sitting on a porch swing, bare feet resting on a wooden banister that ran across the front of the old farmhouse broken only by five steps leading upward right in the center. She didn't look old enough to have a nineteen-year-old daughter until you got close enough to see the heavily etched laugh lines and sagging eyelids that belied the boyish-thin body. Flushed cheeks and three cans of Bud, presumably empty, hinted at how Andrea was coping.

Stephanie bent to give Andrea a quick hug, "I'm so sorry." Dan stayed at the top of the steps while the two women embraced.

"You must be that Mahoney fellow Stephanie mentioned."

Dan stepped forward as the women sat down on the swing.

"Yes. I wanted to offer my condolences."

"Not much good talk will do now. Nineteen years old. She never even had a chance to live."

"I understand she'd just gotten married." Not that marriage equated to living, but it was something.

The derisive snort startled him. "Married, all right. More like a one-night stand gone bad. Her father did the same thing to me. Just took off. Me with a year-old baby in this one-horse town. At least she found out he was a no-good before she wasted much time. And had any complications."

Dan started to stand up for his gender, but then noticed Stephanie's pursed lips. Two against one—not good odds.

"She'd only been home a week and already she'd found a job. That girl was a go-getter. If there was money to be had, she was first in line."

"Where did she find work?" Stephanie paused to pop the tab on a fresh Bud retrieved from a cooler beside the swing.

Dan shook his head when offered one. He was more interested in this job opportunity—hoping it wasn't more mid-afternoon phone sex but guessed she wouldn't tell her mother if that was it.

"She was going to be working for old lady Kennedy's daughter filing and doing research on the Internet. You know, out at the chicken farm."

Buster's place. The car, Amber's body, both within a mile of there.

Did it mean anything? It put Amber in the vicinity and gave her a reason for being there. Penny Kennedy didn't mention any help. Just said she worked for the old coot on weekends.

And it sure painted a picture of Amber as an eager worker—a real hustler—what was it her mother just said? First in line for money? What would she have been willing to do? He guessed they'd never know now. But filing and research seemed legit. Maybe Amber had been turning over a new leaf.

"Did she say how she'd found out about the job?" He wasn't sure where this was leading but he idly wondered if it had been advertised. The operation looked to be pretty good sized. Strange that it would be run by one full-time scientist or whatever Doc's actual title was, a file clerk, and a half dozen Mexican Nationals in the field. For a federally granted program it sure had a mom and pop feel to it. Maybe times were tough in the save-the-prairie-chicken business.

"She met Penny Kennedy at the bank when she was filling in for Stephanie." A nod toward the other end of the porch swing. "Old Mrs. Kennedy was just about driving her daughter nuts. Sending her in to take out the necklace, then forgetting she'd just seen it, and sending her back to take it out again. In and out. I don't think the young Ms. Kennedy got anything else done last summer for running back and forth to the bank with that necklace."

Dan caught Stephanie's eye when Andrea reached down to get another Bud. A slight shake of the head and Stephanie nodded. No need to mention that there was no sign-in evidence to back up Amber's story. Had she told her mother the truth? It didn't make sense that she'd lie. Dan made small talk while Stephanie finished her beer, then they both again offered their condolences and left.

"That's the strangest thing. Maybe Ms. Kennedy is suffering from Alzheimer's, after all, but still…" Stephanie shook her head. "In all my time at the bank, Gertrude Kennedy never came in more than two or three times a year to take the necklace out and clean it. Never. And in the midst of all this traipsing back and forth by her daughter, Ms. Kennedy stuck to her cleaning schedule. The log proves that."

"I suppose it could support Penny's finding the necklace between the mattress and box springs. That would account for some of the running back and forth until Gert forgot where she'd put it. That gave Penny a reason to get your boss involved."

"And that's another thing. When the necklace was found and with the boxes all torn up, I suggested to Mr. Woods that we assign one of the three empty boxes to Ms. Kennedy—just until things got back to normal. Well, he'd hear none of that. He put the necklace in a private safe in his office."

Dan was mentally taking notes. One very expensive necklace had been getting handed around a lot lately. And it gave him an idea. Something that probably needed to be checked. United Life & Casualty had a clause that when an item had been out of the insured's hands for any length of time or a chain of events gave cause to suspect the item might have been open to alteration, an appraisal was in order. Usually an appraisal was done every two years. He'd check to see when the necklace had last been evaluated and then have the home office email the appropriate forms. Just a precaution but he couldn't still that nagging feeling of something not quite right.

"One other thing...I keep forgetting to ask the name of the guard or guards on duty Labor Day weekend."

"We had two during the day—during the week—and only one at night. Weekends and holidays were always the same, one guard. Poor old Sam Bailey had been with the bank for years but this burglary was just too much for him. I think he blamed himself for not detecting the tunnel. But could you really expect a man to look at the padlock every day? The Federal inspectors said they used an exact replica. Slipped the old one off and put their own on—same make and everything. How would he have known?"

"So it was this Sam Bailey who was on duty over that weekend?"

"Well, he was supposed to be but he was recuperating from a bout of pneumonia that had turned into bronchitis—he was a longtime smoker. I remember he called in on Thursday. Mr. Woods took the call."

"So there was a substitute?"

"There was supposed to be but there was some mix-up. Mr. Woods called Tim Echols and he was able to do it Thursday but then there was a truck turnover, big mess, mostly chemicals just north of here and he had to bow out. I'm not sure how it was handled."

"Is this Sam Bailey a local?"

"Used to be. Stayed here long after he lost his wife. Old habits, I guess. Sometimes the familiar is comforting. I heard he moved into Albuquerque to live with his sister a couple weeks ago."

"Did he supervise the other guards?"

"Well, yes and no…the guard during the day he did, but Tim Echols worked the weekend and he was a deputy for Sheriff Howard. I always got the idea that Tim answered to the sheriff."

Dan was quiet. Echols. The ubiquitous Echols. But the sheriff had been up front about it—didn't try to hide his involvement.

"The Feds cleared everyone, Sam shouldn't have beat himself up for something he really couldn't have done anything about. Plus, he was past retirement age. Probably good for him to just kick back."

Dan nodded. Kicking back had a certain appeal and getting out of Wagon Mound was probably good for him. He mentally crossed Sam Bailey off his list of interviewees.

◇◇◇

The emails from UL&C were there when he got back to the apartment. A quick download and a save to the flash drive and he was off to make copies. This time with an almost delirious Simon in the backseat. Stir-crazy probably captured what the big dog was going through. And he could certainly relate.

He took out his cell phone. Dan wasn't sure of a plan but was making one up as he went. First, a call to an appraiser in Santa Fe. United Life & Casualty had used Ortega's in the past and, yes, they would be able to take a look at the necklace that afternoon. Dan made an appointment for four-thirty.

Next, a call to the sheriff. Dan assumed the necklace was at home with Gert but he wouldn't feel right asking to take the necklace without substantial backup—knew that Gert would feel safer with an armed guard so to speak. He caught Sheriff Howard on the way to a late lunch. Yeah, he'd go with him and yes, he'd let Simon ride in the squad car. That was easy. Dan would demand an explanation of that "person of interest" comment later. First things first…now to explain to Gert why he needed to borrow the necklace for a few hours. And get her to sign the release. Dan called ahead then met Sheriff Howard at the Kennedys' house.

"It's company policy and under the circumstances, I'm sure you understand." Dan waited on the steps while Gert signed the UL&C papers and went to get the Barbasol can.

"Actually, it will be a relief. I wonder if old Mr. Ortega—my, I shouldn't say old, he's younger than I am—would keep the necklace at the store? In one of their safes until I get mine put in here?"

"I think that's a good idea. I could probably make a case for UL&C picking up the tab."

"Oh, that would be comforting. With all that's happened at the bank and it's going to be another two weeks before the masons can get the platform built…well, it would be best to know it's being looked after."

"Is Penny here?" Not that Gert didn't have signature authority, she did, but it would be a good idea to alert Penny to the plan. Standing there talking to a very lucid Gert made the Alzheimer's claim seem suspect, but still…and he'd wanted to check out Andrea Medger's claim that Penny had been run ragged taking the necklace in and out of the vault.

"Oh my, no. She's working. She's always working—sometimes six days a week. I think she'd be out there on Sunday if I didn't yammer at her about God setting aside a day for rest. I tell her she needs to slow down but the money comes in handy."

Well, that contradicted the weekend-only claim made by Penny—something about not leaving her mother alone. Didn't anyone in this town tell the truth? And in this case, who was fibbing?

Gert slipped the necklace into a velvet drawstring bag after wrapping it in tissue. "There. I feel so much better already. And with Sheriff Howard helping, I just don't have to worry about a thing." A coquettish smile and Gert and the Barbasol can went back inside the house.

◇◇◇

"Let's drop your car back at the apartment and take this one. I'll follow you." That suited Dan fine. No reason to leave it parked on the street for a few hours. It would take less than five minutes. He took off making sure he was watching the speed limit.

"You know, I have a bone to pick with you." Dan slipped into the passenger-side seat of the cruiser after opening the back door for Simon and then admonishing the dog to be good and get down. This was a good time to confront the sheriff—no interruptions.

"What for?"

"Calling me 'a person of interest' in Elaine's disappearance."

"'Fraid that wasn't me."

"You didn't tell that news team from Albuquerque that I was a suspect?"

"Oh, them. They'll say anything to get a story. They came by the office but I didn't speak to them."

Maybe he shouldn't, but Dan believed him. "No nonsense" pretty much summed up the sheriff.

"Let me get your read on something else." Dan related Tim's reaction to his question about Amber and Emily knowing each other and wasn't prepared for the sheriff's reaction.

After a loud guffaw and a slap to the dash, Sheriff Howard just chuckled. "I'm surprised you're still alive. You sure have a talent for stepping in it."

Dan wasn't sure what "it" was but he thought the sheriff was about to tell him. He was getting a little irked at appearing foolish.

"Rumor has it Amber broke up Tim's marriage…seems he was dippin' his wick where he shouldn't. Amber was a looker and a little too fast for her own good. Emily being a new mom and all…well, not a good time in a woman's life to two-time her."

Dan almost laughed himself. So much for thinking he'd chosen a safe subject. But it was odd that Emily only came into the bank to check on her safe deposit box when Amber was there. If the two had made up, Tim wouldn't have reacted like he did. Something didn't make sense.

"When did all this happen?"

"Oh, not long back. Just before the robbery mid-August or thereabouts. Tim had just started at the Ford dealership."

"So Amber and Tim were a couple?"

"Well, not really...not for long anyway. There was talk that Emily was getting back with Tim."

"So Amber's taking off with a biker over the Bean Day weekend...any truth to that?"

"Probably. Wouldn't be the first time she'd picked up someone. And I'd say that biker if there was one caught her on the rebound."

◇◇◇

Ortega's, opposite Santa Fe's old plaza and one city block from the Saint Francis Church and chapel, nestled into the lower floor of the La Fonda Inn and acted as an entryway to the famed hotel. Rueben Lucero, a university trained gemologist, met them at the door. After introductions he took them to a small office at the back. Dan placed the manila envelope containing Gert's signed release and the bag with the necklace on the edge of a large table.

"This is more private." Rueben motioned to chairs and then sat behind the table and was instantly dwarfed by lamps and magnifying glasses on collapsible arms attached to the wall behind. A black velvet viewing cloth in front of him was covered with intricate instruments. For a moment Dan thought he was in a dentist's office. Rueben lifted the bag containing the necklace and placed it in front of him but before taking it out, he sat back.

"I find this a little awkward."

When it didn't appear that he was going to continue, Dan asked, "How so?"

"Well, it smacks of duplicity—perhaps, things not reported?"

"I'm not following."

"This is the fourth time I've seen this necklace in the last three months. I could only assume that..." He glanced at the card that Dan had placed on the table, "that United Life & Casualty was aware of the alterations taking place."

"No. The company was not aware of 'alterations.' May I ask what you mean by the term?"

"Oh, I dreaded this…I just felt things weren't right." More fidgeting before slipping the necklace out and placing it on the velvet pad. "On previous visits I was asked to extract several of the larger diamonds and sell them, replacing those missing with high-grade Russian zirconia. In the old days no one wore their 'real' jewels, everything was paste as it was called."

"Wait. Let me see if I'm understanding this. You took out several stones, sold them, and replaced them with fakes?" Dan noticed the sheriff was leaning forward.

"Yes. This is a priceless necklace—I don't have to tell you that. The diamonds are the finest—perfect in color, cut, clarity, and carat weight. Every diamond, all four Cs. It used to be that a European cut—giving the stone a smaller table—wasn't as desirable as later designs, however—"

Dan didn't need a lesson in gemology but he sure as hell needed to know who brought it in. "How did you receive the necklace? Was it brought to the shop?"

"Yes, by the family representative."

"And that is?"

"The family banker, Mr. Woods. It's my understanding that he represented Ms. Kennedy—handled all aspects of her estate."

"You have papers to prove this?" Sheriff Howard was standing.

"Yes, of course, excuse me." Rueben left the room and returned almost immediately with a folder. "Here's the first letter asking me to extract approximately one hundred thousand dollars' worth of diamonds, replacing them with cubic zirconia, and offering the store a commission of fifteen percent upon completion of a sale." He handed the paper to Dan who placed it on the table in front of him.

"On the three previous times you received the necklace to extract and sell stones, was it always the same amount?"

"Yes."

"And you were able to find a buyer each time?"

"The approximately three hundred thousand dollars' worth of stones was sold to the same individual."

"And each time Mr. Woods was the one who brought the necklace to you and retrieved it?"

"Yes."

"How was he paid and who was the recipient?"

"Mrs. Kennedy, of course, a check in her name less my commission of fifteen thousand. Each check to Mrs. Kennedy was for eighty-five thousand."

Dan had put off a comparison of signatures long enough. He pulled the recently signed release from the envelope and placed it next to the document that Rueben had handed him. Even Sheriff Howard leaned in to look. To the naked, untrained eye the signatures were exactly the same. Palmer-perfect replicas. What the hell was going on?

Rueben pointed out which stones had been replaced. About half of the total diamonds that made up the platinum chain of bezel set stones attached to an ornate clasp of more diamonds at the nape of the neck. Again, to an untrained eye, the change was indiscernible. The necklace lay there glittering with all its secrets and not divulging a one.

Mr. Ortega himself joined them to sign the forms that placed the necklace in the store's vault for safekeeping. Dan received copies and after more assurances of the necklace's safety, they left.

First order of business was finding a park and walking Simon. Dan kept him on a short lead and brought him back to the squad car long before Simon would have wanted.

"Sorry, fella…we'll go on a long walk tonight." He opened the back door and Simon jumped in. Great dog. He wasn't being fair to him with everything else that was going on.

Sheriff Howard turned onto I-25 and gunned it. It would be dark before they got home. Neither was talkative, but the sheriff put into words what Dan was thinking.

"Gives credence to the Alzheimer's theory."

"Yeah, but every time I'm around her, I just don't see it. The normal forgetfulness of an eighty-five-year-old woman, yes, but not a progressive disease."

"Then you think the signature's a forgery? That she didn't tell Lawrence Woods to dispose of certain stones?"

"Not impossible. I need to talk with Penny. She may be the only one with answers."

"If this was done behind Mrs. Kennedy's back, without her knowing anything about it, would she have a claim?"

"Of course. The same as if the necklace had actually been taken in the robbery. If this was done without her consent or knowledge, she can reclaim market-value of all the diamonds."

"That's good to hear. I like the old girl. How are you going to break the news?"

"I've been thinking about that. I'll want her daughter present—and you."

"Not a problem. Just let me know."

As night closed in, they were getting close to Wagon Mound. And the dread of going back to an empty apartment was almost more than he could handle. Dan checked his cell for messages. Again. Nothing. Not one response to one hundred and fifty flyers. He tried not to be defeated. Something had to work. Someone had to have seen something. It was only a matter of time—he had to believe that.

The yell from the sheriff instantly brought him back to the present. A split second in the headlights, enough time for his brain to register—deer—big—before the car hit it mid-leap, brown body sideways, full brunt of impact collapsing the hood, hooves clattering against the windshield, shattering glass, thrashing legs just missing his head, Sheriff Howard standing on the brakes, fighting the fishtailing cruiser not able to see past the bleeding mound of fur. And then it was over. They were on the side of the road both scrambling to get out; then each pulling on a set of long legs jerking the body back down to the hood, checking for life but finding a broken neck. Both leaning against the cruiser to get their breath knowing they'd just been damned lucky.

"Shit. Look at this car." Sheriff Howard, arms akimbo, surveyed the damage. "Fourth time in two years. If the fucking druggies don't get me, the wildlife will. Boat's looking better and better."

"Civilization is encroaching on their territory. This guy's a beauty. Sad to see him end up this way." Dan thought he saw a retort pass unsaid as the sheriff opened, then closed his mouth. Dan had gotten Simon out of the backseat and was reassuring the big dog who was viewing the inert animal with suspicion and a low growl.

"Hope you didn't want to get home too soon. We need to dress him out and get him into cold storage. You ever field-dress game?"

Well, that went right to his manhood but this wasn't the time to lie, "No, I haven't."

"You'll learn quickly enough. Let's get his head elevated. Grab that side and slide him up about a foot. Steady him there. I'm going to get some tools out of the trunk."

Steady him? Sheriff Howard disappeared and, of course, the buck began to slide downward. Dan backed up and butt-to-butt pushed against the deer. Probably looked stupid but it stopped the animal's momentum. He still only had one good hand. Not a lot he could do with his right wrist in a soft cast.

The knife the sheriff handed him looked like it could do some damage in a fight. Without flicking a finger over the blade, he knew he could shave with it. He watched the sheriff secure the buck to the car's A-posts with bungee cords wound through his antlers. Then a cut around the anus, discarding the testicles, next a slit opening the stomach cavity to the ribcage, more precise cuts dislodging membrane until finally releasing the restraints and with a push from Dan, the animal was rolled onto his side to let gravity pull the intestines from its body.

Sheriff Howard snipped the last bit of sinew and tossed the entrails on the ground. Simon stood sniffing the air but sat down again. The dog seemed confused. Dan was pretty sure he was wondering if that was something to eat but for him Taste of the Wild came in a bag of small uniform chunks, not a steaming pile of gray viscous intestines. If left on his own in the wild, could Simon even survive? Had man bred the instinct for catching and killing right out of certain breeds? Come to think of it, Dan didn't know if Simon had ever seen a rabbit or a squirrel. This was a city dog who lived in an apartment and stayed at Pet Paradise when his owner traveled. And while there he could enjoy supervised play and splash in a doggy swimming pool, but there was certainly no wildlife. Dan made a silent promise to remedy all that. A dog needed to be a dog.

"You gonna help or not?"

"Sorry. What do you need?"

"We're going to have to get the carcass into the trunk. I can roll him off onto a piece of carpet I got back there—that'd make him easier to handle."

"Then what? Don't we have to find cold storage pretty quickly?"

"Yeah. I think we're a couple miles from Doc's place. He's got some walk-in freezers out behind the lab. We've used them before for road kill."

"What will you do with the meat?"

"Orphanage in Las Vegas just about exists on donations like this. Nothing goes to waste out here."

If Dan were being truthful, after wrestling two hundred plus pounds of steaming venison into the trunk of the car, both men were winded. Nothing screamed out-of-shape and made Dan pray he didn't pull something like being forced to lift and balance that kind of awkward sprawling deadweight—all while trying to protect a broken wrist. But after moving a gas can and a number of tools to one side, and tucking in the legs, the deer fit nicely. Both men leaned against the trunk's lid and caught their breath.

"No rest for the wicked. We better get going."

Dan pushed away from the trunk and opened the back door for Simon and followed Sheriff Howard to the front of the car.

"Just need to break out the rest of this windshield. Sure didn't do the car any favors."

The cruiser started but from the clunking and whining, things were rubbing together under the hood that should never touch. Twenty miles an hour was putting the car to the test. Sheriff Howard called in for a tow truck to meet them at Doc's. Dan sighed. It was going to be a long night.

The gate to the ranch was closed but not locked. By now the cruiser was spewing steam and hissing like a pissed-off goose. Dan jumped out, opened the gate and closed it behind them before getting back into the car.

The sheriff pulled up even with the house, "I don't see any lights on. I'm just going to pull around back anyway. Oh, shit." A shudder and the car slowly rolled to a stop. "Looks like we're going to have to drag that deer from here. Probably lucky we got this far."

By leveraging the sprawling body, first backend then front, they were finally able to lower it to the ground.

"Let me go hang on the back door. Just want to make sure nobody's home. Then we'll get this guy put up for safekeeping."

Dan opened the door for Simon but didn't bother to leash him. He didn't think the dog was going to go anywhere not with that fascinating mound of dead wild animal between them. Simon just about had his nose glued to the buck.

"Nobody home. Let's get going." The sheriff grabbed his side of the carpet.

The three of them moved slowly but progress was being made. Dan felt like putting his side down just so he could straighten up but let the wuss-factor make him man-up and keep going. Couldn't let the sheriff see him sweat.

Three yard lights cast an eerie green fluorescent glow across the Quonset-hut greenhouses elongating shadows and giving the area a stalag-esque feel. And the quiet—that seemed abnormal somehow. Dan didn't know what he expected—the comforting chirp and rustle of the several hundred prairie chickens in the last barn? But birds didn't move at night—they hit that perch at sundown and it was lights out.

"I think that's what we're looking for." Sheriff Howard, beads of sweat on his forehead and breathing through clenched teeth, put his side of the travois down and pointed to one end of what looked like a boxcar. "That's the one we've used before."

The deer was now beyond heavy for someone using only one hand, but Dan leaned down and picked up his end of the rug and again started forward. The door to the cooler was bolted shut but not locked. No one seemed to worry out here about break-ins. The sheriff slid back the bolt and pulled the double-paneled door toward him, stepping back as it swung outward.

"Okay, on three…" Dan turned sideways, shifting the weight of the carpet evenly between the two of them, getting a better grasp with his left hand, "One, two—"

"Dan …" Elaine flew through the door. Suddenly there were legs around his waist, arms around his neck, the deer forgotten, "Oh my God…"

He barely saw the sheriff pull his gun, jump into the cooler, and drop to a crouch before hugging this woman to him, whirling her around and realizing that his tears and her tears were smeared across his face. But who cared? He couldn't believe it. Only then did he acknowledge the extent of his fear—that he honestly thought this moment might not ever happen. That in his mind, she was already dead.

"We need to call Jason." She untangled herself and put two feet on the ground but held onto his hand. "What have you told him?"

"I didn't needlessly scare him—only said you'd had car trouble and got turned around in the woods going for help. I assured him there was an all-points out and that we expected good news."

She gave his hand a squeeze, "Thank you."

"Here's my cell, but you need to give Simon a hug before he turns himself inside out." The dog was bumping each of them with his nose while whining his bid to get attention, too.

Elaine dialed before dropping to her knees and gathering as much of the dog as she could into her and hugged him. "I missed you, too, Simon." Then the call connected and Elaine was promising that she was fine, just tired and hungry. A few questions about school, an "I love you," and she handed the cell back and stood up.

It was only then that Dan realized she was standing on her left leg barely touching the ground with her right foot. "We need to get that looked at."

"I think I'll live…especially now." She grinned up at him and he pulled her into another embrace. He still couldn't believe she was here in his arms.

The sheriff cleared his throat, "As a precaution and to cover our bases, I need you to be checked out at a clinic."

"I'm sure I'm fine."

"I'm sure that's true but I need a medical opinion to back it up."

Dan noticed Sheriff Howard's gun was holstered but not snapped down. Did he think they were in danger? It was comforting to know backup was on the way. But he put his arm around Elaine anyway.

"I've put a call in for a lab team to go over this place and a driver to take you to a clinic and then home. But first, we need to talk." He motioned toward the back steps. "Doc travels a lot. I don't want anyone jumping to conclusions just because we're on his land. We're all gonna keep an open mind. Now, Ms. Linden, I need you to start with what you remember of last Friday night."

Elaine nodded, "It was just dusk. I was driving up from my home in Roswell and Bitsy, Gertrude Kennedy's Chihuahua, ran across the road in front of me. I pulled over and got out to get her. I have no idea how or why she was so far from home."

"Penny does office work for the Doc and brings the dog. I've seen Bitsy out at Doc's place, but where you stopped is quite a ways from here—maybe a mile." Dan added.

"I know. I was worried about coyotes or owls. She'd stop when I called to her but run away from me if I got too close. I couldn't catch her. Then, I saw something…even now, I'm not sure what. I was probably a hundred yards away but it looked like a group of people in white lab suits unloading an eighteen-wheeler. Or maybe they were putting things in…"

The sheriff was taking notes, "I'll make this short but I need to ask a few more questions. What makes you think they might have been loading the truck?"

"I don't know. I'm sorry I don't remember exactly what I saw. Mostly because that's when I realized that someone was after me."

"What do you mean 'after you'?"

"Someone on an ATV started chasing me and I ran to an outcropping of rock to lose them and fell. I caught my foot and couldn't move."

"And then?"

Elaine shook her head.

"That's all you remember?"

"Yes. They kept a blindfold on me and only came in once. There were two of them. I could see that from their shadows. But they left food and put an icepack on my ankle. It didn't seem like they wanted me dead."

"But it also appeared that they weren't coming back. That was a lot of food but it wouldn't have lasted forever." Sheriff Howard added.

"But Doc Jenkins, wouldn't he have gone into the storage unit at some point? I mean if he didn't already know I was there."

"Not sure he would have. It looks like the unit hasn't been used in a while. The electric was still connected but the cooling unit isn't working. I'm not sure he would have had a reason."

"But the air was coming on—a circulating fan in the ceiling."

The siren caught them all off guard, but the car barreling toward them up the drive had lights blazing and siren on full blast.

"What the—" Sheriff Howard jumped up. "Rookie…any freaking excuse to wind her up. Wait here."

As the sheriff stomped down the driveway, Dan was glad he wasn't that rookie. The sheriff could probably be a real bastard to work for.

"What are our chances of leaving here? A hot shower—cup of coffee even…just the two of us…we could finish the interrogation in the morning. I suppose they towed the Benz. We can pick it up tomorrow."

Dan ducked the car comment. There was a lot of catching up to do. Some of it not very pleasant. How do you talk about a body swinging from a chandelier or a body burned beyond recognition in your own car? Not to mention that half of some very expensive diamonds from a certain necklace were removed and sold—more than likely without the knowledge of their owner. But just maybe with the knowledge of her daughter. He wasn't looking forward to facing that probability. Elaine may have been gone for seventy-two hours, but the world had kept galloping forward.

Sheriff Howard excused himself to oversee the gathering of evidence and put them into the first squad car with the errant Rookie. But first he made Dan promise to take Elaine by the clinic in the morning—just a precaution but it would put everyone's mind at ease about her ankle. They at least needed to get an X-ray to make certain there was nothing broken. Dan knew he was right. But he selfishly wanted some alone time with Elaine, too. And there would be more questioning, the sheriff reminded them. He'd call and set up a time to meet. Finally, the two of them crawled into the back of the cruiser making Simon move over.

"You've got to be famished."

"Beyond."

"About the only thing open in Wagon Mound is going to be the convenience store. Ham and cheese and some chips?"

"Perfect."

Their driver seemed more than happy to act as chauffeur—probably happy to get out from under the sheriff's scrutiny. If given half a chance, Dan knew he would have turned the siren on, too.

"I'll just be a minute." Dan opened the car door.

Even with the cop waiting in the car with Elaine, it was tough to leave her just to get a couple things. Life was fragile and fleeting. He seemed to think in clichés—sand running through an hour glass, or his fingers—all the images that say there might not be a tomorrow. He had to stop. She was here. She was all right. The nightmare was over…well, he hoped so anyway. He got out of the cruiser and walked toward the store.

Chips, milk, orange juice…he filled a basket. But finding a ham and cheese was a problem.

"'Fraid I'm out of packaged sandwiches. Sheriff was in here over the weekend and bought the last dozen or so in the case. I think he had a crew to feed, you know, bunch of guys pulled some overtime on that accident up the road."

A picture of a stack of sandwiches in a walk-in cooler flashed through his mind. And it didn't give him a very good feeling. But there had been a crew at the site of Elaine's car. Damn. He wished everything didn't seem to lead to more suspicions. He grabbed a frozen pizza instead. This should get a smile; a more fitting homecoming meal.

◇◇◇

Finally, Simon was walked and only one slice of pizza was left— back to normal. Well, more or less. Dan stretched out on the bed and patted the place beside him. Elaine propped pillows behind her back and one under her ankle before she leaned against the headboard.

"This is more like it. Three nights on that cot and I may never be the same again." She rolled onto her side and snuggled into him. "Next time I'll leave a spare car key with you. It would have been so much easier to have just brought the car here. Do you know where it is?"

Dan cleared his throat. Now it was his turn to punch up a couple pillows and wad them behind his back as he sat up. "There's probably some things we need to discuss."

She pushed up to a sitting position, "Such as?"

"For starters, the car was burned."

"Burned?"

Dan nodded then told her about Amber. How Amber's body was first thought to be Elaine's—how he met with the coroner and thanks to Jason's birth, knew what he pretty much had sensed, Elaine was not the burned body they'd found in the car. He left out bound hands and feet and the fact that Amber had probably been alive when placed in the Benz. Some things were probably best left unsaid.

Then he mentioned the bank president's death, the necklace now sans a quarter of its diamonds which had been miraculously found and was never missing in the first place, and how Chet Echols' grandson's former wife—

"Stop. I was gone seventy-two hours and all this happened?" Elaine was sitting up squarely facing him.

"It's been busy."

"And thanks to the removal of the diamonds—the theft of the diamonds, you're back on the case?"

"Something like that. Look, I know it's not what you want."

"How do you know what I want? Obviously Chicago and New Mexico are a couple thousand miles apart and we have some decisions to make, but I've been giving this some thought. I want to throw another possibility in the mix."

Elaine stared at the ceiling before looking directly at him and took a breath, "Dan, I want to work with you. I like trying to figure things out. Yes, I could do without being locked in a freezer but I'd like to be more involved.

I have nine more months on sabbatical. I'd like to put that time to good use."

"What are you thinking of doing?"

"I could take a six month's course of study online and take the national test for private investigators. We could literally work together."

"You're serious, aren't you?"

"I couldn't be more serious."

"Wow. Let's talk, but that's as good a segue as anything." Dan put his feet on the floor, then turned and dropped to one knee. "Elaine Linden, will you marry me? Help me make that life together come true?"

"Amid all the craziness and chaos?"

"Amid all the craziness and chaos until death do us part."

Dan thought she was taking overly long with an answer but then she was beside him on the floor, in his arms whispering, "Yes." They would shop for a ring later. He'd ask the advice of the jeweler at Ortega's in Santa Fe. It had to be special and this was something way out of his league—he'd need help.

"So what do you think about my idea? We could even hang a shingle together—Elaine and Dan Mahoney, Private Investigators."

"You know what? I think that just might be a real possibility." Dan suddenly wished he'd planned better. Champagne would have been nice or flowers or something…something commemorative. Rolling around on carpet that smelled like evergreen car deodorizer in a town called Wagon Mound wouldn't have been his first choice for popping the question.

Then with her mouth still on his, he felt her unbuckle his belt, and unzip his fly. He had a feeling commemorative was just about to happen.

Chapter Fifteen

Sheriff Howard woke them. Seven on the dot. Must have been sitting at his desk waiting until what he considered a decent hour. He sounded chipper enough to have been up half the night. Could they be at doc's place at ten? He wanted to walk Elaine through what had happened and hopefully talk with Doc Jenkins. "Talk" with Doc? "Hopefully"? What happened to warrants and arrests? Dan realized that at some level, he wanted someone or some ones held accountable. He wanted closure. He wanted to wring the necks of those who locked Elaine up—put her through hell. Put him through hell. Anger just below the surface threatened to bubble over.

First stop was an urgent care in Las Vegas. X-rays, reassurance that the ankle wasn't broken, an ace bandage and some 800 mg Motrin with the admonishment to keep the ankle elevated. Yeah, right. He could see Elaine doing that. They needed to backtrack to the farm and meet with the sheriff. It wasn't how Dan had hoped to spend the morning. But he guessed there was no getting out of it. The two of them met the sheriff in front of the gate at ten till. He expected the sheriff to show up with a search warrant and wasn't disappointed. At least that was a start. It was obvious that the doc wasn't too pleased. But Dan had the distinct feeling that he expected them. Who would have tipped him off? It even looked like someone had recently swept the front porch. And if anyone thought it odd that Penny Kennedy was already at work, she attempted to explain.

"Cataloging. That time of year." She smiled broadly and gave Elaine's hand a little squeeze, then waved expansively toward a table literally covered with glass vials and envelopes of seed. It appeared that she was matching the seed to a computer graphic of the plant it came from which she then printed, cut to a uniform three inches by three inches and pasted on the front of an envelope. Once it had been filled with seed and the flap glued in place, it was filed. Boxes with a single letter of the alphabet on the front were lined up underneath the table—most already half filled with seed packets. "These will go all around the world. Five hardy fodder grasses to South America—Chile, actually—and fifteen hybrids to Africa. A game preserve." Her voice just bubbled with pride. "So many animals will survive and flourish because of this work." A beaming smile at Doc Jenkins seemed to complete her little presentation.

Tough for Dan to equate this do-gooder with someone who might have been systematically stealing from her own mother. He needed to talk with the two of them together and soon. Yet, Dan had to admit what he was looking at was a pretty impressive operation and whatever Penny's part was she appeared to be efficient and knowledgeable. But he didn't think any of them, including the two deputies who were there to search the premises, wanted to stand around listening to a dissertation on grass seed.

Finally, Sheriff Howard hustled Dan and Elaine out the back door along with the Doc, leaving the deputies in blue latex gloves to begin their work. But what they might be looking for was a mystery. Contraband? But what exactly? He tuned back into the conversation between Doc and the sheriff.

"I left for Utah on Thursday morning. I don't like flying out of Santa Fe but it's a hell of a trip to Albuquerque. I usually stay overnight either coming or going. Or both, like I did this trip."

"Reason for travel?"

"Conference on preserving our national monuments. I presented a paper on restoring the lesser grasslands of the Great Plains. It was well received, I might add."

"I'll need credit card receipts, air fare verification, proof of registration for both the hotel and the conference—"

"Not a problem. Penny can get those things together for you."

For just doing a little filing on weekends, Penny sure seemed to have a finger on the pulse. Dan wondered if she had keys to everything too and if she ever spent time out here when the Doc was away. That could be worthwhile finding out.

Doc turned to Elaine, "Look, I just want to say how sorry I am that you were inconvenienced. When the sheriff called to tell me what he'd found out here—someone being kept in that old cooler…well, I was just shocked."

Dan was having a hard time with the word "inconvenienced" and he bet Elaine was, too. Afraid for your life, cuts, bruises, swollen ankle—yeah, inconvenienced didn't seem to sum it up real well. And when did the sheriff call? The element of surprise must not be very important.

"Was anyone here while you were gone?" Dan thought he might as well ask.

"Penny holds down the fort when I travel."

"So you're saying she was here through this morning?" At least Sheriff Howard was showing interest.

"As far as I know. The fall is the busiest time of year. We all turn into hunters and gatherers."

"What do you make of the fact that Ms. Linden remembers seeing an eighteen wheeler being unloaded, or possibly being loaded not too far from here?"

" A delivery of fertilizer and grass seed."

"I'm not following."

"I was expecting a delivery toward the end of the week. I have two hundred acres under cultivation—that takes a lot of fertilizer. And I bring in grass seed from other projects. I fertilize and spread seed before the snows—gives me a head start on spring."

"Who unloads?"

"The driver and a sidekick. Along with some of the hands."

"And they all wear protective gear?"

"Have to. You can't imagine the dust factor. Like working in a silo."

"Who brings it up here?" Sheriff Howard's wave of an arm took in the three barns at the edge of the clearing.

"I leave three or four ATVs hooked up to moveable pallets by the road when I'm expecting a shipment. My field crew brings the shipment up here and unloads."

"Would I find any green cards among this 'field crew'?"

"Probably not."

"And if I wanted to interview any of them?"

"It'd be tough. Last week was their last work week for me. A number of them were heading north—Washington State. A cider plant up there picks up the slack when they're through down here."

Without a comment the sheriff started walking toward the cooler pulling on a pair of latex gloves. He slid back the bolt and opened the door, "Take a look inside." He nodded to Elaine then stepped back so that she could lean in the doorway. "Everything like it was when you were here?"

"Not exactly. Someone's removed the slop bucket and all the food."

"Penny was afraid there'd be rats. Food attracts them in a heartbeat. One of our biggest problems out here. She told me this morning she'd tidied up. I assume your boys got everything they needed last night?" Doc had also leaned in to take a look.

"Looks like they better have. I wasn't taking any tidying into consideration." The sheriff looked ticked, Dan thought. "Why don't we go back up to the house. I think at this point I'd like to talk to Penny."

Doc suggested sitting around the dining room table, a rather grand hand-carved monstrosity in white oak. The dining room itself was knotty pine panels washed a light gray. Lids from old tureens many with pastoral scenes but most in blue-and-white dotted the walls. Seemed odd to Dan, but he bet it was right out of *Better Homes & Gardens.* Probably showed what he knew about home decor.

"Anyone for coffee?" Penny paused in the doorway to the kitchen. She was in her bobby socks best, all matching yellow sweater and pullover with an ankle-length brown skirt. Her head full of curls seemed barely under control and was held in place this time by a yellow paisley scarf. Dan always thought of the fifties. A plain Dinah Shore with a Jag instead of a Chevy. There was no eye makeup or straightened hair today. Dress-up must be reserved for bank business.

"Don't have time. I'd like to finish this up." The sheriff flipped open a small notebook. "You were here Friday?"

"Yes, I came out after lunch. It was a regular work day for me—a half day because I was staying the weekend. Sperling Transport had called on Thursday to make sure everything would be set up for the delivery so I needed to be here. "

"Did you meet them at the truck? Show them where to park? That sort of thing?"

"Yes, I always do."

"And the truck was completely full with just your order? Fertilizer and seed?"

"Yes. Just under four tons to be exact. I contacted our field foreman to make sure we'd have the manpower to get the load put away in the barns before dark."

"Do you remember how long it took to complete the unload?"

"Oh dear, an hour and a half…at least. I remember it was beginning to get dark—I hate daylight savings time. I can never get used to it. And I felt a few sprinkles. The last thing we needed was rain."

"Did you go back to the barns with the field crew?"

"Normally, I would have but Bitsy had disappeared. She was with me and I had put her down on the ground for just a second. When I bent down to pick her up, she wasn't there. She wasn't anywhere that I could see. Well, I absolutely panicked. She'd be a quick meal for any number of creatures."

"Did you leave the site to try and find her?"

"I didn't have to. She suddenly appeared."

"And you went back to the house at that time."

"Yes. I usually use an ATV to get around and I tucked Bitsy in my jacket pocket and followed the crew up to the barns."

"And the driver and his helper in the eighteen-wheeler took off at that time?"

"Yes."

"When did you leave?"

"Right after they did. I like to get home at a decent hour to fix our dinner—As you know, I live with my mother."

Dan didn't think there was anyone in the room who didn't know that, but he watched the sheriff make a note before he asked, "How often do you go to the walk-in cooler?"

"I never do. Unless I'm taking inventory or checking in a shipment of supplies, I don't go into the backyard even. I walk Bitsy out front."

"And you, Doc?"

"I spend most of my time in the office. I can't tell you how long it's been since that cooler has been in use. A year or two, maybe. Frankly, I was surprised that there was still electricity to it."

"And Amber…" Penny paused to dab at her eyes. "I'm still in shock. I called her mother this morning when she didn't come in to work…I never imagined…it's just so awful." More dabbing at her eyes and a quick blowing of her nose.

"Did she work Friday?" Sheriff Howard referred to his notes.

"Yes. She was here before I was—eight or so. She left a little early—about four-thirty. She needed to go into Las Vegas to shop. Grocery shop, and, well, pick up some Budweiser for her mother…and I remember she was going to get some Advil. She hadn't been feeling well. Headache and runny nose…she thought it was some upper respiratory sinus thing."

"Did you notice anything unusual? About her work? Anything happen Friday?"

"No, typical day. We're just about to go under with all these packets to make up. We both ate a sandwich at the table and kept on working during lunch."

"So, nothing out of the ordinary?"

"Not really…unless you count the number of phone calls she got."

"More than usual?"

"Yes. I've kinda had to get on Amber about phone calls every once in awhile, but Friday it was just out of control."

"Any idea who from? Same person? Different people?"

"Well…I hadn't thought about it. Two were from her mother—one requesting the beer-run. And the others I thought were some guy—not from anything she said but she excused herself to take the calls in the kitchen. Once, I heard her raise her voice and another time, it looked like she'd been crying."

"But no comments?"

"No. Complained about having to pick up beer for her mother—the two weren't close. Said she hoped she could shake the sinus-thing before Monday. That was it."

"Did Amber leave before the truck got here?"

"It would have been about the same time. I stopped work when the foreman came up to the house to get keys to the ATVs. Amber had been gone maybe fifteen minutes, not more."

"And what did you do then?"

"I got a ride to the site."

"On an ATV?"

"Yes."

"I'd like to take a look at that site. Doc, can you and Penny take us down there?"

"Sure thing. Transportation's right outside the door."

Dan assumed that would be several ATVs and wasn't wrong. Elaine was limping but gamely got on behind him and Dan followed Doc and Penny with the sheriff bringing up the rear.

The site wasn't much to see—a clear path the truck had taken leaving a dirt road and pulling off onto the grass, then tracks going forward again. "Where does this go?" Sheriff Howard pointed in the direction of the road.

"Hooks back up with County 5 'bout a mile from here. I had this detour cut in when I bought the place. Easier for deliveries."

"Pretty secluded back here—I can't even see the highway."

Dan got the distinct feeling that the sheriff was thinking out loud. Was he thinking that this would be a good place for any kind of delivery—fertilizer, drugs, or something else? Were they that far from where he and the sheriff had heard the gunshots a couple nights ago? The warning that was answered by someone deep in the trees. An involuntary shiver tickled across his shoulders. The place gave him the willies. And he guessed he wasn't the only one as Elaine slipped her hand in his.

"What kind of bird do you reckon that is?" A sweeping glance from the sheriff took in the tops of several pines.

"I have no idea. I'm not a birder. Are you?" Doc looked uncomfortable, Dan thought.

"Just an amateur."

Now everyone paused to listen. A moment of silence, then a whistling roll of sound ended in a series of chirps—but it came from the opposite direction of the first call. Dan didn't know birds but he doubted that one had feathers. Everyone waited expectantly but the two calls seemed to be it.

"Any idea what that was?" The sheriff asked.

"Not something on the wing. I'd guess hunters checking in with each other."

The sheriff frowned, "Any problems with squatters? Or others you might not want using your land?"

"It's hunting season—always have to chase a few off this time of year. The land is posted private but that doesn't seem to mean much. The boys keep an eye out for anything else. We're isolated here that's always an invite to take advantage."

"I don't need to tell everyone not to touch anything." The sheriff pointed to a water bottle and a wadded burger wrapper. "I'll get the boys down here later."

"So I didn't see anything after all. I mean there apparently was nothing to see." Elaine sounded dejected. "I don't know what reason there could have been to abduct me."

Dan was beginning to feel the morning had been wasted. "I agree. Someone went to a lot of trouble to just get your car."

"And Amber…do you think she left the property or was she…detained here?" Elaine turned to the sheriff.

"Time frame would have her still around here—if Penny was accurate about when she left work. Seems like there's a piece of the puzzle that should be apparent but I'm not seeing it. I need to get the boys out there in the woods, too—do a little bird hunting. I'll call if anything turns up. I may need you later, but you're free to go now."And with that the sheriff walked back to the ATVs.

◇◇◇

Dan opened the car door, then paused. "How about coming with me to pay a visit to Gert." He wasn't willing to let the whole morning be a wash.

"You haven't told her about the theft?"

"Finding you kinda got in the way of things."

"Oh? Is that a complaint? Maybe I should disappear again."

"Not on your life. You're not getting out of my sight. I'd asked the sheriff to go with me but I doubt he can get away anytime soon. Come on, let's go break the bad news. "

Gert was raking the yard when they pulled up, but insisted they all go in for a nice cup of tea. And it wasn't until this ritual was complete and they were sitting around the dining room table that Dan broached the subject of the necklace.

"I was able to meet with Mr. Ortega himself. I'm sorry I didn't get back to you yesterday."

"Oh my, finding Elaine safe and sound was more important than a report on the necklace. I just knew you had gotten turned around in the woods when you went for gas. It's so easy to do." Gert leaned in to pat Elaine's hand. "Welcome back, dear."

Penny must have come up with that story and it was actually better than having to explain what really happened.

"Now, I'm sure you're going to tell me I'm dreadfully under-insured. And if my premium goes up, well, that's all a part of owning such a unique piece of history. How do you put a price tag on keeping your dearest possession protected?"

Dan wished she didn't look so chipper…and trusting and hadn't referred to the necklace as her "dearest possession." To say this wasn't going to be easy was an understatement. Big time.

"I need to treat this as a deposition. May I use a recorder?" A nod from Gert, and Dan placed the small compact Sony on the table between them and turned it on. "I have a list of questions that we'll need to address."

"Of course."

Dan took a breath, "Before we could even begin the appraisal, Mr. Ortega informed me that this was the third time he'd seen the necklace in as many months."

"How could he have seen the necklace?"

Dan paused, then "It was brought in so that a certain number of diamonds could be removed and sold. He was also instructed to replace those taken out with Russian zirconia."

Had he thought she might have been behind the ruse? It had crossed his mind but not this kind of duplicity, double dipping—sell the diamonds piecemeal and declare the necklace stolen for full payout. The gasp put his questions to rest.

"Who…?" Gert grasped the edge of the table with both hands, her voice was barely a whisper and for a moment, Dan wondered if Gert's heart was strong enough for what was turning out to be a shock.

"Mr. Ortega had no reason to think it wasn't being done per your instructions. Mr. Woods from the bank brought the necklace in all three times." Dan took an envelope out of his jacket pocket, "This gave him full authority to do what he thought was your request." Dan placed the copy of the contract that she had supposedly signed on the table in front of her.

Gert leaned in and studied the signature but didn't touch the paper. "I've never seen this and I certainly never signed it." Gingerly, with an extended index finger she pushed it away from her.

"Is that your signature?" He had to ask.

"Yes, but it's clearly a forgery. I never signed this…this falsehood, this lie."

"Before we go further, I want to assure you that the necklace is covered for theft. Those diamonds will be replaced by equivalent gems and the necklace's worth restored. We simply need to make certain that the sales—three separate sales—of diamonds removed from the necklace were not authorized by you."

"I understand. This is simply a part of your job." There was a tremor in her right hand.

The worst part, Dan thought as he watched Gert's mouth pull into a prim, straight line. Her hands, tightly folded, now back in her lap.

"But it won't be the same. The diamonds that are gone are a part of history. The necklace was there; turn of the century, Teddy Roosevelt...of course, the *Titanic*. Louis Tiffany handpicked all the stones—big ones, smaller ones. No, there's no replacing that."

"I agree. That is truly what has been lost—a slice of time." Dan leaned his elbows on the table and met Gert's stare. "Was there anyone else besides yourself who could have had access to the safe deposit box?"

"Penny, of course." Involuntarily Gert's two hands flew to cover her mouth. "You couldn't think...you don't...Penny... maybe Mr. Woods used some sort of master code and got into the box and took the necklace...but Penny? That's not possible." She looked over at Dan, "Mr. Woods would have had access to my signature. It's going to be difficult to prove his involvement now. But I don't think stealing diamonds is a reason for suicide."

"Mr. Woods' death has been ruled a homicide."

A stifled gasp, "Oh, my. I didn't know."

"I also need to ask you about another incident. When the claim was originally filed, you stated that the necklace was in your safe deposit box at the time of the break-in."

"That's true, it was."

"Last week Penny came to me with the necklace. She told me she had found it in the guest room—your guest room here at the house. It had been put between the mattress and box spring. She said that you sometimes put it there?"

"Never."

"Not even if someone came to the door and you needed to get it out of view quickly?"

"No." Gert was now sitting bolt upright.

"Penny told me that she thought you had put it there and had forgotten about it. The rest of the story you know—she asked Mr. Woods to 'find it' using the excuse of confusion caused by the break-in for it having been misplaced. He offered to safeguard it at the bank but you opted to bring it home."

"Mr. Mahoney, stop right there. I've heard enough. I am not senile. The things you're saying simply did not happen. To the best of my knowledge the necklace had remained in the safe deposit box after I had removed it to clean it." Gert pushed back from the table and stood. "I'm saddened that you feel you need to point a finger at Penny. Yet, I've not known you to be a dishonest man. If I am to believe you then I must acknowledge my daughter is lying. That she has been stealing from her own mother. I need to do some thinking. Leave the necklace with Mr. Ortega. When I've gotten to the bottom of this, I'd like you to take me to Santa Fe to meet with him. Until then, the necklace is safe."

Gert walked them to the door. "I appreciate your candor. I imagine the personal stories could make your work difficult." Another quick squeeze of Elaine's hand and she opened the door.

"I'm sorry I had to be the messenger—"

"I needed to know. If circumstances are, in fact, what they appear…well then, I have decisions to make."

A hug seemed to be called for but Gert's ramrod straight spine and pursed mouth made him hesitate. Instead he followed Elaine to the car. The old girl had grit. How many people could take that kind of news and not fall apart? Elaine turned to wave before getting into the Cherokee, but Gert had already shut the door.

"I'm glad that's over. I'm sorry for Gert—there's no win-win to any of this. Do you mind driving? I need to check something." Dan handed the keys to Elaine.

He needed to make a quick call to Santa Fe to reiterate that the diamonds were paid for by check—one made out to Mrs.

Gertrude Kennedy for eighty-five thousand, and one for fifteen to Ortega's. And he needed to know dates. All three times were the same—and all three occurred in August. One on the eighth, the next on the fifteenth and the last just four days before the break-in. Bingo. Checks leave a trail. And yes, the store had made copies. UL&C would require them for their records.

Wow. That close to Bean Day…did someone have advance knowledge—get as much as they could from the necklace before they would declare it stolen? And recoup the entire five-hundred thousand? Eight-hundred thousand total wasn't a bad haul. For the first time in a long time, Dan felt he was getting closer to the truth, and he wished it didn't point a finger at those who stood to gain the most.

Chapter Sixteen

"Hello."

"Stephanie, Dan Mahoney. I need your help. Can you get into the bank this afternoon?" A quick explanation—he needed to prove that Gert Kennedy wasn't behind selling diamonds out of the necklace and then trying to claim the loss of the entire item. He had to back up and give a quick overview of what he'd found out at Ortega's but after some exclamations of shock, Stephanie said it wouldn't be a problem. She was just going out the door. She'd been called in by bank management to box up Mr. Woods' belongings. Maybe he could meet her there? She could get everything for him—copies of Gert's accounts—monthly reports going back to June. Not a problem. She would have access to whatever the bank would have sent out in the mail.

Stephanie met them at the door and explained to the guard what they wanted. She made copies of Dan's driver's license and business card, then Elaine's drivers license and university ID. The three of them waited while the guard cleared them with his boss…whoever that was. Finally they followed Stephanie back to Lawrence Woods' office.

"I'm sorry, but they can't be too careful." Stephanie walked ahead and opened the door.

"Not a problem. I expected as much." Dan looked around. This was not the bare-bones room he'd waited in a week ago. The floor was littered with bubble wrap, stacks of newspapers, packing cartons, cardboard boxes yet to be set up and rolls of tape—masking, cellophane, and scotch tape in dispensers. She certainly had her bases covered. And she'd need every bit of packing material if she boxed up everything he was looking at.

Desk top, chairs, benches, bookcases—there wasn't an uncluttered surface in the room let alone a place to sit. Knick knacks—plaques proclaiming Wagon Mound Bank employees winners of good citizens' awards, baseball trophies, basketball championship two-handled cups on wooden stands with twenty or so names engraved, framed watercolors, a couple of oils and pictures, some framed, some not—but all telling a piece of Wagon Mound history.

"Where did all this come from?"

"Storage. Mr. Woods put everything in storage when he came. We hardly recognized the place—bare walls, empty showcases. He was Spartan and expected the bank to reflect his taste. There was quite a row over it. This is our town." Stephanie's hand swept in a circle. "Its citizens needed a place to show off what they are all about. Like this stack here. Pictures of Bean Day celebrations dating back to the 1950s. We don't have a library or a city hall or anywhere that this memorabilia can be on display. It made sense to use the bank. But not to Mr. Woods. God rest his soul."

"Do you mind if I look through these?" Elaine pointed at the Bean Day pictures.

"No, of course not. It's a wonderful step back in time. There's so much history in this area. We'll just be out here at my desk." Stephanie picked up several folders and went back down the hall. Dan looked at a few pictures, then left the stack with Elaine. Seemed a shame the town had been deprived of viewing their heritage. He had a feeling things would be different from now on.

"Oh this is so terrible." Stephanie sat behind her desk and leaned forward as Dan sat down. Then in her best stage whisper, "It's exactly what you thought. Everything was set up to double-dip. But the money didn't go into Ms. Kennedy's account." She paused and looked around her then leaned even closer. "Eighty-five thousand was deposited into Ms. *Penelope*

Kennedy's account. Copies of the checks show them signed by Gertrude Kennedy but I'm certain those signatures are fake." She sat back and folded her arms. "And each time, on the exact same day, ten thousand dollars went into Mr. Woods' account, a transfer made by Penny Kennedy. Must have earned himself a little bonus."

To say Stephanie looked smug wouldn't quite capture it. Dan thought she'd be fighting the idea of panty hose for some time to come—even if the perpetrator was dead. There had really been no love lost.

"Let's take a look."

"I made these copies for you. This is Penny Kennedy's account. All three times the checks went into her account. Each check to Gertrude Kennedy was signed over to her daughter—more forged signatures, no doubt. But this is the odd thing, the money was transferred out all three times within hours."

"Any idea where it went?"

"Caymans."

"Islands?"

"One and the same."

"Penny Kennedy's name was on the transfer?"

"Yes—along with our very own bank president's name."

"Lawrence Woods took the necklace to Santa Fe for the stones to be extracted and sold, then he helped Penny Kennedy transfer money to the Caymans, and made an easy ten grand for his trouble."

Stephanie nodded and sat back arms folded across her chest. "And poor Mrs. Kennedy never had a clue. Is it any wonder that this bank was under investigation?"

"Wow." It was tough for Dan to get his mind around a plan so devious—could Penny have been planning on a life that didn't include Mom? He found that hard to believe. A spinster living with her elderly mother and a Chihuahua...not the profile of a criminal. Was Lawrence Woods the mastermind? Sell the diamonds but claim a loss for the entire necklace after the break-in? Or because Dan didn't want to believe Penny could do something so ugly to her own mother, he was refusing to see the truth?

"Stephanie, do you have a copy of Penny Kennedy's monthly statement for August?"

"I know what you're thinking and you're right—the deposits don't show up. They're only recorded on electronic bank totals as deposits for each of those days. Obviously for Ortega's benefit. The jewelry store would have needed signed, deposited checks for their bookkeeping."

Dan sat back. An interesting paper trail, to put it mildly. Certainly seemed to get Gert off the hook.

"Am I interrupting anything?" Elaine, holding two framed photos, stood behind Dan. "I think this is interesting." She placed the photos in front of him. "Do you recognize anyone?"

Dan pulled the first photo closer. It was a picture from a newspaper of about twenty bikers lined up under a banner that read, "Bean Day Festival, Sept. 14, 1980." There were an assortment of bikes, mostly Harleys with a couple Triumphs thrown in. The group looked young; several riders had passengers. Those were sure the pre-helmet days—a couple bandanas but nothing more substantial, Dan noticed.

"Do you see him?" Elaine was leaning over his shoulder. "There. Who does that look like?"

Even Stephanie came around the desk to look. "That's Sheriff Howard." Her index finger landed on a bike third from the left.

"A much younger sheriff but you're right. I'm not sure I know what's so unusual about the sheriff doing a little riding." Dan wasn't following.

"Wait. That's not the interesting part. Take a look at this." Elaine pulled the bottom framed photo out and placed it on top. "Who's that?"

This time he recognized the person and understood Elaine's excitement. Under a banner that read "Wagon Mound's Biker Babes"—right in the center was Penny Kennedy. Astride a Harley, leathers, a bandana holding a head full of curls in check, young, slim—even a grainy photo couldn't hide sheer youth. She must have been in her early twenties. And the man sitting on the bike behind her with both arms around her, chin touching the top of her head? Sheriff Howard.

"Did you ever hear that these two were chummy?" Dan turned to Stephanie.

"I was only twelve at the time. I have no idea. Sheriff Howard has been married all the time I've known him. Of course, until he lost his wife a year or so back. He was actually born and raised in Las Vegas, New Mexico. He's not exactly a local."

Dan guessed the term "local" was reserved for those being born within the city limits—didn't seem to extend out into the county and certainly not to a neighboring town. There were rules and then there were rules. Out here they seemed pretty cut and dried.

Dan sat looking at Penny on a bike. Was she a rider? Or was this picture just posed for the photographer? And if she was a rider, what were the chances she could have pushed a piece of paper under his door and taken off on a Ducati? *It's not what you think.* Was he just trying to read something in or did the line sound more like what a woman would say? Penny certainly had a reason for wanting him out of the way.

And the sheriff. Now there was a question mark. A few hundred thousand would buy a pretty nice boat and retirement home…keep milking the necklace and replacing the stones with fakes…but he had no proof that the once-happy couple were even back together. The photos in front of him were over thirty years old. And then the thought he didn't want to dwell on—was Lawrence Woods' death a result of getting involved with the necklace? Or the tunnel? Because it just didn't feel like the two were connected.

He was bound to report what he knew—that the necklace had been looted to the tune of three hundred thousand dollars. This wasn't the usual case for UL&C. Messy to say the least with criminal charges looming unless Lawrence acted on his own without Penny's knowledge. But there he went again trying to excuse Penny. Of course. Penny's name could have been forged on a check and a transfer to open an off-shore account. But that wouldn't explain how or where the necklace was found. Who was telling the truth there? Dan only had second-hand information shared by a dead woman with her mother that Penny Kennedy just about drove her nuts asking to take the necklace out of safe-keeping because her mother was senile. And there were no notes or signatures in the log books to even see if the dates that the necklace showed up at Ortega's were the same as when Amber was supposedly being pestered. The hard facts were Lawrence Woods and Amber Medger were dead. Both murdered. And even if his knowledge was inconclusive, Dan needed to let someone know.

Chapter Seventeen

"Are you saying we might have an entire day to ourselves?" Elaine looked elated.

"Looks like it. What do you want to do?"

"What if I wanted to go into Santa Fe and look at rings? I remember saying 'I do' the other night."

"Perfect choice. Lunch, maybe a movie—" And then his cell rang.

"Sheriff Howard. Yeah, we'll be here. Not a problem." He turned the phone off and slipped it back in his pocket. He didn't have to say anything. Elaine moved to hug him.

"It's okay. We'll have plenty of time to shop. I'm going to take Simon for a walk. The sheriff didn't say he wanted to see me?"

"Didn't say what he wanted."

"I won't be long." Elaine clipped the leash in place and was almost knocked down by an exuberant Simon who was completing a circle of half jumps. "We need to give you more attention." She made him sit before opening the door.

Dan watched the two of them move across the lawn scattering leaves before stepping off the curb and heading down the street. Elaine not even limping with Simon glued to her side. That was one resilient lady. Funny, but moments like this were what made being alive pretty worthwhile. He leaned against the railing breathing in the crisp fall air and only went inside when they were finally out of sight.

Dan heard the sheriff on the stairs and turned and held the door open before he had a chance to knock. That was quick. Dan hoped this was a positive visit.

"Thanks. Did I catch you at a bad time?" Dan shook his head and moved back as the sheriff stepped inside, walked around the corner of the bed and pulled out a chair at the kitchen table.

This didn't look like a short visit or a happy one. The sheriff hadn't cracked a smile. "Get you something?"

"No, on duty…that is, if you were about to offer a beer—which sounds pretty good about now."

"Fresh out. Iced tea?" The sheriff looked tired. Had he always had that furrow etched between his eyes?

"That'll work."

The sheriff waited until Dan had placed two glasses on the table, then he leaned back and stared at Dan full on. Dan knew enough not to flinch or say anything but he was beginning to feel uncomfortable.

"What made you think there might have been something in those unused safe deposit boxes at the bank?" The sheriff's stare was so intense Dan could feel it.

He cleared his throat, "A hunch. Nothing else added up. By reason of elimination, no one lost anything. That is, nothing was stolen due to a robbery but there was a painstakingly complete tunnel that said something made that kind of work important, maybe even necessary. Guess I've been toying with the idea that it could have been a drop for something. Drugs, maybe. We still don't know how long the tunnel was operable. We just know they chose safe deposit boxes over a couple million plus in currency."

The sheriff broke eye contact and rubbed his forehead with the tips of his fingers.

"You were right. But I wish to hell you hadn't been. I lost a good kid—a promising kid. Twenty-three years old, just graduated from college and all he wanted to do was get into law enforcement. Been a deputy just six months."

Dan waited while the sheriff took a long swallow of tea and moved a napkin to soak up the ring the sweaty glass had left.

"Now he's dead. And there wasn't one damn thing I could have done to stop it because I just plain never suspected."

Dan was lost. Had the kid been in a car accident? He hadn't heard of any but what did this death have to do with the unopened boxes?

"You've lost me."

"I sent him in there to dust for prints and vacuum the insides of the boxes—the ones, as you pointed out, that hadn't been opened. The robbery was an innocuous chore, a thankless one because I believed it was going to be a dead end, and it took his life. He went to Urgent Care three days later but they sent him home. Said he had the flu. His pregnant wife rushed him to the hospital yesterday morning and now he's gone. In six days. Gone."

Again, Dan waited. None of this was making sense. How or why were flu symptoms connected to the bank?

"You know what he had? What killed him just inside a week? What some sick, son of a bitch kept in those locked, unmarked boxes? Ricin.

Yeah, you heard me. Ricin. This kid breathed enough of the stuff he vacuumed up to contract ricin poison by inhalation. He never had a chance. You inhale the stuff and you're a goner, check out within days. A little on the skin and you have a fighting chance." The sheriff leaned forward elbows on the table. "I gave the order to use the vacuum. I sent that poor unsuspecting kid in there to check the boxes."

Dan sat back. Didn't this just about make the whole thing a brand new ball game? Who would keep ricin in a safe deposit box?

"I gotta quit hiding behind thinking that this is a sleepy little western town. I've lived in this area all my life. We don't have terrorists, or murderers on the loose. Worst we ever get up here is discovering a pot farm in the national forest or somebody's ninety-year-old grandfather dies of exposure bringing his sheep in in a snowstorm."

Dan was pretty much speechless. Another death. He was feeling a part of the sheriff's guilt—it had been his idea.

"Just a heads-up. The FBI Joint Terrorism Task Force and U.S. Department of Homeland Security are involved now. I don't know who has first dibs on you, but you'll be hearing from somebody. In the meantime I gotta help plan a funeral."

The sheriff stood, dumped the rest of his tea in the sink, and let himself out.

Chapter Eighteen

"Terrorism? Terrorists in Wagon Mound, New Mexico?"

"I think the Feds have to allow for anything. Ricin has been a terrorists' tool before. Doesn't mean it was one now. And just for the record, I don't remember the Unabomber living in a thriving metropolis."

"So, who do we know who fits a Unabomber description?" Elaine handed him a second cup of coffee and joined him at the table.

"I think we can rule out Gert."

"Dan, be serious."

"I am, sort of. But by virtue of the necklace, Gert's in the lineup. Personally, I think we can rule out Gert's involvement with anything that's happened—especially anything with the necklace. I've narrowed suspicions to Penny or the bank president or Penny *and* the bank president."

"And your best guess?"

"Toss up at this time. Might not be too difficult to prove motive, though."

"For?"

"Penny. A fifty-something spinster seeing her inheritance within reach with only a very robust mother in the way. And if you knew that whatever was taken would be replaced by the insurance company…Well, you wouldn't really be hurting mom but more like helping yourself to what was already yours. And a bank robbery conveniently covered everything up. Of course, finding the necklace was a little risky. She obviously didn't know I'd have it appraised."

But ricin? Dan could understand Elaine's problem with credibility. It just seemed so farfetched. Keeping a toxic weapon in a bank vault in Wagon Mound, New Mexico, made the questions of who did what to the necklace absolutely pale in comparison. Whatever was going on was a lot bigger than an insurance claim.

And the Feds seemed to agree; they didn't waste time calling. He was commanded to meet them at the bank at nine sharp in the morning. Bring credentials, any notes, or photos, and be prepared to spend half a day. If he'd thought things were starting to fall into place, he'd been dead wrong.

The bank was positively bustling. A number of people, probably all locals, were wandering in and out. Dan guessed more from curiosity than any need to do business. The bank was open but chaos looked to be in control. Plain clothed guards seemed to occupy every corner including the front sidewalk. Dark glasses, dark suits, phones in their ears. It reminded him that the problem at hand was not simple burglary. The death of three people made it a lot more than that—was the death of old Chet number four?

Stephanie glanced up and gave him a quick smile over a stack of folders before Alice whisked him back to the prez's old office. This time the room was without clutter and boxes with a couple half-way comfy couches. Looked like the Feds could command a touch of luxury. Ditch the Quaker austerity and add some overstuffed. It didn't mean they were any more punctual. He glanced at his watch. A quarter after.

"Sorry to keep you waiting." The man who stepped inside the room was more than a little overdressed for Wagon Mound. Some unknown salute to the recently departed but impeccably dressed former bank president? Dan doubted it but the crisp, pin-stripe shirt, and navy merino wool suit with power tie in red…pretty dressed up for this community. But the damnable thing was the man looked familiar. Dan knew he was staring but just couldn't quite place the face. Unless…

"Yes, we've met before. If you could call it that."

"At Jeeter's place—the chop shop. Didn't recognize you without the bandana and mustache." Dan recalled the man who had stuck his head in the door but was now totally transformed into a Federal mucky-muck. Things were getting more interesting.

"You got it. Sorry I didn't stop to introduce myself at the time. I actually am Will Ferris, Jeeter's brother. Gives me first dibs on jobs out this way."

Dan couldn't be sure but he thought that was meant to be funny. Sarcastic, maybe? He offered a half-smile, "Good camouflage."

"Yeah, works for this job anyway."

Will took the chair behind the desk and motioned to one in front. "Coffee? Anything before we start?"

Dan shook his head and watched as Agent Ferris opened a manila folder.

"I need to ask some routine questions first—results of your investigation involving the item insured by United Life & Casualty. Where that investigation stands at present." He looked directly at Dan and smiled. "I'm not going to remind you that anything you say could be held against you. You know that."

"Am I under suspicion?"

"Of course not. Just a precaution until we cross the t's and dot the i's. I need to know what you know. You may think you have reason to be personally involved with finding the person or persons behind certain recent activities. The abduction of your fiancée, the rollover…am I making myself clear? This is federal territory now. I would remind you to stick with why you're here. Respect boundaries. There's some indication that that's difficult for you to do." A slight downward nod of the head toward the open folder. Then a stern countenance and stare, hands clasped.

They had a file on him. Dating from when? Probably longer back than he cared to know or cared for them to have. Fifty-two years of age and Dan felt like someone had just popped his knuckles with a ruler. Well, two could play this game. It was obvious there would be no give and take—what's mine stays mine mentality was at work here. And that was just fine with Dan.

"Where do you want me to start?" Two could play this game, and Agent Ferris wouldn't get anything that wasn't public knowledge. Not unless he wanted to share.

"Let's start at the beginning, Mr. Mahoney…your trip to Wagon Mound and why."

The recorder was switched on and Agent Ferris leaned back in his chair. Yeah, this was going to be a long one, Dan thought. In fact it was a little before one when Dan finally left the bank. And didn't leave anything behind he hadn't wanted to. Just facts. He'd reiterated the saga of the necklace stopping short of sharing the pilfering of diamonds and possible fencing operation headed up by a disgruntled daughter and the local banker. Because, of course, that last was just conjecture and he needed to find out for himself. And soon.

Nothing was mentioned about ricin, or empty safe deposit boxes or the death caused by cleaning one of them—and he didn't ask questions. He didn't even stay around to chit-chat with Stephanie, even though he sensed she would welcome a break. He was feeling more than a little claustrophobic and fresh air was a welcome change to the stuffy confines he'd sat in for over three hours. And he didn't rule out it was tough to look at that chandelier and not see a body. He felt for Stephanie.

"I'd like to talk with Penny, without Gert." He hadn't meant to just open the apartment door and blurt it out, but he was feeling some urgency. And he hadn't heard that the sheriff had followed up, talked with either Gert or Penny or both. Of course, now he might know why.

"Well, hello to you, too. Can I tag along? We can eat these in the car." Elaine pointed to a plate of sandwiches.

"Sure. Wouldn't have it any other way. I expect Penny may still be cataloging seed shipments. And I wouldn't mind another visit to the ranch. In fact, let's take a chance that she's there and just drive out."

◇◇◇

They were not only in luck—there was the Jag—but right beside it was the sheriff's county-issue SUV. Dan allowed himself a "hot damn." Maybe, just maybe there would be some answers. Finally. He grabbed his briefcase and headed for the front steps.

Penny opened the door and quickly covered her surprise with a short, self-conscious laugh, and some comment about hoping Elaine was feeling back to normal. But Dan had to ask if they could come in. It didn't seem to be a popular idea. Then Sheriff Howard stepped into the hallway, uniform awkwardly unbuttoned one extra button at the neck, no t-shirt, and lacking the obligatory regulation necktie. Could it be that they'd just interrupted something? A little shifting of eyes, nervous patting of her skirt and a tug on her pullover sweater. Without it being spelled out, Dan knew the two of them had been making out. Making out? Is that what you called it over fifty? Or sixty-plus if referring to the good sheriff. Dan was only ten years or so behind and, yeah, making out worked.

"The Professor isn't here right now. He had to run into Santa Fe." Penny paused. "Can I take a message?" Still no one had moved—just a tight-knit tableau in the hall blocking the entrance to the living room.

"I'm not here to see Buster. I'd like to take a few minutes of your time."

"May I ask what this is about?" Penny's hand fluttered up to her neck.

"I have a few questions concerning the necklace. They're not ones your mother can answer."

"Oh, I see." She didn't invite them in but just moved back out of the door, then turned and walked toward the kitchen. "We can talk in here. Is there anything I can get you? I've just made a pot of tea."

Dan and Elaine shook their heads. Still nothing from the sheriff as he brought up the rear. His shirt now buttoned correctly. Everyone took a chair. Dan waited until Penny had poured a cup of tea. If shaking hands were any hint, she was not looking forward to the discussion. There wasn't an indication one way or another that she'd talked with her mother. He imagined it would be more than a little difficult for Gert to confront her daughter—possibly it hadn't been done. So, now it was up to him. He took a deep breath.

"Let me just lay it out. Facts and supposition, and you can help me with that second part."

Penny nodded and seemed to be shrinking in her chair, eyes big, face the color of chalk.

"Here's what I have," Dan paused. "Before I start, I need to record this conversation." He reached into his briefcase and pulled out the recorder and placed it in the middle of the round dining room table and pressed On.

"Oh, I don't know…I'm really not comfortable…" Penny glanced at the sheriff who must have given her some sign because she just gave a little shrug and clasped both hands in front of her. Resigned, Dan thought. He hoped he'd finally get the truth.

He cleared his throat. "UL&C has a policy that when an insured item has not been in the insurer's possession for any length of time be it one hour, one day or longer, that item must be reappraised. I've taken the liberty of having Ortega's in Santa Fe perform the appraisal and submit their findings in writing." Dan removed a binder from his briefcase. He inched it toward Penny. "To save us some time, let me summarize. Approximately three hundred thousand dollars of diamonds have been removed from your mother's necklace and sold. Monies from these transactions briefly found their way into your bank account before being sent to the Caymans—to another bank account in your name."

Dan paused but there was no comment from Penny. He did note the look of surprise on the sheriff's face. "And what was probably a handler's fee of some sort—ten thousand appeared siphoned off for Lawrence Woods up front. Mr. Woods was the go-between, the person representing Gertrude Kennedy—only Ms. Kennedy never authorized such representation. The signature on the letter requesting the sales had been forged. It would appear that you and Mr. Woods were milking a cash cow for your own benefits." The barely audible sound of sucking in air made Dan glance quickly at Penny, but the sound had come from the sheriff.

"You said you had nothing to do with these shenanigans— that it was all Lawrence Woods' doing—"

"I did it for you." Penny pushed back her chair and stood, grasping the edge of the table with one hand and pointing at the sheriff with the other. "All for you. I knew we would never have a life together being so much in debt. We would have been saddled with over a hundred thousand in medical bills. Dear dead Emma. How could we have gotten out from under that? And what were you going to do about it? Nothing. You were just content to keep on working, keep on living in this god-forsaken town—"

"You're blaming me for embezzling? And from your mother? No wonder I looked good all of a sudden—you needed a cover-up." The sheriff stood abruptly catching the edge of the table on his holster sending the pot of tea sloshing over Penny's hand. "I'm a law-abiding citizen—a man who's served his community, worked toward a better good—"

"Oh, really? Everything you touch turns to shit. Look what you've done." Because of the scalding tea? Not entirely, Dan thought. Penny was holding her hand and crying, then seemed to fold into the chair.

Elaine quickly scooped up towels from the kitchen and filled a bag with ice. "Here, this will make it feel better."

Penny unbuttoned her cuff and pushing the material back held the ice pack in place. But not before Elaine had seen the tattoo—the stem of a four-leaf clover. Not a tree trunk, a stem. And this put Ms. Kennedy in the cooler putting an ice pack on *her*.

Deftly Elaine wrapped a towel around Penny's arm tucking the ends under on each side. She hoped her hands weren't shaking because something told her that she needed to be careful with this information. She couldn't just accuse—pain, blindfolded, a lack of sleep and food…who would believe her? Could she believe herself? She hadn't even remembered the tattoo until now. In trying to move on and not dwell on what happened that night, she'd repressed an important clue. But what did it mean? Who was the other person in the cooler? Not Sheriff Howard, she was certain of that. She quickly glanced across the table. The man was livid, jaw clenched, red splotches of color dotting his neck. They'd be lucky if he didn't have a stroke. No, she'd bet her life that he had no idea what his girlfriend had done.

Penny seemed not to notice Elaine taking any extra time with the ice pack but continued to sob. "Don't you see? This is my inheritance. Mother wouldn't have been cheated. She would have gotten full value. We could have gone away, bought a boat—"

"So it's okay to screw over insurance companies? And put my job in jeopardy? This is one hell of a way to say you love me." The sheriff paused and turned to Dan. "So what happens now? Will your company press charges?"

"Pressing charges will fall to the insured. It will be up to Gertrude Kennedy. She has several options. Press charges, sue to get the three-hundred-thousand back, or simply take a loss on the money and insure the necklace at its current, lesser value exonerating United Life & Casualty of any claims. She may have a case with the bank because of their president's involvement. I can't speak for her but I will meet with her in the morning And then, the Feds may have a say about prosecuting because of the bank involvement   hiding money taken from an account without the owner's permission or knowledge for an out-of-country transfer and deposit." Dan put the recorder and binder back in his briefcase. "I'll keep you posted."

He left the house hearing Penny entreating the sheriff to just listen to her, give her a chance. Dan doubted that would happen. His grandmother used to say "there's no fool like an old fool," and he knew the sheriff didn't relish being duped.

Chapter Nineteen

Dan turned the Cherokee toward town. Questions. Just when he thought he might be getting closer to answers. For starters, he was convinced that pretending to find the necklace was a mistake. Penny should have just left that part alone. But when he wouldn't leave town, she had to try something else. "Finding" the necklace was her ace. She counted on UL&C recalling their agent. Yet, Penny and the necklace were only one part of the puzzle. It didn't explain Amber's call to check Dan's itinerary so that Chet Echols could put him out of commission. And it didn't explain Amber's death and the bank president's death—somehow that was tied to the ricin. But why was he so sure of that? And, if so, how were they connected? And locking up Elaine? How did that fit in?

"You're quiet. Are you okay?" He realized Elaine was staring at him.

A half glance in her direction, then full attention back on the road. Nothing like a rollover to improve your driving habits.

"Still too many unanswered questions."

"And here's something else. I remembered something this afternoon. I can't make sense out of it, but I know it happened. I'd forgotten about it until now."

Dan waited. Was that all? "Want to share?"

"You'll think this is crazy but what if I told you I think Penny was one of my captors?"

"Why do you say that?"

"The one who put an ice pack on my ankle had a tattoo. I thought it was a trunk—"

"A chest of some sort?"

"No, no, like a tree—a tree trunk. Only now I know it was a stem, the bottom part of a four-leafed clover."

"Penny has a tattoo?"

"Yeah, and not a little one either. It's about the size of a silver dollar."

"I never noticed."

"How could you? She always wears long sleeves. She only rolled her sleeve back today when she got scalded."

Now it was Dan's turn to be silent. What part would Penny play in abducting and hiding Elaine? And who was her accomplice—or the other way around?

"You didn't hear their voices?"

Elaine shook her head, "No one said anything."

"You were blindfolded, possibly drugged—certainly suffering a twisted ankle and in pain…not good indicators for making your memory foolproof."

"I know. I'm even doubting myself."

"Tell me again what you do remember."

"Well, just before I fell I heard a scream—not just one, more like a series of frantic cries. You know, like someone was terrified."

"Guess we can assume that it was Amber and she was afraid for her life."

"I don't think abducting me had anything to do with men unloading a truck. It probably *was* a load of fertilizer and feed. I think someone thought I saw something else—something happen to Amber."

"Bound, gagged, stripped, thrown into a car that was set on fire—what had she done? What could warrant a death so brutal?"

"It smacks of anger. Whoever did it didn't like her very much. Why do you think they used my car?"

"Maybe for no other reason than to buy time. Didn't think the body would be identified so quickly—wanted me to think it was you. Or, hey, maybe just because it was handy."

"And maybe they thought you would leave. That killing me would be the last straw."

"Didn't know me, did they?"

"Dan this is all so dangerous. Solving the necklace's disappearance is such a small part of it. The bad guys are still out there."

He didn't want to tell her he was thinking the same thing. He wasn't sure they were any closer to a solution than they had been this morning.

"Are you sure this is the business you want to get into?"

"Yes, I'm beginning to like the danger…a little."

"Well, you have a front-row seat and plenty of time to decide."

"Are you up for stopping by Gert's? I'd rather do it now and not wait."

"This won't be easy."

Gert met them at the door and didn't invite them in. "It was Penny, wasn't it?" She looked tired, Dan thought. All eighty-five years seemed etched in wrinkles around her eyes. "I'm afraid I haven't confronted her. I've waited on more evidence…something concrete."

"I understand. Apparently, she didn't act alone. Lawrence Woods was a part of this."

"That ninny. He wasn't right for this town. Stood out like a sore thumb. Not hard to believe he'd be on the take."

"But she did it for love…I'm not sure that makes a difference but she was trying to help the man she loves." Elaine offered.

"I don't think he needed money. Certainly not now."

"With the medical bills from his wife's illness? I think they were exorbitant and him being so close to retirement." Elaine added.

Gert looked perplexed. "Who are you talking about?"

"Sheriff Howard, of course."

"That was over thirty years ago. He dumped Penny to marry that snippy little Emma Waites. Penny was devastated. She'd had a dress picked out. They were engaged, you know."

Elaine just stared, then glanced at Dan. He looked as lost as she was.

"But you seemed to indicate that Penny does have a boy-friend."

"Used to, anyway. And with benefits, I'm sure. Isn't that what they call it today? You'll excuse me talking about my own daughter this way, but Penny was never good at keeping her knickers up."

"Who would this boyfriend be?" Dan finally found his voice.

"The bank president, of course. God rest his soul."

"Lawrence Woods?" Incredulous. Dan just stared. It was shock enough to think of Penny as a biker babe, but a cougar? Why, there had to have been fifteen years difference in their ages.

"One and the same. Started last year right after he moved to town. She had lots of free time and a place to meet. She pretty much runs that laboratory out there by herself. Doc Jenkins travels a week out of every month and she keeps things going. There were plenty of overnights, I can tell you that. No, there was no way she stole from me to pay some poor man's debt. I'm afraid it was just plain avarice. I think that bank president saw a way to get quick money. I'm just positive it was his idea, his pressure for her to act. I don't think their romance would have ever amounted to anything. So, to Penny's way of thinking she was just dipping into her inheritance—the fact is, I'm not dying quickly enough."

Gert paused. "I don't think they knew that I'd guessed what was going on. But there were too many whispered phone con-versations when she thought I was asleep on the couch. I might be from a different generation but there are some things that don't change. And, Mr. Mahoney? It's not Alzheimer's. I'll keep in touch. Insure the necklace with the remaining stones. I won't register a claim. I'm just so sorry that a member of my family had to cause so much heartache for you."

◇◇◇

"Do you think the second person in the walk-in cooler could have been Doc Jenkins? Five eleven, slightly built, a stoop to his shoulders?" Things still weren't adding up, Dan thought.

Elaine put a cup of hot chocolate on the table and pulled out a chair. "I've been wondering about that and I don't think so. The other person seemed young, bigger, bulkier—I don't think that's how you're describing the Doc. But I'm not sure. There was just something about how the person moved—bent down placing the food on the floor. Quicker movements, less deliberate than an older person would make. Of course, I could only see shadows."

"Damn. Once again, if there's an answer, it only turns into another question."

◇◇◇

This wasn't a night for sleep. Dan covered his insomnia by pleading some alone time to complete the paperwork on the necklace. And then just sat there and watched Elaine as she slept. He was a lucky man. He didn't need to remind himself that there could have been a much different outcome. And it made him angry—not so much that he still had aches and pains where he didn't before but that someone had the audacity to endanger the innocent.

The necklace was accounted for—a headache for UL&C, but there was an end to his involvement. It was difficult to see Penny with Lawrence Woods in a romantic way but it made sense that the president could have taken advantage of her. Maybe even suggested a way to get easy money. No wonder a visit to the bank meant wearing makeup.

But he was ducking the real meaning of solving the theft—he could leave. There wasn't a reason to stay. Other than a big part of him needed to see justice done. And ego wouldn't let him leave the outcome to the Feds. More importantly, he bet he knew someone else who felt the same—someone who also had a stake in the outcome.

Chapter Twenty

He knocked on the door to the sheriff's office at eight-twenty. He hadn't shaved, but a shower and clean clothes made a sleepless night less apparent. Dan stepped through the door after a gruff "Come in" and could see the sheriff wasn't in much better shape.

"Good time to talk?"

"Look, about yesterday—"

"No explanation needed. I'm just looking for a second opinion." Dan moved to stand in front of the sheriff. "I'm assuming you haven't gone to the Feds, or am I wrong?"

"You have to ask?" The laugh Dan got said it all—Sheriff Howard wasn't any more enamored of letting someone else call all the shots in his own backyard than Dan was. "Pull up a chair. How can I help?"

"Probably not do more than just listen."

"You got it. Shoot."

"Some of this might tread on sensitive issues—"

"Nothing sensitive here and I mean that. But before we start I just want to say thank you."

"Thank you? For what?"

"Not telling the Feds the whole truth about the necklace. If they'd gotten ahold of Penny, that story about stealing for me—for our future together…well, I don't have to tell you I'd be fodder for a review board. And it's a little late in the game for that."

"Some things best go unsaid. No need for anyone to know who doesn't have a need."

"I appreciate it. Just want you to know that."

Dan nodded, then reiterated how Gert thought the boyfriend was none other than the late bank president, and how Elaine had seen Penny's tattoo earlier while she was locked up. Making it look very much like Penny knew more about the abduction than she'd reported—maybe even knowing something about Amber's death.

"Let me interrupt here to say the boyfriend *was* Woods. Penny came clean yesterday—seems Woods had a wife somewhere and he didn't want to be put in the position of getting cleaned out. But it was going to cost him to get free. I was a good cover. Sort of one boyfriend stand in for another. I never suspected." The sheriff stopped and cleared his throat. "Penny and I had had a relationship at one time but I married someone else—I'm not proud of what I did but I guess vindictiveness knows no limits. As I just said, a hint that I'd been in on the theft and my career would be over—pension and all. I think she planned to hold that over my head in case she got caught with the necklace. The whole thing could have been Woods' idea. I really don't know. And tattoos? She's got more than that single four-leaf clover."

Dan watched as red crept up the sheriff's neck. Dan would just bet he had first-hand knowledge of Penny, probably not restricted to the forearm.

"But the Clovers are a gal's group of riders. More than one Clover in the community or, at least, there used to be. A good clue but doesn't necessarily point a finger at only Penny."

"Any way we could get a list of names?"

"I doubt the group keeps a roster."

Another dead end. Dan looked at his notes. "But the ricin, what do you make of that? Obviously, it was important enough to keep in the bank. I'm willing to say it was the reason for the tunnel—and maybe the reason Lawrence Woods was killed."

"Could be. Black market toxins fetch pretty good prices— at least that's what I'm told. It doesn't take a lot to make the stuff, it's just so dangerous to handle. Few are willing to take it on. Head to toe body protection and I've still heard of people getting sick. Small doses are lethal—a hand full of castor beans and you're in business."

"Castor beans? Ricin comes from castor beans?" Dan wasn't sure he'd heard correctly.

"Yeah. Why?"

"Because I know where there's at least one plant." He quickly explained that Doc had given him a tour of the greenhouses. Said something about using the castor bean in research.

"Interesting. Remember how last August several government agencies received packets of ricin in the mail? It was pretty much a nationwide scare aimed at those who were most likely to vote yes for a bill allowing fracking in the southwestern United States."

"Any evidence that the bill targeted New Mexico?"

"No, none that I remember reading about, but a fracking operation would more than disrupt the lesser prairie grasslands— pretty much put Doc out of business."

"I don't remember that any group took responsibility."

"Don't think anyone did. Of course, it was treated as an act of terrorism. Wouldn't that be something if ol' Doc Jenkins was sending out packets from Wagon Mound, New Mexico?"

"He had the operation in place for it. They send seed worldwide."

"You up for a chat with the good Doc? I'd like to question him, not just throw him to the wolves. He's been a top supporter of this community. I want to hear what he has to say."

Dan was more than up for a chat. For the first time he felt like answers were right in front of him—maybe not clear quite yet, but there.

"I'm assuming you carry a little fire-power?"

Dan figured that would include the .38 strapped to his calf. "Yeah."

"Tell you what, if you're going to cover my back I'd like to know there's a chance you could do some damage. Let me make a copy of your permit and driver's license and you stick this in your belt." The sheriff unlocked a drawer and slid a 9mm across the desk.

◇◇◇

Penny opened the door and, if looks could kill, as the saying goes, there'd be a couple bodies on the porch, Dan thought. Frosty didn't begin to describe the atmosphere.

"Hello, Penny, is the Doc in?"

Dan had to hand it to him, the sheriff was cool and business-like. And just when it looked like Penny was going to refuse them entrance, Doc Jenkins came down the hall.

"Hi, boys, what can I do for you? I just bottled a fresh batch of brew, a couple longnecks have got your names on 'em."

Somehow drinking before noon meant nothing to this man and remembering the coffee, Dan allowed as how beer would be his beverage of choice—regardless of time of day. "I'll take one."

Once again, in less than twenty-four hours, they were seated around the same oak table. Dan deferred to the sheriff to get things going.

"Just want you to know this visit is unofficial. Just friend to friend."

"Anything I can do to help. Just name it."

Dan wondered if the Doc was aware of Penny's transgressions. Somehow, he thought not. And there didn't seem to be any reason to enlighten him.

"Guess there's no good place to start." The sheriff paused. Collecting his thoughts? Dan thought so. "I lost a deputy last week from ricin poisoning. Seems like a cache of it was being kept in the bank—safe deposit box. He came in contact with the powder when he was lifting prints."

"Whew. That's powerful stuff. Deadly, as you know, and not something the public knows much about." Dan noticed the Doc looked genuinely concerned as he spoke.

The sheriff nodded in Dan's direction and he leaned forward, elbows on the table. "When I took a tour of your greenhouses, you mentioned doing research on the castor bean—coming up with a new feed?"

"Yes, but it wasn't worth following through with the plan.

That stuff is just too dangerous to work with. And it doesn't take much to have a lethal dose."

"But you were raising plants here."

"A few but I didn't have the room to grow them to maturity. I did what everyone else does—I ordered beans online."

"There are on-line suppliers?"

"Mr. Mahoney, castor beans are not a controlled substance. If you don't alter them, they're as safe as can be. They're a naturally occurring lectin—a carbohydrate-binding protein. I'd say there're a few hundred growers—all legit—who'd be glad to send you a packet or two."

"Just out of curiosity, what kind of investment are we talking?"

"You can get more than you'd need to do some damage for twenty bucks. It only takes a few grains the size of table salt to take out a full grown man."

"You know I'm going to have to give this information to the Feds."

"Not a problem, sheriff. I have nothing to hide. My failure at producing a viable feed is well documented. Taxpayers are always looking at ways to cut the 'pork' out of special projects and our government was hoping I could come up with a cheap alternative to grains and alfalfa. Those chicks can put away the calories."

"What kind of set up does it take to make ricin?" Dan was curious.

"Initially, just stuff you'd have in the kitchen. Coffee grinder, filters, a blender. You could walk right into the middle of a lab and not know what you were looking at. Purifying it causes a bit more of a problem, but a liter of manganese heptoxide will purify the ricin from eighteen castor beans."

"Tough to get this manganese heptoxide?"

"Not if you have access to a bunch of depleted car batteries."

Car batteries. Dan sat forward. Who did he know with a yard full of old cars? Someone who had to sleep in the garage and hadn't gone into the house—not for any sentimental reasons involving his grandfather's death but maybe because the place was toxic. Probably couldn't even go in without full protective gear.

"Sheriff, could I talk to you for just a minute?" Dan pushed back from the table and walked to the front door. When they were out of earshot, he told the sheriff of his suspicions. "Tim Echols fits the profile. And Emily could be in it with him. Or maybe that's why she moved out…he could have set up the excavation of the tunnel—he was a guard. And he had reason to scare me away and someone who could do it."

"Worth looking into." The sheriff ducked back into the dining room and offered their apologies, then followed Dan to the cruiser. " I think you're on to something. Sure won't hurt to look around out at his place."

The sheriff deftly guided the cruiser back to the highway and they rode several miles in silence. Something was eating at the sheriff, Dan just didn't have a clue as to what.

"Something wrong?" Might as well ask, Dan decided.

"Yeah…well, maybe…if your suspicions pan out, then I have myself to blame—for a lot."

"How so?"

"I lost sight of being a good cop. I always treated Tim Echols as if he were my own. I was blinded by trying to help a home-grown kid. It was my recommendation that got him into the police academy. I don't have any kids so supporting a local boy… well, ol' Chet was a friend of my father's. My family came from around here before we moved up the road to Las Vegas. Chet took Tim in as a youngster—his daughter was an unwed mother with more problems than she could handle without trying to raise a baby, too. And Chet did a good job—with some help from the community. Whoever said 'it takes a village' got that right."

A couple more miles of silence, then—"Ol' Chet was a pillar of the community. Minor celebrity and all that. Sure, we'd all heard the Hollywood stories one or one thousand times, but to do what he tried to do to you…well, looks like he was just trying to help his own. I guess blood's thicker than water."

"What do you think went wrong?"

"Whatever goes wrong today for young as well as older folks—greed—get rich, get what you think is owed to you."

Dan knew the sheriff was thinking of Penny. "And they all think they can get by with it. Never get caught. As long as I live, the arrogance of the criminal mind will always astound me."

"So how'd Tim get mixed up in it all?"

"Can't tell you that. Connections are made electronically today that could've never happened just a few years back. The tunnel could have been his work. The cutting tools? Laser cutters and blowtorches? All part of a good car repairer's inventory. Tim would have had access, but I'm wondering if the tunnel hadn't outlived its usefulness. That as a drop it wasn't finished."

"Why do you say that?"

"Well, and I know what you're going to think, that I'm trying to make excuses for Penny…but I wouldn't put it past that snake of a bank president to seize an opportunity to line his own pocket, set up a robbery and talk Penny into declaring the necklace stolen. There wouldn't have been any good reason to uncover that tunnel otherwise. It could have been there for years. But an extra few hundred thousand? And knowing the tunnel operation was coming to a halt, he had the time to loot the necklace before using it as a decoy and going for the whole banana. Problem was, they didn't count on you."

"I gotta say you're making sense."

"Yeah, and it wouldn't have taken much romancing to turn Penny's head. She wasn't getting any younger. They don't call 'em the weaker sex for nothing."

Dan silently thanked his lucky stars that Elaine wasn't with them. That way of thinking could get a guy in real trouble nowadays. And nothing was farther from the truth.

"I gotta feeling that Lawrence Woods got crosswise with whoever was behind the tunnel operation. Don't think his double-dipping was appreciated especially after it put Wagon Mound in the spotlight. I'd hate to think Tim did Woods in… but it's a real possibility."

The obligatory junkyard dogs still on chains bayed a chorus of warnings as Dan and the sheriff got out of the car.

"No knocking on the front door unless you don't value your extremities." The sheriff unsnapped his holster.

"Tim lives and works in the back. I'll see if he's there." Dan was headed in that direction when the first shot rang out. And it was from something big. His guess was an AK-47.

"Dammit. Grab some cover." The sheriff was already prone wiggling his way underneath the bed of a rusted out truck. "No heroics. Let's see who it is and what he wants. I'm calling for backup."

Dan slid down between a panel truck and a flat bed with one wheel turned on its side. He couldn't see the sheriff and only pinpointed his position by voice. Backup had a really nice ring to it. He eased the 9mm out of his belt and held it steady. If there was some way he could work his way around to the side, get a bead on Tim without him knowing it. It was going to be tough, Dan dropped to one knee still afraid to give his location away.

And that's when the blue Sonata roared into the yard. The driver braked hard, then just left it running as she ran toward the front steps of the mobile right through the dogs who were turning themselves inside out trying to follow. Emily. And in a hurry and not in a very good mood if Dan could judge by her demeanor and how she was pushing dogs out of the way.

"Emily. Stop. Don't go in there." The yell came from Tim Echols who stepped from the garage door still holding the assault rifle. But he was too late.

The blinding flash, lightning-bright in intensity, was followed one nano-second later by an explosion so violent that it hurled empty propane tanks through the air in a rain of slivered glass and bits of metal. Dan was knocked against the side of the panel truck and buffeted to the ground face first—debris in his hair dust up his nose and a trickle of blood oozing from his ear. And he knew he was the lucky one. The dogs and Emily had to have been obliterated. And the sheriff? He had been closer to the center of the blast than Dan. He could only hope he'd escaped.

But his bigger worry was Tim. Would he come looking for them? It was pretty certain that he'd escaped serious injury.

protected by the metal building. But now Dan could feel his skin start to blister. The heat from the fire was at a meltdown level. He had to move; he had to find the sheriff.

Pushing to a crouch, Dan stood against the truck thankful for its paneled sides. In the swirling particles of dust and ash it was difficult to see as far as the garage. But his hearing wasn't impaired. A 4 by 4 truck roared to life just beyond the drive, driven no doubt by Tim. It careened around the Sonata and bolted up and over the low ravine separating junkyard from county road.

Dan couldn't wait. He started yelling the sheriff's name and moving in the general direction where he'd last seen him. He didn't get an answer back but dropped to all fours to scramble under the smoke checking under vehicles. He tripped over the pair of legs before he saw them. The sheriff wasn't moving and Dan grabbed his ankles and pulled. If it was really true that adrenalin kicked in under adverse conditions, he needed a jolt of it now. The sheriff outweighed him by seventy-five pounds and getting him up and out of there was going to be challenging. He had the sheriff in a sitting position when two hands reached in to take one side. Dan hadn't seen the fireman but, boy, what a welcome sight.

"Got the wind knocked out of him." Dan shouted, indicating the sheriff. "But somebody should check him out."

The young man leaned close and yelled. "Lucky for you we train about five miles from here. We saw the fireball and thought it was an exercise. We've got a full crew here and an ambulance. We'll get the sheriff to a hospital in no time. Anyone else injured? "

"This is it for outside. A woman on the porch was too close to the center to have survived. I doubt anyone was inside."

The fireman nodded and between them they carried and dragged the sheriff back through the yard of trucks and junked cars to the emergency vehicle. By the time they got there, the sheriff was coughing and wheezing, taking gulps of air but definitely looking like he'd live. And against some pretty loud protests, the EMT folks were ushering him into an ambulance.

He could be out of the hospital in an hour, but it was best to not take chances. The retreating wail of the siren was a welcome sound. The sheriff was on his way to help if he needed it.

The fire burned hot and several smaller explosions kept the crew at a distance. The pump truck was in place but depending on the accelerant, the fire was not going to be an easy one to control. Dan lost track of time but knew a couple hours had passed. He stayed out of their way. Finally he watched as they bagged Emily's remains and placed her in another emergency vehicle. There had been too many deaths.

He texted Elaine to say he'd been held up. Understatement, but he didn't give details. He'd left the Cherokee at the sheriff's office and would have to bum a ride. Guess it was about time to make that call to the Feds. But then again it looked like he didn't have to. He watched as four cars pulled up behind the fire tape and several officers got out. Dan walked toward the officer nearest to him. They'd want a statement and he might as well get this over with.

◇◇◇

Elaine went with him in the morning. Dan had a feeling he wasn't going to get out of her sight for a while. The sheriff had been taken to Santa Fe—nearest hospital that could handle possible inhalation of toxins. More of a precaution, but a good one Dan thought. Seems they were right about Chet's place being a lab. The hospital brought back memories but he knew the sheriff would get top-notch care there.

He'd tried to make the trip to Tim's sound like it was all in a day's work but she knew better…knew that he'd put his life in danger…again. She was tired of worrying about him. And that was all right. He agreed. He was tired of worrying about himself and it kinda felt good to have someone care so much. It was time they were together without murders, threats, duplicity… just the two of them. And it might be a good thing to have her see the worst side of his business—might take the edge off of her wanting to hang that shingle, though he was beginning to think working together might have merit. Perhaps more pressing, he still hadn't made good on that promise of a ring. He needed to take Elaine to Santa Fe.

The sheriff had already called him before eight, chafing at the bit to get out of Christus St. Vincent trauma unit. Tests were negative and his lungs were clear but a meeting had been arranged for nine in his room—the sheriff, Dan, Elaine and Willis Ferris, Federal Officer. Dan didn't have a choice, he'd be there. And he felt good about being included. Agent Ferris might have chosen to simply debrief the sheriff.

It seemed the meeting was the only thing detaining the sheriff. He was out of bed, fully dressed and sitting at a corner table when Dan and Elaine walked in. It was pretty obvious that he didn't plan on being there much longer.

"Guess I owe you another thank you."

"Can't accept that alone—you were a community effort. There's a young fireman by the name of Mike who did the majority of the pushing and pulling. It's just good to see you up and around."

It took another five minutes of small talk before Agent Ferris appeared. And to give him credit there were no slaps on the wrists for not involving him first before going to the Echols place alone. He'd fully expected a reprimand for letting the suspect escape. And then Dan found out why.

"You'll be glad to know one of your local officers stopped Mr. Echols for a non-functioning taillight. Being up-to-date on APBs he recognized Mr. Echols as being wanted for questioning. He brought him in around seven last night. After some time spent chatting with the suspect, I think I can lend a little closure to the ordeal this community has suffered."

He certainly had everyone's attention. A quick look at his notes, then, "I know you figured out that the bank safe deposit boxes were a place for the safekeeping of contraband. Manufactured ricin was packaged and kept in a safe deposit box and the tunnel allowed for twenty-four hour access. The tunnel had been operative approximately four months. A packet of ricin had been mailed to a local senator's office in Santa Fe, and traced to a post office in Taos. I've been out this way undercover for the past two weeks. I was led in this direction after that take-down in Tupelo—"

"Mississippi?" Was ricin some new nationwide terrorist threat, Dan wondered.

"Yeah, maybe you read about the case? Elvis impersonator ordered a hundred red castor beans from eBay and processed ricin in his kitchen? It was a crude operation but he represented the Save America group and managed to get a couple envelopes to local senators. Mr. Echols' ricin was a good deal more sophisticated. And more deadly. It appears that he was recruited by Lawrence Woods."

"I'm not sure I can get my mind around why Tim would take a chance on producing something so deadly. And Woods? He was in on all this?" This from the sheriff.

"We don't think Mr. Echols' involvement was political. But, yes, the bank president's was. Echols simply refined the stuff and made a lot of money providing both the product and the repository—with the help of Woods. There is evidence, however, that the operation was winding down—the bank's usefulness had been outlived or to be on the safe side, the group was seeking a new place for safekeeping. Anyway, as you know, Mr. Woods was relatively new to the community. What wasn't known is that he had ties to Save America and volunteered for duty out here away from any spotlight, probably to set up the ricin operation. There are always the Tim Echols who are eager to make big money doing something illegal."

"Any idea who killed Woods? Or why?" Dan asked.

Agent Ferris cleared his throat, "Now this is where things get dicey. I have no idea what Mr. Woods was raking in by providing the bank as a receptacle, but it wasn't enough apparently. That's when Woods and the Kennedy woman—or maybe it was just Woods—decided to stage a break-in. Put the tunnel to one last good use. The two had been pilfering the stones in that necklace for a month prior to the robbery. The necklace was gravy. But with the theft of the necklace came you." He gestured toward

Dan. "Knowing this could mean trouble, Tim's grandfather was tasked with scaring you off. The results weren't quite what they had planned on. Tim had paid to have that truck built and had had a movie deal until he needed the truck elsewhere."

"How much of all this was Penny in on?" Dan needed to know.

A shrug. "We're not sure whose idea it was to sell off the necklace piecemeal and then attempt to collect on the whole thing, but we know it was 'found' mostly to get rid of you. But, of course, by then Ms. Linden was missing and the plot had thickened a bit."

"Lawrence Woods was murdered, for one thing." Dan added.

"According to Echols it seems Lawrence Woods was killed simply because he demanded more money to be quiet. But knowing the low profile Save America likes to keep, I can't imagine they were thrilled with a staged robbery involving their once-viable repository. Things would have gone more smoothly if his death had been accepted as a suicide. Don't think the killer was planning on a murder charge."

"Tim killed him?" The sheriff asked.

"Mr. Echols is not admitting to anything. He gave us as much information as he did as part of a plea bargain—he'll be naming those from Save America that he worked for."

"Do you know why Amber was killed? And why it was done the way it was?" Elaine asked.

"A nasty love triangle if there ever was one. Amber and Emily had been best friends until Amber made a move on Tim. Yes, he was divorced, but Emily still seemed to feel she owned the territory. Tim and Emily decided to kill Amber after Amber found a bag of white powder in the glove box of Tim's car. It seems she tasted it. Yes, you heard me correctly. I think Amber assumed that the powder was some kind of narcotic and just dipped a finger in. Tim saw her do it and knowing that she would in all probability die and possibly lead authorities their way, he and Emily decided to kill her and dispose of her body by fire—destroying any evidence."

"When he found out she was already showing symptoms, Tim lured Amber away from work early and he and Emily met her at the ranch. Tim seems to think that because she had been exposed anyway, killing her was humane, not a crime. I'm afraid our laws say otherwise. By the way it was Emily and Tim who put you in the walk-in freezer. They assumed you saw them with Amber. They did a pretty good job of covering their trail. I'm betting Amber's car was sitting in that junk pile outside the trailer."

Willis paused, "Blowing up his grandfather's house was a last ditch effort to get rid of evidence and kill anyone who snooped. The mobile had been converted into a lab and was pretty toxic. He and Emily had been on the outs and Tim thought she was looking for money. Didn't count on her showing up yesterday." A turn of a page and, "That's about all I can share at the moment. You'll each get a copy of my report." He turned to Dan. "If your office needs more, let me know. Any questions?"

The group was silent. Funny, Dan thought, how things fell into place so easily. Made sense even in retrospect. He stood, shook hands with Willis and the sheriff, handed Willis a card with the home office address, and they were out of there.

When he checked his phone, he was a little surprised to see a message from Gert Kennedy. Could he meet her and her lawyer at Ortega's in Santa Fe? At one?

Damn. Just when he thought everything was all wrapped up. Must be some glitch in the policy, something she disagrees with. But having her lawyer there? Could there be a problem they'd all overlooked? There was just enough time to get from the hospital to the Santa Café for lunch before one. He even splurged on a glass of wine to go with the fried Calamari with cilantro oil dip.

Elaine opted not to go in when they got to the jeweler. She said she needed downtime. Dan thought she'd had enough cloak and dagger for the time being. And he didn't blame her. It was a lot to digest. He promised not to be long and she just looked at him. He had some work to do in the trust department. Note to self, he really had to get some brownie points back.

Chapter Twenty-one

"Please, sit here beside me." Gert pulled out the chair next to her. "Rueben has something he wants to show us." Gert was beaming and had just taken the liberty of patting his knee. What was going on here? Her lawyer, a Mr. Anthony Padilla, stood just behind her chair. Had they discovered another problem with the necklace?

"I suppose I should make a disclaimer of sorts. I want you to know the decision has been made and I won't take no for an answer. I've spent the last few days coming to terms with all that has happened. "

She paused and looked around the table. "My daughter may be incarcerated for her part in the duplicity involving the necklace. I am, however, being assured that a good lawyer will be able to present a strong case that Penny was duped by a man in authority and be dealt with leniently. It would appear that moving the money through the bank to offshore holdings was not something Penny either initiated or was aware of." Here she glanced back at her lawyer. "The money from the sale of the stones already taken from the necklace will provide for representation. I will sell the house here and join my niece in Boca Raton, Florida. I've always wanted to live by the ocean and, frankly, now's my chance. I cannot think that Penny would want to stay in this town but that will be her decision. I am no longer responsible for her choices."

Gert reached for the glass of water Mr. Padilla had set in front of her before continuing. "And I've decided to sell the necklace—the stones that are left. Tiffany has bid on the setting and quite generously, too. I think mother would agree with my decision...under the circumstances. But I know she would support what I want you to see now. Rueben?"

Dan watched as the gemologist emptied a small velvet bag over the black cloth in front of him on the table and a ring tumbled out. Not just any ring, Dan recognized the center cushion-cut, heart-shaped sapphire from the necklace only now it was outlined with diamonds that also dotted the band—tasteful, spell-binding, probably set in platinum.

"You want UL&C to insure this ring for you?"

"Oh my darling man, no. I want you to give this ring designed by Rueben to your lovely fiancée."

"But I can't—couldn't—" Dan was speechless.

"Of course you can. Nothing would make me happier. It would go a long way in alleviating my feelings of responsibility for all that has happened. And what better way to pass on a legacy—or perhaps begin a new one. It will look exquisite on Elaine and would work quite nicely as an engagement ring, don't you think?"

Dan could only nod.

To receive a free catalog of Poisoned Pen Press titles, please contact us in one of the following ways:

Phone: 1-800-421-3976
Facsimile: 1-480-949-1707
Email: info@poisonedpenpress.com
Website: www.poisonedpenpress.com

Poisoned Pen Press
6962 E. First Ave. Ste 103
Scottsdale, AZ 85251